THE FALL OF VALOR

> . . . *Being unprepar'd,*
> *Our will became the servant*
> *to defect.* MACBETH II: I

THE LOST WEEKEND
BY CHARLES JACKSON THE FALL OF VALOR

CHARLES JACKSON

THE FALL OF VALOR

A NOVEL

RINEHART & CO. INC., NEW YORK · TORONTO

The lines from the song "Let's Remember Pearl Harbor" on page 212 have been reprinted by permission of the publishers: Copyright, 1942, by Republic Music Corporation.

To
RHODA
again

. . . But were the coming narrative to reveal, in any instance, the complete abasement of poor Starbuck's fortitude, scarce might I have the heart to write it; for it is a thing most sorrowful—nay, shocking—to expose the fall of valor in the soul. Men may seem detestable as joint stock-companies and nations; knaves, fools, and murderers there may be; men may have mean and meagre faces; but man, in the ideal, is so noble and so sparkling, such a grand and glowing creature, that over any ignominious blemish in him all his fellows should run to throw their costliest robes. That immaculate manliness we feel within ourselves, so far within us that it remains intact though all the outer character seem gone, bleeds with keenest anguish at the undraped spectacle of a valor-ruined man.—HERMAN MELVILLE, *Moby Dick*

CONTENTS

BEGINNING

REMEMBERING THE INSTRUCTIONS in her last letter that morning, John Grandin went around pulling down the shades. A letter from his wife still seemed a very unusual event, somehow; though he had received half a dozen in the past week, it would be a long time before he would be seeing her handwriting again. In spite of the bright morning, the living room suddenly became so dark that he had to turn on one of the lamps for a last look around.

The solid wall of books opposite the windows facing the Drive was such a familiar sight he scarcely saw it any more, like a family photograph which one rarely looks at after the first few weeks, though its every feature is only too well remembered and can be traced or seen in the dark; he could lay his hand on Hazlitt, for example, by reaching along the third shelf to the left, just so far and no farther, like the pianist whose unseeing finger finds the right key by habit. The ash trays were empty; the slip-covers had been pulled down and smoothed out; the magazines were neatly arranged on the converted butler's tray which served as coffee table in front of the big sofa. He was satisfied that the place was in order and clean. Only the hearth was untidy; last evening he had burned a number of themes unclaimed by careless or indifferent students, and their weightless blowy ash moved restlessly behind the firescreen. He removed the screen, took up the brass-handled tongs, and poked the more substantial masses farther back into the fireplace. Having thus carried out Ethel's instructions about cleaning up, he inserted her letter between the pages of the book he was taking along for the train trip and stuck the book in the pocket of his jacket. Finally, he looked in at the door of the study which, too long, had been his literal retreat—where intense concentration and the expenditure of hundreds of solitary hours had helped to stave off the mounting depression which lately threatened to swamp him.

He saw, here also, the rows of books lining the study wall, the always-littered desk which no one was allowed to touch, the couch where he slept alone. He should be a happy man: only yesterday he had received official appointment to the Committee on Administration as faculty adviser to the students beginning next semester and Scribners had enthusiastically accepted *The Tragic Ideal* for November publication. Following on the heels of his having been raised to a full professorship, these things meant substantial recognition of all he had been working for, all he had been giving of himself, the past sixteen years. He had wired the news to Ethel last evening, and was eager to hear what she had to say about it when he would meet her this afternoon on the Cape. As if his wife and two sons weren't enough, now more than ever he had everything to live for; yet the satisfaction was nothing in view of the inexplicable anxiety which accompanied his nights and days. His happiness, his success, his marriage itself, seemed founded on sand. What man's wasn't? But in his case he was sometimes tensely aware of some unnameable force which momentarily menaced the whole structure of his planned life. He gazed about the dark study where the work had been produced (at what cost in concentration his wife would never know) which might or might not do something for him in the scholastic world. Though this had been their home for many years and he would shortly be returning to it again—willingly enough, doubtless, when their holiday was over—he was glad to be leaving the place. In some vague way he connected his unrest with the apartment, particularly with the study, and his confinement and isolation there. It was due to an unhealthy preoccupation with self, a denial of the life around him. The burden would lift when he got away; what he needed was a vacation with Ethel, the island and the open air, walking, swimming, the sea and the sun. As he slammed the door and locked up, he heard the heavy tongs fall inside with a loud clang—against the hearth fender, probably. He started toward the elevator, then changed his mind. He unlocked the door and came back in.

He picked up the tongs and replaced them against the side of the hearth, leaning them against the black marble slab that supported the mantel. Once more he looked restlessly about. Standing in the nearly dark familiar room, he puzzled over his nameless apprehension.

Though outwardly his life had been going well indeed, John Grandin had lately found himself living under an emotional suspense. For hours, sometimes, he had a sense that something was about to happen to him, something untoward, perverse, impossible to fit into his comfortably ordered life; then the feeling would pass and he would forget it until it came up again. It interrupted his work, interfered with his attentions to his family and to family duties, left his mind far from at rest. Working of an evening in his study—or even of an afternoon, in broad daylight—he would lift his head, his senses all aware, and catch himself in the act of expressing the baffling thought: When will the blow fall? What would he do when it did fall, what kind of blow would it be? For months his thinking had never been wholly his own, for something or someone seemed to be thinking for him and through him. In the back of his mind lay a vague and fearful uncertainty, a reminder of doom, so that he found himself wondering, even almost casually (it had become so habitual by now): Now what was it I was feeling or supposed to feel bad about?—as if he had lately passed through a harrowing experience which, though he had deliberately put it behind him, still lingered in his mind, sent reverberations of its unpleasantness into his everyday thought, and somewhere lay dormant but still menacing, still liable to waken again. When it intruded itself actively, he could almost have declared for his own peace of mind: Very well, I'm guilty, they've found me out, the police will arrive any moment now, Ethel will leave me, the children

e to show for it, he would take
t people ever had.
all and pulled the door to. As
the firetongs fall with a bang
ounded all along the hall; but
ight. He descended in the rick-
ed to the bus stop on the corner.

II

the middle of the small low-
d been her bedroom during her
furnished now with a double bed
when she came home to her par-
band. Her bags were packed and
still she remained in the room,
if there was something she had
her father back the car out of the
rn. She went to the window, called,
ght down," and yet remained.
ken the children downtown, to be
e should go. But they had already
hey were to stay with their grand-
ould probably miss her very little,

telegram she had received from her
gain. She was glad about the new
by for him that his book had been
book which had been keeping him
but she couldn't help wondering if

little in his life and had littl
to his grave more than mos

He stepped into the h
it slammed shut, he heard
again, a harsh clank that s
to hell with it now, he tho
ety cage of the lift and walk

ETHEL GRANDIN stood ir
ceilinged room which ha
childhood and which was
for those rare occasions
ents' house with her hus
she was ready to go, but
frowning uncertainly as
forgotten to do. She hear
garage and sound the hor
"Just a minute, I'll be ri

Her mother had ta
out of the way when sh
accepted the fact that t
parents in Maine and w
if at all.

She picked up the
husband and read it a
appointment, and hap
taken by Scribners, the
from her for so long;

will be taken away, I'll lose everything and have to serve my term—and I'll feel better . . . But what he would lose, or why, was the mystery.

He attributed it to the war. Everywhere in the world the blow was falling. Safe in his study, with no connection whatever with what was going on abroad, it would yet reach him and fall. At times, hearing in the midnight quiet of the house the voice of his conscience, he would step to the door of his study to listen for the heavy sleepful reassuring breathing of Ethel in her bed, or go into the children's room to see if they were all right or (absurd thought!) still there. Even as he felt in the dark to see if they were tucked in and covered, his fears vanished, he forgot the unfounded apprehensions, and he would tiptoe from the room with a sense of gratification keener and more moving than any other he had ever experienced in his life. Returned to his study, the sense of the blow that was yet to fall would also return; or it might hold itself off, to rise up again in an unguarded moment during the middle of a bright afternoon several days later, giving him no relief; for relief would only come when the secret was out (if secret it was), the nature of the crime named and accepted. There was nothing he had "done," nothing to feel guilty about. Perhaps in the course of time, he thought, he would come through it and live it down.—But what in thunder had he to "live down"? Simply that he had been a better teacher, a deeper student, a more honest man than his fellows; and had striven for truth more than for success. It was a thought tainted with vanity, he could not have brought himself to express it in so many words, but all the same he knew in his heart that, though he had done

little in his life and had little to show for it, he would take
to his grave more than most people ever had.

He stepped into the hall and pulled the door to. As
it slammed shut, he heard the firetongs fall with a bang
again, a harsh clank that sounded all along the hall; but
to hell with it now, he thought. He descended in the rickety cage of the lift and walked to the bus stop on the corner.

II

ETHEL GRANDIN stood in the middle of the small low-
ceilinged room which had been her bedroom during her
childhood and which was furnished now with a double bed
for those rare occasions when she came home to her parents' house with her husband. Her bags were packed and
she was ready to go, but still she remained in the room,
frowning uncertainly as if there was something she had
forgotten to do. She heard her father back the car out of the
garage and sound the horn. She went to the window, called,
"Just a minute, I'll be right down," and yet remained.

Her mother had taken the children downtown, to be
out of the way when she should go. But they had already
accepted the fact that they were to stay with their grandparents in Maine and would probably miss her very little,
if at all.

She picked up the telegram she had received from her
husband and read it again. She was glad about the new
appointment, and happy for him that his book had been
taken by Scribners, the book which had been keeping him
from her for so long; but she couldn't help wondering if

his new duties at the University and the extra work and time which they would entail might not come between them even more.

A photograph of her husband stood on the dresser. It was a good likeness and she loved the picture; he had always seemed to her a very handsome man. He had thick sandy hair with a slight wave, and a full mustache of the same sandy color. The forehead was almost his best feature, it was high and clear, with a real distinction. The eyes were light brown: honest, and very young looking. His nose had substantial manly nostrils and the mouth was wide and firm, with full and rather sensual lips. She remembered well how those lips parted slightly when they kissed her—when they covered her own mouth completely —and how an intoxication swept through her then as if that moment were almost enough. She gazed at the photograph of the only man she had ever loved or wanted in her life and wondered how long it had been since he had kissed her like that. Weeks? Months? Could it really be months? It was well that she didn't know. Had she known exactly she might have had real reason for despair. As it was, she could still go on from day to day in the hope that tonight might be the night, or at most tomorrow.

Because she had been brought up in a loveless house, Ethel Cameron had wanted only one thing from life: love. During all her adolescence she had seen her parents living in a waste of days, useless to one another, strangers, living as solitarily together as if each lived alone, getting nothing from marriage and thus giving and getting nothing from themselves. In her teens she had made a private promise that when or if she would one day meet the man she loved, she would give herself to that man to her fullest bent and live solely for him. This she had done. But she had come late to love. Perhaps even it was her fault; perhaps he was too old for her, or she too young. She was twenty-three when she first met and fell in love with John Grandin and he was ten years older. Or maybe he was the one who had come to love too late. Which may have been why (she didn't know; she really knew nothing about these things apart from herself, or about how it was with other people) he had retired early into a kind of separate life of his own, leaving her so unsatisfied in love that sometimes she thought she couldn't bear it. The children should have made a difference but they did not; much as she loved them, it was the love of her husband she wanted even more. She had had it so intensely during their first few years that now her life seemed almost dangerously empty.

It was ten in the morning; in another six hours they would be meeting at Woods Hole on the Cape, after a separation which to her seemed weeks longer than a week; by nightfall they would be in the same bedroom, possibly (at last) in the same bed. Her heart sank at the thought; and instead of feelings of love, she discovered in herself an unexpected anger.

The horn sounded again from the drive below. She picked up her two bags and ran downstairs.

III

THOUGH HIS luggage was already at the station, having been taken down the evening before when he picked up his reservation, and he had no other thing to carry but the book in his pocket, John Grandin decided at the last moment to take a cab, feeling already a holiday mood and anxious to induce as quickly as possible the sense of light-heartedness and irresponsibility befitting a vacation; almost (for cabs were not his habit) a reaching for recklessness and luxury. Yes, "luxury" in the Elizabethan usage too, he told himself, welcoming the thought: an indulging of the senses. Civilians had been asked not to use taxis except in emergencies and ordinarily he observed these conditions, just as he and his wife conscientiously observed all the wartime regulations. But this was an occasion, and different. He waved no to the bus about to pull in at the curb, and hailed a cab.

The day had begun hot. It was June 25, 1943—full summer, with a real summer haze lying over the city, though the season was not yet a week old. He sank back in the taxi as if already in a deck chair and told the driver Grand Central. With a racing of the motor, the cab pulled away from 116th and the Drive.

It was a vacation well earned, much needed, long looked-forward-to, and all the more precious because it was to be short. Other men in the English Department were to be off till September but he had signed up for summer school again, and not entirely because he liked teaching: there was a shortage of men during the war and he had volunteered to help out. As the cab swung down Riverside Drive in the early damp June morning, with the buildings across the river already trembling in waves of heat, the one troubling thought in John Grandin's mind was that he must be back in two weeks.

The thought did not bother him long; for meanwhile

there was to be the holiday with his wife, their first together in some time, away from the children, in a seaside place they had never visited before. Ethel had left a week earlier to take the children to her parents' home in Maine and was to meet him this afternoon at Woods Hole, where they would board the boat to Nantucket—to arrive at Sconset, the hotel folder assured them, in time for dinner. For the duration, Dune House could not send a car; the island bus would meet them at the pier.

"For the duration"—it had a finality, a suggestion of everlastingness, out of all proportion to its literal sense; and the worst of it was, no one needed to complete the phrase. What it referred to was universally understood—as if, in these changing times, only one thing had "duration."

It was the second summer of the war, for other countries the fourth (the seventh for still others): it lived with one now. Sheltered civilian though he was, he felt it keenly, and was increasingly fretted by tiny, irrational, but disturbing obsessions he could not shake, petty irritations of which he was ashamed, in view of the realer upheavals abroad. All life was changing alarmingly fast, including one's very vocabulary. A blouse was not a man's shirt or a woman's waist but the jacket of a uniform; a battle was no longer an engagement between two armies met in the field but the overrunning, by land and sea and air, of whole nations, so that one spoke of the Battle of France or the Battle of Italy—not, as in the old days, the battle of provincial localities such as Soissons or the Marne; and terms like *for the duration* had come to be part of daily speech, so familiar as almost to have lost their original meaning. Added to this was the encroachment of the war on the classroom, in the form of more and more students in uniform or fewer and fewer boys. John Grandin looked out from under the gaily striped awning of the open cab, its scalloped edges flapping noisily in the hot breeze, and willfully did not see the line of destroyers idling on the Hudson, the ugly transports and freighters riding high in the water, awaiting the portentous cargoes that were to be taken, under armed convoy, to secret foreign ports. He saw, but did not think of them. Instead he thought of the Nantucket steamer and wondered what it would be like . . . A man with an accordion would come round, there would be shoeshine boys, pennants would fly and hats would blow away. . . .

. . . And Ethel would be dressed attractively and sensibly in a fall suit, against the possible chill of the ocean breeze, with no flapping taffeta or whipping silk; and later, on the island itself, in a linen shirt and skirt, scorning the halters and shorts, the slacks and dungarees, that other women affected at vacation resorts. During the trip over, she would speak of the boys or question him about the apartment, characteristically avoiding any mention of what would be uppermost in her mind: their holiday together.

The book was crowding his pocket. He pulled it out. Apprehensive that he might leave it on the seat and forget it, he kept it in his hand. Instinctively, from old habit, he held the book upside down, its cover and title against him, so that no one might see what he was reading when he should walk through the station. Why he did this, he could not have said. He would have done the same had it been a popular novel, the diary of a war correspondent, or a learned work on philosophy or metaphysics.

The taxi was moving through Columbus Circle. The city air was close and thick, heavy with damp. What it needed was an island breeze, Grandin thought: Manhattan was hardly one's idea of an island. The motorman of the old-fashioned trolley that rumbled noisily along beside the taxi wore a blue shirt, and his back was black with sweat. Scarcely a man was to be seen in the street with a coat on. Several persons had already lined up at the ticket window of a movie. Imagine going to the movies so early in the morning, he reflected, or in the daytime at all; but of course all they wanted was to get inside, out of the heat, in a place that was air cooled.

The choice had been either two weeks at this time—the last in June, the first in July—or three full weeks later on, between the closing of summer school and the start of the fall semester; but after they consulted the calendar, there had really been no choice at all. A full moon was due a few days hence; it was this which had decided his wife, and himself as well.

Had it been a mistake? Because he did not like to be ruled by such things, he thought with some distaste of the sentimental notion which had done him out of a longer holiday later. But anxious to please, anxious to make her happy (which of course meant his own happiness too), he had gladly given in to his wife. Ethel must have a full moon. Like a romantic schoolgirl she believed that a vacation was not a vacation without a moon; and though she did not express the idea in words, he recognized that her anxiety to be in Nantucket when the moon was full implied a compliment to their relationship, a tacit but perhaps wishful declaration that they were still lovers.

The driver turned down Broadway. He was driving fast, but the air that rushed through the open taxi was no breeze at all. The cavern of the street was like a vacuum, breathless; the flags hanging everywhere were as lifeless as if struck in metal; in another hour the asphalt at the crosswalks would begin softly to give underfoot, showing the print of one's sole, so that the pedestrian would be all but obliged to hurry to the safety of the curb, lest he leave his shoe behind in the hot grip of the muck.

The past week alone, without Ethel, had been a dismal and restless period. Ordinarily they spent scarcely a dozen evenings together a month. With nothing to do—with the certainty that he would soon be at his books—she went to bed early, to doze off over a magazine, while he sat up. Half an hour later he would hear the splashing thump as the magazine slid from the bed, and Ethel, aroused, would turn off her light for the night. Left to himself, with no possibility of interruption now that his wife and children were asleep, he was content to sit in his study midnight after midnight, poring over the delights that would never be exhausted, never begin to be rediscovered or examined enough, no matter how long his days should last. (Though he had smiled at the picture, how well he had understood the man shown in a recent *New Yorker* drawing who, while referring to an open volume, composed a letter which began: "I'm afraid Professor Witherspoon has erred in his quotation of Verlaine. That line, if memory serves, goes rather like this . . .") These nights of reading and study were perhaps his moments of greatest happiness, tinged though they were with an anxiety to get the utmost out of the hurrying hours. At such times he had a prescience of the shortness of life and grudged the hours for sleep. But with Ethel away, even though he had been ignoring her for so long, he had oddly not known what to do with himself; something was lacking, the quiet rooms were too quiet, he was not comfortable there alone. There was no point in going out for an evening walk; the Drive was crowded with sailors and girls and he would only be depressed by the meaningless love-making unrestrained everywhere—a natural accompaniment of the war, of course, but he wanted no part of it, wanted not even to see it. To his surprise he discovered that, though home, he was homesick; ruefully he remembered that during the week just ended he had telephoned Maine five times. True, he had waited till evening when the rates were lower, but it was an expense he could ill afford—besides being, again, an infringement of wartime regulations. Why had he called and what had he got out of it? What had they talked about? What, for that matter, did they ever talk about? It had been a need for communication merely; but the language they were accustomed to using between them, if language it could be called, was not the means for communicating anything.

. . . In moments of time-out such as this, he was given to intense and searching introspection (so far as he understood or was able), honest with himself and willing to face unflattering facts. . . . How much was their marriage founded on habit, how much on love? But how much difference did it make?—Or if love, what kind? Of Ethel there had never been any doubt from the beginning; she was the woman with human needs and human gifts, giving and needing love as the heart gives and needs blood or the lungs air. He had fallen in love with her ten years ago, and though he loved her still, he had always had other interests as well, interests which, the older he grew, were inclined more and more to absorb him entirely, so that he couldn't honestly say whom or what he had ever been able to give himself up to more wholeheartedly than to his work. He had been a good husband to Ethel, faithful and loyal, but his was a life of the mind. He was glad and lucky to be loved, it was what he needed and wanted, but he looked forward to the time when their marriage would become habit even more. Middle age was so much easier than youth; life was more peaceful and better ordered; there were fewer interruptions to his increasingly consuming interests, less effort between him and his wife, almost no need to "keep up." Perhaps time had shown their marriage not to be the ideal promised and expected when they had been bridegroom and bride, but who could say it was less sound or secure than most? That this was nothing to pride himself on, however, he was only too well aware. One can take small credit for contentment.

But as he recalled the almost childlike pleasure with which Ethel had made preparations for the holiday, his heart was touched and a wave of tenderness such as he had not experienced in many weeks swept over him. How could he have gone so long taking their relationship for granted, doing nothing about it, allowing Ethel to wait—and wait —for whatever halfhearted attentions he had time or thought to give? He had fallen into the habit of neglect, the only sin. In working too hard or studying too late, he had lost all track of what they meant to one another. With a sense of relief and gratitude he realized how the vacation was well timed for them both. Nothing so rekindled their interest in each other or renewed the novelty of a love long-accustomed-to as separation, a change of scene, a chance stay in a hotel room, or a visit to just such a holiday place as they would arrive at tonight. Away from home and the children, the two of them alone together in a strange place, the promise of a full moon—it would be like being young again, and he could again be the kind of husband that made Ethel a happy wife.

The taxi had turned off Broadway and was heading east as if toward home—toward Nantucket and a moon and reunion with Ethel. . . . And now unaccountably it occurred to him, by an act of perception more emotional than mental, that it was he who had chosen these two weeks in preference to the longer holiday later without a moon. As if in secret league with his wife, he it was who wanted, who was banking on, the full moon. Aware of a sense of guilt because the intensity and absorption of his studies too often excluded other pleasures, he welcomed (if the truth were known) any stimulus to love. A hotel room, particularly in a summer resort, could be virtually an invitation to erotism, not the less so when a man's companion was his wife. The atmosphere or evidence of strangers in the room before them, the absence of the children and home responsibilities, the locked door, the sense of others sleeping or making love in the adjacent rooms, the automatic scrutiny of the desk clerk which debated whether they were or were not married, the speculating eyes that followed them out of the dining room or the understanding glances of those in the parlor-lobby when they said goodnight and ascended the stairs, had their stimulating effect. Or was all this imagined on his part—the trappings of philandery, promiscuity, the traveling salesman, the unfaithful, or the young unmarried? Whatever it was, imagined or not, it added a pleasant zest to stopping in a hotel, and he went back to his original thought: A hotel room with the white night outside, the moonlight laying across the bed a white blanket alive and luminous with their own movements; or a beach bathed in the dazzling white haze of the moon, the surf prismatic with tumbling cascades of glass; perhaps a silent honeymoon couple lying somewhere near by in the sand; and he and Ethel— The cab had stopped.

"Sorry, Mac." The driver turned his head. "Can't go on, for a minute. Got much time?"

John Grandin leaned forward. "What's the holdup?"

"That." The driver pointed; and he saw what had halted them.

The taxi had stopped on East 44th, no more than a short block from Grand Central but on the wrong side of Madison. Up the avenue from the south, stretched out till it disappeared over the small rise of ground that was Murray Hill whence it came, moved a strange parade of oddly assorted men, two abreast, ambling along the sidewalk in a formless double column which cut off, for the moment, all east- and westbound traffic. He glanced at his watch. "Do you think they'll take long?"

The driver shrugged. "No telling. Sometimes they're quarter of an hour or more."

It was eight-twenty-five. The Cape Codder left in twenty minutes. He may well have had plenty of time but he liked being early. Besides, he had to get his bags from the checkroom. "Perhaps I'd better—"

"Sure, you better walk. Only a step from here, anyway."

"Thanks." Grandin paid, tipped, and left the cab.

He did not mind having to walk the rest of the way. It was, as the driver had said, only a step. What he minded was the interruption; particularly the nature of it. It threw him off.

With other pedestrians, a few of whom now and again left off watching and broke through the marching barrier as if they had no time for this sort of thing and must be about their business, he stood on the sidewalk and watched the parade. He wanted badly to dart or step quickly between the advancing pairs and so be on his way, but he could not bring himself to do it.

It was not a parade in any formal sense. The men were not marching in correct formation along the street but rather shuffled or ambled up the sidewalk in a long straggling group, barely keeping double file. They were men and boys of many ages. Some were in shirtsleeves, some wore sweaters in spite of the heat, a few were well dressed; they carried proper suitcases, or rolls of clothing, or paper bags; and it was clear to even the most casual observer that these men were on their way to the Induction Center on Lexington Avenue—that for them, in short, this was The Day.

It was a sight so discomforting that John Grandin found himself embarrassed. Nor was he the only one. Others in the crowd around him watched the procession with an awkward expression which plainly said they would rather not have seen it. There was a strange silence in the street as the men passed along. Only the very young, only boys and young girls, greeted the draftees with smiles, laughter, or the catchphrases of the hour. The laughter rang hollowly in Grandin's ears. He felt an impulse to plunge through the double column and get on, get away, get out of here—but he stood rooted to the sidewalk, touched with a melancholy respect.

How different this seemed from other wars, other years. He remembered the gaiety of embarking soldiers in the past, the excitement and emotion of the frankly adoring crowd, the wave of solidarity that went out from everyone, till the cheering throng and the departing soldiers themselves were one great loving people, united in a wave of mass affection which for the moment was stronger, more enveloping, than any other emotion in life. It was not so here. There was a look of sheepishness on the faces of the crowd. An embarrassment and faint shame had fallen over the entire street.

Most touching of all was the appearance of the men themselves. It struck straight to his heart, it troubled and upset him. They were sheepish too, and silent. They straggled along hangdog and silly; they stared at the sidewalk in a ludicrous grin, or straight ahead, unseeingly, with jaw set; and occasionally one or two would send a bold defiant glance directly into the eyes of a bystander, as if to say, Go ahead, laugh. And it was by no means comforting to think that in a very few weeks all this would be different, the men would be changed, they would become proud and disciplined and alike, they would fit and belong together so that, in the mass, one could scarcely tell them apart, their native individuality, good or bad, lost in the necessary great machine of which they were to become each a resigned anonymous cog. John Grandin felt so uneasy that he could watch them no longer; and when the final pair of draftees had at last straggled by, he broke into a run toward Grand Central as if he barely had time to catch the last train on the timetable, the last to anywhere.

IV

THE TRAIN down from Boston was hot, noisy, and dirty. Ethel Grandin rode in the daycoach, not because there was no Pullman (she hadn't inquired about that) but because it would have seemed extravagant to pay extra fare for a trip of only three hours; she disliked anything that suggested ostentation or luxury. Her luggage was piled in the rack above her head; one bag remained in the aisle, to the annoyance of passers-by, but that was something she could do nothing about. Each time the conductor came through he frowned darkly and seemed about to reprove this thoughtless passenger for cluttering up the aisle with her baggage; but after one look at the self-contained lady sitting coolly in her seat virtually surrounded by servicemen, he changed his mind and went on. In her lap were the sandwiches she would eat for lunch, and a detective story called *Holy Murder* which she tried at intervals to read. The thickset private who all but leaned against her shoulder and the two sailors sprawled in the seat facing her— one of whom rested his feet on the dingy plush upholstery between her and the soldier—eyed her parcel of sandwiches now and then, her book, or, more frequently, her legs.

That the book did not hold her interest was more her husband's fault than the storyteller's; taking over her thought more and more, he stood between her and attention. She put the book aside and watched the passing landscape, but the soldier thought she was looking at him and returned the look; so she directed her gaze along the car instead, a little above the heads of the two sprawling sailors. One of them, a dark unshaven fellow, was about to fall asleep with his cheek against the windowpane and his mouth open; the other was a blond child in no more than his middle teens. It was he whose neatly polished shoes continually brushed her skirt—purposely or not, she couldn't make out; and when he caught her eye he gave her a sly, insolent, yet boyish smile.

Alan and Ted would have engaged both sailors in conversation at once, and the soldier as well; her husband would have done the same; but she could not bring herself to look squarely at these young men, much less converse with them. Like many women, Ethel Grandin loved the war, loved the fact that her country was in it, loved servicemen and the uniform; her eyes filled up with tears and her breast nearly burst at the sound and sight of martial music and a parade; but if a soldier or sailor accosted her on the street—or sparred for an opening to familiarity, as this boy seemed to be doing—all thought of the uniform vanished instantly and she could only regard him as what he was in actuality: a fresh kid.

Some women would have laughed, thinking it funny, or cute; others might have been flattered. But she was not flattered and she did not think it cute. On the contrary, there was something distinctly unpleasant in the idea that he might think she would be interested in him. She stared with a fixed stare at the far end of the car, determined to think of other things and thus wipe him from her mind.

She was glad she had remembered to send postcards to Alan and Ted during her few minutes in Boston; she must get some more in Woods Hole, and again in Nantucket before leaving for Sconset. She had not wanted the children with her and had only considered the idea at all because her husband had suggested it. She knew well why she preferred to meet him alone today; indeed, in her present confused state, it was the only thing she could be sure of. This was not because in the romantic sense she wanted her husband all to herself; it was because this holiday—possibly even this night—was to decide an issue in their marriage which (in her mind, at least) had reached a crisis. Had the boys been present to take the attention of either their father or their mother, this issue would not be resolved.—But what the "issue" was, or how one could resolve it, she did not know. If she did know, she would be able to meet her husband with a confidence and purpose she was far from feeling.

His hint that she bring the boys with her had not helped any. She was glad he was devoted to their sons, it was something she had always been proud of. So many men were indifferent to their children, particularly when they were little, but he had loved them from the first, had tended and taken care of them, and had shown an

interest in them equal to the interest he brought to his
work. In so far as the children were concerned, she could
ask nothing more. But lately—increasingly so during the
past year or two—Ethel Grandin had begun to feel she
was being left out; he loved the children more than he
loved her, had more need of them in his life, paid more
attention to them than to herself. Time after time recently she had felt a curious sudden pang as she saw him
respond so completely to one of their sons, saw his look
of affection, his entire gratification and satisfaction with
them. The pang was not jealousy; it was the feeling of
being unwanted. She would have given much to know
that he was as pleased with her as he was with them,
and as loved. She had been, in the past.

From the first he had been the only man who had ever
understood her; but did he understand her now, or know
her feelings at all? She remembered so clearly the first
evening he had taken her home from a party, and why.
It had been an embarrassing evening, with several silly
people spoiling what might have been good talk. She
had no social gift in the sense of being able to make
conversation about nothing with men and women she
didn't care for or know well. Present had been a woman
with a flair for dramatics who at one point in the evening began to entertain them all with palm reading. She
took Ethel's reluctant palm in her own, gazed at it with
wide-eyed amaze, and gasped: "Look at that Mount of
Venus! Did you ever see such a Mount of Venus in your
life? I ask you!" Acutely embarrassed, Ethel Cameron
found herself murmuring: "I've been told I have a mur-
derer's or a suicide's hand." The woman gazed at her

darkly, held her speech for a dramatic moment, and then replied: "Well, it's not a *mur*derer's hand."—Of them all, John Grandin had been the only one who understood that Ethel had improvised what she had said (just as the palm reader had improvised her remark about the Mount of Venus) in an effort to take part, help out, give the woman something to go on. It had been silly of her to have suggested such a thing, but she had felt called upon to say something. Neither she nor John Grandin was foolish enough to attach any importance to the woman's reckless interpretation, but they were both incensed by its stupidity. In a few moments they had left the party together; and an hour later (incredible to think of it now, since he had been, till then, such a stranger) they were making love.

That night he had become the single soul in the world whose destiny (oh far more than the children's) was irrevocably linked with hers.

V

COMFORTABLE IN HIS Pullman chair, John Grandin thumbed through *Life*. There was an article about a typical middle-western town, chosen, perhaps, because it was the only town in the middlewest which a survey showed to be "typical"; there was a four-page spread celebrating a new movie; there was a layout illustrating what fashionable women were wearing, these days, while tending their Victory gardens. Picture-of-the-Week was a full-page photograph of four marines lying face down on a South Pacific beach, the pants and shirts tight with the already swelling bodies. He turned from this quickly to think of other matters.

He wondered what the new class would be like in the fall, the class to which he would become official adviser, the individual members whom he would come to know through many a personal conference. He was honored that he had been chosen in this capacity, honored that he should have been considered wise and sympathetic and interested enough to give youth that most difficult of all things, "advice." He felt the responsibility keenly, and hoped with all his heart that he would at least be able to give each of these young people something of what they *thought* they wanted.—He was honored, also, that the work on which he had been spending so much time and thought for so long had at last been accepted by a publishing house. Heaven knew they would get little out of it in the way of financial return; it was a "prestige job" merely, as they said in the trade; but perhaps the few hundred who would be able to bring to the book a tithe of what he himself, after hundreds of hours, had brought to it, would acclaim the work for what he intended it: a serious study of a serious subject, and one worth having been done. He expected no substantial honors from *The Tragic Ideal;* but he did expect—and want—an increase of standing in the profession, and perhaps half a dozen understanding letters which told him their writers knew what he had been driving at, had many times had the same ideas themselves, but had not thought themselves up to expressing these ideas half so well: surely the best tribute a writer can have—all he writes for, in fact.

Forward—at the far end of the train, so to speak—
Ethel stood waiting for him. He wondered whether, as a
surprise, she had changed her mind and brought along
one of the children, after all. It was a vain thought because,
though he had several times hinted it would be so nice
for the boys, she had insisted this was to be his and her
holiday and no one else's. She would be flushed and hot
after the trip from Boston, but her look would be eager,
her whole bearing youthful, as young and attractive and
erect as ever; for her figure was still that of a girl, and
even her face gave little hint that she was over thirty.
After being away from her—seeing her without the children, especially—he was always struck by how young she
looked and congratulated himself on her appearance,
the more so because he was not unaware that in the
frankly appraising eyes of other men he was a very lucky
husband. He was; yet how surprised they would be if they
could know how sometimes a hot and helpless exasperation
amounting to anger rose up in him as he watched the fasti-
dious way in which she ate an olive, or as he saw her
licking an envelope (the little tongue darting in and out
like a lizard's), or when she asked the garageman questions
which she could not hope to understand nor he explain.
. . . But perhaps they would not have been surprised after
all; for these were the unspeakable things in any marriage
—unspeakable literally, because, while a man could speak
of any number of characteristics or habits he did not like
in his wife, he could not say to her: I hate the way you
eat an olive or lick an envelope. To a woman in love with
her husband, this would be the equivalent of his having
said: I hate everything about you—I hate you.

The enormity of the thought astonished him, and then almost made him smile; for of course no such thing was true. It was merely one more instance of the precariousness of marriage, of the misunderstandings to be watched for and the dangers to be skirted. Which is exactly why one did not speak of those tiny exasperations which could seem, at times, to overshadow one's whole happiness. For that matter, the episode past and the cause of the exasperation removed, the anger was nonexistent too, even in memory; and a man could be astonished at the thought. as he was astonished now, and promise himself that the next time it arose, he would be reminded that he had smiled about it in retrospect and could do so again. He got up and went down to the Men's Room for a cigarette.

Luckily he had not brought his book. It would have been impossible to read here. At least half a dozen men were ahead of him, squeezed together on the black settee that ran at right angles to the window or on the small leather seat near the door. With the exception of a good-looking lad in khaki, they were mostly middle-aged. He found a place to stand, out of the path of anyone who might wish to enter the lavatory, and lighted a cigarette.

Of the men present, the one who stood out most prominently was the youth, and not entirely because of the uniform. Rather he was conspicuous because of the concentrated attention and admiration of the others. Grandin did not know what branch of service the young man was in, and so during a pause in the conversation he put the question into words.

One of the men looked up sharply. "Can't you see?

He's a paratrooper!"—and there was a silent exchange of surprise that he could have been so ignorant.

He noticed, then, the patch on the boy's shoulder. He marveled that they should have known to a man. So far as he recalled, he had never before seen that little red-and-white symbol; even if he had, he would not have known what it stood for. Army and Navy insignia (so generally known, it seemed, to all) he was totally unacquainted with—like the mysterious tables of a racing form, who played end for Notre Dame, and batting averages.

The paratrooper was handsome in a lean-faced way, clean-cut, obviously of good family. He spoke readily of himself. After intensive training at a Georgia camp he was on short leave to visit his family at their summer home in Nantucket, where he had spent every summer since he was a child. Here was by no means the cutthroat young villain with an appetite for violence who, one heard nowadays, made the ideal paratrooper. This lad had aristocratic nostrils, fine hands, well-kept nails and teeth. He was personable and well bred, and he talked freely and well, without diffidence, certain that he was interesting to the older men.

That he was not reticent was manifestly not his fault. The others pressed such admiring attention upon him and plied him with so many questions (calculated, usually, to show the knowledge of the questioner) that it would have turned the head of a less disciplined youth. Though nothing was known about him beyond the few facts he had himself disclosed, the paratrooper was already regarded with some awe as a hero. When details of his training were given out, the men exchanged glances and nods among themselves, murmuring audibly to one another, "Nice boy," "Some life," "Must take nerve," and again, "Nice boy," while the young man, pleased, pretended not to hear. John Grandin was touched and disturbed to notice how intense in the crowded little room was the feeling of admiration, even affection, for this youth whom they did not know. It was the uniform, of course, plus the danger; plus the fact that they were not young.

The book he had brought along was lying on the floor by his chair, face down as he had left it. He picked it up, lowered the shade a trifle, and made himself comfortable to read.

He did not know why, of all the volumes in his library, he should have chosen *The Collected Poems of A. E. Housman* for his journey. But it was a book he could always read and reread again, stay with for as little or as long as he liked, dip into anywhere and find something satisfying. So many pages were turned down at the corners and so many lines marked that he was distracted, at first, wondering what particular notion or response in the past had made him cite a certain passage or verse. Phrases were underscored which puzzled him now; try as he might, he could see no reason for most of them. He leafed through the volume, turned back the bent corners, and after a while was able to ignore the markings and enjoy himself.

Enjoyment was hardly the word; he was in for a surprise he would not have believed possible in a book so familiar. The theme of the poems he remembered well, yet suddenly it seemed as if he had never really paid attention; certainly he had never felt its impact so strongly. Reduced to one of its simplest terms, this theme was that there was beauty and a lofty irony in the idea of youth stricken in untimely death, particularly on the battlefield; and it was sounded over and over with a delicate perfection that had once been breath-taking in its art. Verse after witty verse, so satisfying before, now struck him with repulsion. Beneath the grace of the most lightly turned stanza lay a cynicism bitter beyond even the poet's wonderful words: morbid, macabre, necrophiliac—polluted with an amorousness, a virtual lust, for the grave. The verses smelled of rot; no felicity of phrase could mask the underlying sordid horror. The crowning offense, the very climax of the insult, lay in the fact that the theme of dead youth was strummed not only with charm but with wit. Epigrams! His intellect reacted with violence, he who believed in the freedom of art, without regard to subject matter, without restrictions political or otherwise; and he could only come to the shocking conclusion that in wartime such a volume should have been suppressed.—He went down again to the smoker.

There was the same group admiring the handsome communicative paratrooper; but now, to his surprise, a large blond soldier in khaki and heavy GI boots sprang up and offered him his seat. The courtesy was so unexpected that for a moment John Grandin did not know how to deal with it. Of course he declined; he would have felt ridiculous indeed to take the place of a serviceman. Besides, the gesture was so patently that of youth to age, a young man's politeness to an elder, that he was by turns amused and embarrassed. In their brief exchange he got the impression that the big soldier was probably from one of the daycoaches, come up to see what a Pullman was like, and not enjoying it much; he was uneasy and awkward, and seemed to sense keenly his anomalous position. Grandin further noted that the fellow had blue eyes, tawny curling hair bleached on top as if by long exposure to the sun, a well-tanned face; and he was, by any standards, enormous.

One of the men left and he found a seat by the window, next to the soldier. He felt the pressure of the thick shoulder against his own; he did not like sitting that close to other men, especially strangers, but there was no room to pull away. The paratrooper, primed by his admirers, still held forth. The soldier listened with the others; he followed the paratrooper's words with aloof but polite attention, his hands clasped tight over a wide knee, his elbows rigid at his sides, as if trying to take up as little room as possible. John Grandin felt his tension and he wanted to say: Relax, soldier; so long as you're in uniform, you're more than all right with this crowd.

There could hardly have been a greater contrast between the awkward private and the confident, rather sophisticated paratrooper. The difference was so marked that the latter drew all the admiration, and the men paid small attention to the uncomfortable fellow too big for his clothes who sat hunched up on the settee. Whatever exchange of conversation there may have been between him and the others, or between the two soldiers, must have proved unsatisfactory, for the paratrooper dominated the little room as before, as if he were the only uniform present. His cigarette finished, Grandin dropped it into the cuspidor and went out; and as he left, the blond private flashed him a painfully polite and eager smile.

The train was moving slowly through a fashionable parklike community and from the window he saw many pairs of white figures leaping about a series of tennis courts which, unless one looked sharply and concentrated on a certain court and quartet of players, might have been taken for a Manhattan playground alive with tenement children. Tennis balls zigzagged across his vision, blurred by the moving train till they resembled streamers of white tape; and John Grandin was reminded of the continuous tennis match outside his classroom which had had such a distracting effect on him all that spring. . . .

On one of the first warm days of April he had become aware of the *denk-dunk* of tennis balls being batted back and forth beneath the room where he lectured. It was a pleasant sound; far from interrupting him, it brought a rather poetic accompaniment to his talk which was quite in keeping with the warm sunshine streaming in and the first sensual stirrings of summer which could be felt on the air. Each morning he meant to go to the window and look out at the players when class was dismissed; but for several days, in the intervals of changing classes, he forgot to do so. Then one morning about a month ago he stepped to the window. Twelve young men were playing on the three courts below; they wore white tennis shoes, thick white socks, and white shorts, nothing more; their shoulders were already bright pink with the beginnings of their summer tan. Involuntarily he moved a step back into the dark of the room and stood erect, looking obliquely down through the window at the thrusting lunging arms, the play of muscle across the lean backs, and the almost formless legs that seemed to have been fashioned cleanly and sparely, like pistons or driving rods, for action only; and he surprised in himself a stern disapproval. In his day, even on a campus that was not coeducational, shorts—or at least shorts only—had not been allowed. His irritation did not spring from priggishness. On the contrary, it arose from a full awareness of the Greeklike charm of the scene below: it was a Puritan disapproval because the sight was much too attractive, too pleasant to look at, there was work to be done, and this was no time for play. The vivid scene below started up a swarm of sensual images in his mind, images of youth, exercise, the outdoors which he had ignored too long, and impatience for summer to come. In short, it distracted him. Hundreds walked by the courts and gave no more than a passing glance at the players; but for the single passer-by who might be too absorbed by the spectacle—or for the one who, standing at his classroom window, was thrown off from his work—the costume was regrettable. Depressed, he went back to his desk in the semi-dark room to await the next students; and for days, thereafter, the *denk-dunk-denk* of tennis ball and racket continued to provide a kind of soft antiphonal background to his lectures. He wondered if the students were aware that he kept to his theme with difficulty; and for the remainder of the term he did not once go to the window to look down again at the players. . . .

VI

A DOOR BANGED and banged at the rear of the daycoach; torn tabloids drifted or slid along the gritty linoleum of the aisle; a hot breeze smelling of coal gas swept through the car. The young sailor with the wise look recrossed his legs and slumped farther down in the seat, resting almost on the small of his back, shifting his buttocks under him in a suggestive fashion till the flyless front of his dark pants was stretched tight across his abdomen and groin. He folded his arms. Ethel Grandin knew he was looking at her with a grin, challenging her to look back. She scanned the aisle for a vacant seat. The car was full. She closed her eyes, like the sailor nodding against the windowpane, and pretended to doze.

Ethel Grandin not only loved her husband, she was still in love with him. There had never been anyone else and there never would be. It did not belittle either his love or hers to say that she loved him because he had been nicer to her than any other man she had ever known. This was the simple truth; and for a woman who had an inborn timidity of the male, it counted for a good deal. Curiously enough she possessed a real affinity with men and vastly preferred their company to women, but she was by nature afraid of them and had been afraid ever since, at thirteen, when she came home from school one noon with her underpants mysteriously bloodied, her mother had grasped her by the shoulders and dreadfully, savagely, threateningly muttered: "From now on don't you ever dare let a boy touch you, do you hear? *Don't you ever dare!*" The overheard conversations of other girls, much later, had somewhat cleared up the meaning of what her frightened mother had been unwilling to explain; but the fear of men took root, persisted, and she couldn't truly say she had wholly got rid of it to this day. This timidity did not matter so long as she had—and knew she had—her husband's love. Not knowing, her confidence in herself was rapidly vanishing.

With him she had never been afraid, not even from the first. The fact that it was she he had chosen established her as a woman of importance, if only to one man; and his passion had awakened undreamed-of possibilities. At the difficult beginning of their love-making he had been the soul of tact and caution, so unlike other men she had heard of. Under his caresses she opened up to him and for the first time in her life came into her own: alive, aware, confident of the future and her role in it. In a matter of weeks she changed. No one could have told her in her teens that she would one day sleep with a man she was not married to, but she had slept with John Grandin, wanting it as much as he did, with no sense of sin whatever (despite her mother's fearful warnings), scarcely even a sense of surprise, except the surprise of discovering that the act of love was by no means an easy matter.

At first this had consisted of hours and aching hours of straining together, yearning for the next step yet dreading what it might be, then fancying in herself a hopeless despairing inadequacy. She remembered one terrible night when suddenly she had broken away from his embrace and turned to the wall, to sob out her grief and shame alone; and when he, astonished, had pulled her to him again and tenderly whispered, "Darling . . . what's the matter," her tears flooded his shoulder as she poured forth her misery because the act of love had gone forward so painfully, with no hope even yet that it would be attained: "I'm not right for you, there must be something wrong with me . . ." But he had comforted her, whispering, "Darling, don't you know I love you besides that? It doesn't matter about tonight . . ." Only much later did she realize fully how gentle, controlled, and considerate he had been. Regardless of her reticences or inexperience, most men would have carried through quickly, brought the matter home and achieved their satisfaction, with small regard for the girl they might be hurting or losing. Not he; he had loved her enough to wait. By some almost feminine intuition he seemed to know how it was with her, and he couldn't have been kinder or more patient with her ignorance. It was one of the things she had always been grateful to him for. At that most important moment of her life he had not failed her; and the result was: she fell in love with him, and had never fallen out of love since.

The pleasures of love had soon turned into the solider pleasures of marriage. About sex she had known nothing. Even in college, when the girls in the dormitory talked of such matters, she had left the room—priggishly, perhaps, but she couldn't have helped herself. Whatever she knew now she had learned from her husband; and once the step was taken, there had been so much to learn. Perhaps it was an immature or a childish thought, but with a man who loved her, a husband of one's very own, it was for the first time wonderful to be a grownup, free to abandon oneself to love without fear of parental disapproval, without their even knowing. And she had been good for him; she knew she had always been good for him. To deny this now, or to reproach herself because it had been otherwise, would have been to deny all that had been between them in the past. Because of this, what had been happening lately had confused and humiliated her, so that she was

fast losing the belief in herself which she had found only
in her marriage.

Where had she failed? For somewhere in their marriage there was failure. How otherwise could she have
reached such a state of uncertainty? Her husband seemed
to be going from her, a fact she had only fully realized this
week. Had he lost interest? Didn't their love mean to him
what it did to her? Fatigue of marriage was a deadly thing,
but others had weathered it before and they could
weather it too—provided they knew what the matter was
beyond mere fatigue, restlessness, boredom. She had as
much to give him as ever but he seemed to have forgotten
it was there. In what way was the failure hers? She had no
means of knowing because she had no clue. She only knew
that this week—this week in Maine away from the husband whose presence (because she loved him) prevented
her so often from speaking her mind—she had been able
to review the past few years of their marriage as if in a
new light, and the conclusions she had arrived at were
frightening and upsetting. In spite of the dreadful uncertainty of many many nights alone in her bed while her
husband sat up in his study, she had still thought—because
it had become her habit to think so—that she was happily
married. Now she had discovered bitterly that her role in
his life was little more than that of housekeeper.

VII

IN THE CHAIR behind him, someone was talking about
swing. "You ought to study the new forms," the voice said,
"you really ought. Why, Lionel Hampton's recording of

Central Avenue Breakdown is as complicated and intricate as anything in Bach, père *or* fils. People don't realize!" John Grandin picked up his copy of *Life* magazine.

It fell open to the Picture-of-the-Week, the full-page photograph of the four dead marines, and this time he looked at it carefully and thoughtfully. The bodies lay face down on the beach, very near to the water's edge, at rest at last in the sand that was so soon to pack them in. The beach was strewn with the broken fronds of palm trees, and in the background could be seen the bare stalks of the trees themselves, pitifully ragged and ravaged. A few feet beyond the inert bodies, the small last wash of the breakers slid nearer and nearer and spread itself in the sand. The palpable stillness of the scene, its unutterable loneliness, shrieked of the fury that had raged across the beach a short time before. But the fury was over, now, and all that had remained was the cameraman. Graphically, beyond the power of any words, the solitariness of death was brought home with a peculiar, a melancholy beauty—the collective dying that had become four lonely deaths, infinitely moving because each marine was now unaware of the photographer, of the beachhead won or lost, of the waves sliding close by, of each other, and of the unknown spectator, unmoved or unstrung, who regarded them from the comfort of a parlor-car chair. He closed the magazine and picked up his book.

Suddenly he was ashamed of his reaction against the poems and the poet, ashamed that it could have been so violent; it had gone against every tenet of his background and taste. Who knew better than he that the theme of death-in-youth was more "suitable" to poetry and had always been more attractive to poets than any other theme in human experience; and while the heart was wrung, the aesthetic sense was exalted and satisfied. Let the artist make epigrams, even, if he chose, so long as the result was beautiful like its subject . . . *Here dead lie we because we did not choose To live and shame the land from which we sprung. Life, to be sure, is nothing much to lose; But young men think it is, and we were young* . . . For centuries poets had been half in love with easeful Death; and the fact that the musèd rime was well turned or the phrase felicitous by no means denied, but enhanced rather, the ironic or tragic emotion of the artist. Even so rugged a poet as his beloved Walt Whitman, who scorned the dandified decadence he had been complaining of, had celebrated the beauty of death in many a challenging manly chant . . . And was it Bach père or Bach fils, he asked himself with a smile, who had composed *Come, Sweet Death?*—His spirits lifted; he had, for the time being, recovered.

There was a stir in the car. A number of passengers had risen to look out the windows; John Grandin rose with them. The train was rumbling over a long steel bridge. Below, moving slowly down the river to the Sound, was a submarine. For a moment it was directly beneath the train, at right angles to the bridge; then it slid into full view, longer, slenderer, riding higher in the water than he would have expected. It had been painted almost a pearl-gray and looked brand new. He wished Alan could see this; yes, and Ted too; Alan might have known her type and tonnage and could have named, perhaps, her sister craft. He could see several men in dungarees and undershirts standing along the narrow deck; their red arms flashed in the sun as they waved upward at the train. One man jumped up and down and clowned for his admiring audience; a few others stood silent, with arms akimbo, possessed by who knew what grave, envious, or scornful thoughts? The passengers remained standing at the windows for some moments after the submarine had passed from view on its way out to sea; and when they resumed their places, two or three involuntarily exchanged glances.

. . . Alan collected in a notebook the names that pilots gave their bombers, and had added some of his own: *Hell's Angel, The Avenger, All-Out Alan.* He passionately hoped the war would last long enough for him to get in. Ted, who had never heard of peacetime, believed it would last forever. He went into the diner and found a seat.

The steward placed him at a table facing a couple just finishing their meal. They were about his own age. The man shot him what appeared to be a hostile glance and in the next instant said pleasantly, "Lovely day." He introduced himself and his wife as Mr. and Mrs. Howard; or rather, he added, Sarah and Bill.

Though somewhat given to facetiousness, Mr. Howard was friendly, natural, and very attentive to Mrs. Howard. As Grandin took them in, he gathered the impression that here was a man in love with his wife, a longtime lifetime love. There was about him a buoyant spontaneity, almost an animal good nature, that would probably keep the Howards in love with one another till Kingdom Come. His wife was about forty, tall, with a large and rather petulant face. The eyes and eyebrows wore an expression which seemed to indicate a perpetual disdain, as if she lamented that nothing was good enough, why did one have to put up with things, what *ailed* people? She was a woman loved and so made no effort.

"This cake is plain stale," she said to her husband. "But of course if we complain, they'll only tell us there's a war on."

"Now Mama," Mr. Howard said.

On the way back to his chair, Grandin stopped in the smoker for a cigarette. A bluff hearty man came in chewing a toothpick. Catching sight of the paratrooper he exclaimed, "Why Jimmy, how are you, boy? Didn't think we'd be seeing you this summer a-tall. Drop around to the Srail Club some afternoon and we'll open a keg of nails."

"I've only got an eight-day leave, Judge, I won't be coming out to Sconset. Not much, is it?"

"Oh I don't know," the Judge said slowly, looking slyly around the group. "Eight days wouldn't be nothin' a-tall in Sconset. But for Nantucket it's plenty," and he winked broadly at Grandin.

The paratrooper protested with spirit; and as if by prearranged mutual agreement, the two of them fell into a lively argument as to the relative merits of their respective towns on the island, an argument that seemed to be a virtual routine, almost a ritual, practiced by old-time residents of Nantucket. Though good-humored enough, the discussion continued at such heat and length that Grandin, on finishing his cigarette, was glad to get back to his Pullman chair.

The moving landscape beyond the window was in-

viting, typical, and rural. It was not the kind of New England he had known in Maine, during his few visits to his
wife's parents, nor in Williamstown, where he went to
college. Here were long rolling fields, very little forest,
great sandy wastes studded with pine scrub, and always
there was the feeling of the sea somewhere, not far away
—almost the sound of the sea itself. Unaccountably John
Grandin felt a nostalgia for the Atlantic island he was yet
to know. He leaned back in the comfortable chair in the
hopes of a nap.

Gazing idly along the car with half-closed eyes, he felt
himself already very near asleep, assisted in this by the
swaying motion of the train. Passengers came and went in
his dimming vision but he scarcely noticed, now, who or
what they were. He wondered what the hotel room would
be like; he thought of Ethel. . . .

. . . At the recollection of the way her knowing hands
would suddenly grip him across the small of the back at the
climax of their love-making—the way she would cry out
the single syllable of his name in a half gasp, half whisper
—his legs went limp and his heart jumped. At such times,
all else was right for days after; he was a different husband
then, happy in his work, happy with his home, his children, his wife, seeing his wife in fact (then and only then)
as the ideal companion of his life, the woman he loved
because she made of him a man fulfilled. Sex, ignored,
stood like a chilling stranger between them, too important,
too demanding; satisfied, it became one with the other
comforting pleasures of ordinary existence, scarcely
thought of; the tensed atmosphere of their life together
cleared up, humor was restored, a perfect balance in the

routine of their relationship once more maintained itself,
so that it almost seemed (then and only then) as if their
love had little to do with sex. In all his life he had found
no better, no other love. How unfair, then, to make love
to Ethel only when circumstance chanced to place them
together in the same bed or room, as it would tonight.
They loved one another, they had no one else, and life
was so short. It was so easily within his grasp to give Ethel
the happiness she wanted and needed, and thus re-establish his own happiness too; cruel to make her wait, and
wonder, and so seldom know. What a waste to spend his
nights poring over the same familiar books while his marriage went stale, forgotten by him, a rebuke and a humiliation to her. For the first time he was glad he had not
insisted that she bring the children with her to Sconset,
for now the holiday ahead seemed to promise him the
opportunity of recapturing the wife he had been too long
without. With a kind of excitement like youth, he dwelt
on what their night together in the hotel room would be
like, their week, their two weeks. Eagerly he welcomed
the chance to make it up to her, to wipe out his long indifference. Love-making could be a habit one could fall into
again as much as the habit of neglect; and when Ethel
returned with him to New York, he would abandon his
couch in the study and move back to her room, their old
room, where he had once belonged.

Curiously his new resolution seemed to give him the
first peace of mind he had had in many months. Certain
of what the night held in store for him, he was content
now for the tiresome trip to run its course, even if the
train were hours late in arriving. He pressed deeper into

the comfort of his chair, then relaxed his every limb and muscle in the effort to induce sleep. Drowsy, he was about to drop off, but through half closed eyes he saw the familiar figure of the big blond private who had offered him his seat in the smoker appear at the end of the car and start coming his way.

. . . Odd that he should have thought of the fellow as familiar; he had seen him only once before, and then for only a few moments. Now he realized he had not noticed, or for that matter missed, the presence of the soldier during his last few visits to the smoker. Perhaps he had been there, perhaps he had not. But in encountering him again, he experienced a recognition, a comfortable sense of friendliness toward him. It may have been the young man's awkwardness, his appearance of being out of place, which had aroused his unconscious sympathy. He watched the fellow moving clumsily along the aisle, his great shoulders slightly raised, his arms outthrust to catch his balance as the car moved and swayed around a curve. The face looked typically American, the very personification of the American boy—the contemporary hero; so much so that he ceased almost to be an individual: he was the epitome of a type.

As he reached Grandin's chair, the towering figure gave a lunge and the hand caught hold of the luggage rack above Grandin's head just in time to prevent his crashing against the window. From this precarious position he looked down and smiled. John Grandin could not, for the moment, smile back; he was too struck by what was surely the most utterly winning smile he had ever seen in his life. When he recovered, the soldier had already gone on.

He sat up, awake now. After a moment he picked up the magazine and turned again to the Picture-of-the-Week.

Violence in a tropical setting was a commonplace, nowadays, so that an island beach, far from being the romantic image that men longed to escape to, had become a symbol of death. Characteristically he speculated on what these boys had been through or left behind, boys who could not have dreamed in the safety of their beds in their parents' homes that they would end up in this out-landish way, riddled with bullets on a beach they never heard of—young men who had so much to give to love and who would never make love again. That marine in the foreground hugging the earth with an almost amorous concentration, the booted feet toed in and the left arm cushioning the cheek for his long assignation—he would like to have been there with him, to lug the death-heavy fellow farther up the sand out of reach of the creeping tide, there to cover him over with a blanket, perhaps, and to stay with him through the night.

. . . But what need had he of blanket or vigil? Five minutes after the picture was taken, no doubt, the medical corps had hauled away the body, along with dozens of others, and the photographer had sent off the film to his paper, wondering whether this one would turn out to be the lucky shot out of hundreds of similar shots which he had been sending home since the campaign began. He closed the magazine and put it away for good; and as he did so, he was aware of a desire to turn back to the picture again and again.

VIII

ETHEL GRANDIN was aroused by a cry in the car. An infant
a few seats away had set up a piercing catlike waul, and
the distraught mother tried to shush her child with loud
hissing sounds like escaping steam. The young sailor
caught her eye and gave her a wink. "Some fun, eh lady?"
She smiled politely, then picked up her book and pretended to read. There was nothing on earth she had to
say to him—small talk, even with intimates, came hard
with her—and whatever he might want to say to her
would, she felt, be embarrassing and familiar.

If her husband had already become indifferent or
preoccupied, what would he not be like when he assumed
his new faculty duties next semester, giving so much of
himself in conference with the individual students of the
new class? And if the new book were to become a success
(which of course she hoped for), his interests would be
further drawn to other fields, fields in which she could not
follow him, in which she had no part. She had read the
manuscript and been impressed by its scholarship, but
what had impressed her even more was that she did not
know this man. And yet, though it was bitter proof that
he lived in a world of ideas and interests far from her own,
it did not seem even remotely to explain why he had lately
been ignoring her so utterly.

Defensively, she had tried to become as aloof as he.
As a kind of test, she had taken to going to bed without
kissing him good night. She merely said "Good night" and

left the room. Surprisingly, he had protested. It was unheard of; didn't he count for anything, didn't she want to
kiss him good night—didn't husbands and wives always, as
a matter of course if for no other reason, kiss one another
good night? It seemed to have become a symbol to him
(as to her) of their growing estrangement; if they abandoned the good-night kiss they might as well openly admit
failure and give up. So she made it a point again of going
up to him before she left the room and kissing him on the
mouth. But an artificiality had crept into it which puzzled
her. She felt none of the old pleasure, because of some
withdrawal in him which she could not but reflect. Indeed,
she experienced an involuntary impulse to draw back at
the moment, or kiss him coldly as a sister or cousin, so that
there was no satisfaction in it for either of them beyond
the observance of the formality; and after a few nights of
this, the good-night kiss was abandoned again as a failure
—with what feelings on his part she would perhaps never
know.

It did not even seem to be resignation; yet a self-
conscious and curious pretense constrained them both,
now, as the indifferent good nights were said. She had only
contempt for those husbands and wives who constantly
kissed one another in the presence of others, as if publicly
to declare, out of some basic insecurity or make-believe,
that they were still in love or that a nonexistent love still
flourished. This custom, so prevalent in American life,
seemed to her suspect; in the privacy of her own living
room, with no one looking on, she could no more have
brought herself to do such a thing if her feelings were not
in it than she could have flown; and from hating herself

for keeping up the pretense, she would have despised her husband as well, had she suspected he was playing up for her benefit or his. Now when she left the room for bed with her book or magazine she merely said "Good night" in strained tones which may or may not have been lost on him; and he, behind a mask of casualness better than her own, replied from his chair, "Good night—sleep well." How these good nights had changed from what they had been like in the past, only he or she (out of happy memories that recalled moments far different) could have said.

Ethel Grandin had no patience with women who complained that they had given the best years of their lives to their husbands. Of course they had!—and why not?— and what else did a woman want or expect to do? For that matter hadn't he, if the phrase must be used, given his best years too? They had been wonderful years, but time was fast slipping away; in the phrase equally common, she was getting no younger. If the marriage she had been building on for so long was to come to nothing, what would become of her? She was thirty-four, not old; but life would offer her no second chance. Nor did she want another, provided her marriage could be restored. If she must face the fact that she was no longer needed or wanted—children or no children, she would rather die.

Could she leave him—take the boys and leave? It was impossible. Regardless of her unhappiness, it wasn't right to think of herself before the children. Alan and Ted loved their father; and for her to deprive them of his love because he had become indifferent to her was the kind of selfishness it was not in her to give in to. It was impossible also that she could ever love another man. She was the kind who gave only once, and all; there was nothing left for her if she was not wanted by the one man she loved. The uncertainty of whether or not he still loved her was undoing her; interiorly she was going to pieces, developing a self-distaste which very possibly contributed to their dilemma as much as his own indifference, for he was a perceptive man and saw these things. She was never able to keep from him her smallest emotional reaction. From knowing her so well, he had acquired an intuition of her slightest mood or change of mood; and his growing knowledge that she was afraid must have made him despise her the more.

If she wasn't still in love with him, it wouldn't matter; perhaps then she could accept the situation, fulfill her duties as a mother, and go on for the children's sake. But passionately she loved her husband: she had belonged to him too much, and been a part of him too long, not to.

During the spring they had had a small quarrel, a quarrel in which each of them, as if by secret agreement, had skirted the real issue that was too dangerous to uncover. Irrelevantly she had found herself saying: "What about me, I've got to get *some* happiness out of life, I can't go on like this!" And he had answered, sarcastically but all too truly: "The trouble with you is, you can't accept the plain facts of life. Look at other people! Who do we know that's happily married? Not one couple. Take your own father and mother. Do you think for one moment they're happily married?" "That makes no difference," she had cried helplessly, "I don't care about 'other people,' no, not even Papa and Mama. I won't *be* like other people—life's too short!" He took his time to light a cigarette and then answered: "Tolstoy says the chief cause of unhappiness in marriage is because people have been taught to think marriage means happiness. The more happiness we expect from marriage, the more we suffer. We expect the impossible, and aren't prepared for the usual." "Rubbish!" "Tolstoy rubbish? Now, really! He also says—" In anger she cut him short: "To hell with Tolstoy, I'm talking about me!" But, defeated, she had left the room.

In spite of his mysteries or aloofness, he was an honest man, more honest than most; he always had been. Sometimes, without her being prepared for it in the least, he struck straight at the heart of the matter with a statement utterly disarming in its candor—a statement, indeed, which might have been the climax of an hour's discussion instead of (as it seemed) a single isolated thought, almost an irrelevant one. Apropos of nothing that had been mentioned before, he recently said: "Darling, if I forget, why don't you come to me? I get busy or tired, I work too late, it's my fault entirely; please believe me, all I need is to be reminded, occasionally. You know I want you." Though casual enough, this little one-sided conversation had been unprecedented in its boldness, in its revelation of his own turmoil, and in its truth for them both; and it remained one-sided for the simple reason that it had said everything, leaving nothing whatever for her to say. She found herself completely at a loss for words; she was genuinely touched, so much so that her heart went out in pity for him far more than for herself. The simplicity and honest appeal of the revelation barely allowed her, at the time, to register its true meaning. Only later did she fully realize what he had so plainly said: it could be up to her as much as to him. But out of some unshakable pride she couldn't have done it, regardless of how many nights, sleepless, she had waited for him. She had to know she was wanted for herself, not because he thought he ought to want her; she couldn't bear the feeling (oh, shameful!) that he might be going to bed with her just to be nice. All the strictures of her virgin days would have come back had she thought so, and more than ever she would have become a woman unloved and cold.

It was long past time to eat; she unwrapped the sandwiches. Assuming an expression in which nothing could have been misconstrued, she said to the boy opposite to her: "Wouldn't you like some of this?" He pulled his feet down from the seat, sat up, and leaned forward with a grin of anticipation. "Okay if you can spare it, lady." "Certainly. Wake up your friend, maybe he'd like some too." "Nah," the boy said, slapping the air with a downward gesture of the hand, "leave him lay. He's full of booze anyways." The private was getting off at Middleboro and expected to eat there, so she and the young sailor ate alone. In spite of his smiles and grins, she did not converse with him further.

One of the things that had lately seemed to come between her and her husband was the war, which was odd because they were completely united both politically and patriotically. While she thrilled to victories abroad, avidly read details of the agonizingly slow progress in the Pacific or pored over maps or photographs in the papers, he became increasingly depressed. He seldom discussed it; she knew he suffered as if personally over the wanton slaughter; but the extent to which he had been keeping his feelings to himself was brought home to her by an episode which occurred a few weeks ago. Though he knew nothing about this—didn't know she had discovered it, that is—it had revealed to her his tragic and even morbid concern, or perhaps his sense of guilt for being out of it, his identification with all that was going on abroad without him.

One morning when he was at class she had gone into his study to tidy up. She knew how he hated having his study cleaned; the regular cleaning woman, for example, was not allowed in the place. On the other hand, a man could let his workroom go just so long; there came a time when someone had to step in and clean up for him, his preferences in the matter notwithstanding. She opened the windows and vacuumed the carpet; she dusted the mantel, emptied the ash trays, and put back books and papers strewn about the floor or left lying in a disordered heap next to his favorite armchair. The desk was forbidden ground; he was right in refusing to let anyone disturb the papers and reference books he had been using. But if she were careful to dust around the edges without leaving evidence that she had done so, his worktable would be the more efficient for it. She finished dusting across the back and sides of the desk, and then, to complete the job, she picked up the desk blotter to dust underneath.

It was a sizable affair, mounted, with leather corners; on its rectangular expanse were a number of scraps and notes meaningless to her. She lifted the blotter by its substantial binding and, carrying it flat so that nothing would be disarranged, set it on the couch where he slept. As she did so, she uncovered a clipping which had been tucked under the blotter out of sight—some months ago, from the looks of it, though its subject was timely enough.

It was a photograph from a newspaper, two or three columns wide, neatly cut out with a pair of scissors which had eliminated the unnecessary caption, for the picture spoke all too plainly for itself. It showed a battle-exhausted marine lying in a burlap bunk fast asleep, his right arm (as if by habit) around a heavy Garand rifle, a packed kit of some kind resting on his chest, and his left hand relaxed and limp on his stomach—the only part of him which did not seem, in spite of his dead sleep, tensed and ready for instant action. He wore a wrinkled shirt open at the throat and loose tropical shorts exposing thick bare thighs and knees, slightly hairy and probably dirty. He had a couple of days' growth of beard so that a potential mustache of some size and width was plainly outlined. His eyebrows were raised, his eyes closed in sleep; his nose was short, almost pug; the mouth was wide and attractive, with tightly closed lips; the chin was strong. He was a very rugged, masculine, and mature-looking young man, possibly a good deal younger than he looked; but the chief effect of the picture was one of utter exhaustion, with the fellow passionately at rest (perhaps dreaming of home, she thought sentimentally), yet prepared to spring to automatic action the moment the siren started screaming. Dustcloth in hand, she stood looking down at the picture, absorbed and moved. The relaxed curling hand showed a dark fuzz on the back; the rifle must have rested heavy on the weary shoulder and in the crook of the arm. Her heart went out to the dog-tired marine, dead to the world, and, for the time being, blessedly at rest and safe: she would like to have lifted the rifle gently from off his shoulder, oh carefully so as not to disturb him, and then stand by to see that the alarm of the siren, which would so rudely ruin everything, was not sounded. The photograph had a compelling beauty; realistic in the extreme, yet poetic, it evoked the *Drum-Taps* poems of Whitman of which her husband was so fond (*O Tan-Faced Prairie Boy*).—And at this reminder of her husband and where she was, she put the clipping back on the flat of the desk and replaced the blotter as before.

If he had been so moved by a picture in the paper as to go to the trouble of cutting it out and saving it (the picture was a very moving one indeed, no one could have blamed him), why hadn't he said anything about it? But that was a secondary consideration; the first was that her husband was troubled and secret. She knew he had long been obsessed by the war; she did not know what private thoughts or emotions possessed him during those midnight hours spent in his study. As she settled the blotter and looked to see that his desk was as he had left it, she knew instinctively that she would never speak to him of finding the clipping unless he spoke of it first.

The memory of that discovery puzzled and disturbed her more than she could easily have said; she hated knowing anything about her husband which he had not told her himself: it was as if she had uncovered an emotion so private that she had no right even to know of it. Here was one more instance of the fact that they were drifting away from one another: living together as closely as ever, yet worlds of emotion apart. Whatever saddened or troubled him, she wished she knew of it. But this was something

he apparently did not want, else why would he have kept
to himself such a simple thing as a clipping from a newspaper? More than ever she dreaded meeting him this afternoon, and at once hated herself for the thought, for this
was what they had been looking forward to for so long.
The whole unspoken intention of the holiday had been
to bring them together again in a kind of second honeymoon—they had even purposely chosen a period in which
there would be a full moon. But as the train neared its
destination she had the awful feeling that two individuali-
tics (formerly one, but now separate) were moving rapidly
toward one another out of an almost chemical necessity;
and inevitably, beyond her power to control it, there was
bound to be but one result when they met: collision, and
explosion.

IX

"Woods Hole—all out!"

In the pleasant confusion that followed, everyone forgot everyone else. The friendships of the journey were
abandoned in the business of the moment, the matter of
luggage and things to attend to. John Grandin felt a kind
of excitement he had not felt in years, the excitement of
arriving at a new place. Added to this was the pleasure of
knowing that in a few moments, only a very few moments
more, he would be seeing Ethel.

The boat was in from New Bedford. Riding high at
the end of the pier, sending up great gusts of black smoke
into the bright midafternoon air, it shut off all view of the

wide seascape and the open sea beyond. Curiously it resembled a piece of stage scenery, a prop boat in an operetta; if one ventured behind the painted canvas, stage hands would be discovered, shooting craps among the slats and ropes. Heedless that it might be illusion, the passengers streamed off to the steamer.

John Grandin stood in the cinder path, waiting. The Boston train was due at any moment. The Howards passed. Catching his glance, Mrs. Howard gave him a meaningless exaggerated shrug, as if in answer to a question she hadn't quite been able to get—one of those pointless gestures in passing which are yet a kind of social exchange.

Down the track in the opposite direction from which he had come, rolling slowly along under the great willow and cottonwood trees, its chuffing panting engine sending the hanging branches swinging upward, came the train from Boston. With gigantic sighs and groans it rolled to a stop. In the pleasantest agitation, he waited while the passengers climbed down. Seeing that the Nantucket boat was under steam, they hurried along the pier as if they expected the gangplank to be thrown back on the landing at once. Grandin stood watching for his wife. As the crowd thinned out, he was gradually filled with misgiving. Was it possible she had missed connections in Boston? The last of the passengers had left the train; workmen had begun at one end to sweep out. Bitterly disappointed, he looked up helplessly at the empty cars. There was still no Ethel in sight.

Worse than disappointed, he was angry. His chagrin turned at once to anger that Ethel should have been so careless as to miss the train in Boston; it was so unlike her. *Now* what was he going to do? Wait all night in Woods Hole till the next train in the morning? He gazed miserably at the steamer, its decks crowded to the rail, and felt helpless to decide what ought to be done. It was a bad start for the long-promised holiday, perhaps even a bad sign—or was there going to be any holiday at all? He could never have anticipated such a turn of events as this; he did not know when he had been so disappointed. Husbandlike, it did not occur to him to worry; his only feeling was one of anger that she had been late in Boston.

Unwilling that anyone should be witness to his disappointment, he turned his back on the steamer, took Ethel's letter from his book, and pretended to read it, as if looking up some information. At this moment of his exasperation, his wife stepped out from behind the last car. Smiling faintly, she came up the cinder path. All his anger at once fell away as he realized what had happened; in her confusion, she had got off the wrong side of the train.

"I didn't know," she said as she came up. "They opened the doors at both sides and—how was I to know?"

He laughed. "Darling, I'm not blaming you. I'm only too glad you're here at all!"

"Thanks." As he kissed her, she stiffened slightly, her shoulders back. He knew she had never really liked being kissed in public but he paid no attention and kissed her again.

"If you knew what a bad moment I had, when everyone got off and no Ethel."

"I'm glad," she said.

But as they started toward the steamer, he sensed that something was wrong.

He refused to bother his head about it now; there were too many other things to attend to. He was only aware of irritation again because, as always, she had picked a fine moment to be difficult. Maybe he was imagining it. But now he heard her clear her throat. No, he wasn't imagining anything. There was trouble ahead; and his heart sank as he realized it would be hours and hours before he would even know what the matter was.

He tried a joke. "It isn't the book, is it?"

"What isn't the book?"

"After all, I only brought one."

It didn't work. Ethel was looking straight ahead at the gangplank and seemed not to have heard. He felt as though he were walking alone.

"Or maybe it's the new appointment."

"What new appointment?"

"Really, Ethel."

"Oh, the *appoint*ment. Congratulations!"

He checked their bags with a porter on the lower deck and then they went up the stairway. No band played; there was not even the accordion man he had expected to find, like the one on the Coney Island ferry. The boat was astir with people finding themselves places. Children ran everywhere; even dogs seemed to be on the loose, free and unattended. He found chairs for themselves against the wall of the closed salon on the promenade deck, rather than along the outer rail. Though it was hot here, he was sure it would be breezy enough when the boat sailed.

"How are the boys?"

"Fine. They sent their love to you."

"Your father and mother?"

"All right."

The boat was underway. It pushed slowly and silently from the pier, giving the illusion that it was the pier and the mainland that moved off, while they remained stationary. Presently the engines started up more vigorously and a steady but not-unpleasant throb began to make itself felt throughout the length of the steamer.

"What do you think," he said. "I found that old rubber-lined bag we used to carry diapers in. Remember? The canvas one? Thought it might come in handy for wet bathing suits."

"Good idea."

He leaned forward and covered her hand with his. "Are you glad to see me?"

"Are you me?"

"Of course! If you knew how I felt, back there, when you didn't get off with the others."

"Yes; you said."

He released her hand. "What's the idea, Ethel?"

"What's what idea?"

"Oh Lord."

The fact that she didn't protest made him know he was right. Something was wrong. He sat back and looked at her. She wore a smart plain brown suit, a close-fitting brown hat like a beret, and alligator shoes. Her legs were sleek and attractive in what were probably her only nylons. She did not at all appear to be the mother of two boys, and herself over thirty; but her hazel eyes looked coldly past him and her face was set in an uninviting mask which made her seem, for the moment, far older. She cleared her throat.

"Okay. Tell me, Ethel."

"Hm?"

"What's the matter?"

"Why, nothing."

"I asked what is the matter?"

She opened her bag and drew out matches and a pack of cigarettes; but after several tries in the blowing wind, she said, "I'm afraid you'll have to light it for me, if you will." Her *Thank you,* then, was as clipped and polite as if they had just met for the first time.

An aproned boy came around shouting that the cafeteria below decks was open for business. They were not due to arrive at Dune House till seven-thirty; probably later, since it was now nearly five o'clock.

"I'll go down and get some sandwiches," he said. "What would you like?"

"I'm not hungry."

"We ought to eat something. It'll be hours before dinner. Ham? Cheese?"

"I don't care, anything."

Standing in line in the corridor below he thought of that habit of hers, the nervous slight clearing-of-the-throat. Ten years of it had taught him what it meant: an "issue" was brewing. It was so characteristic that Ethel herself was unconscious of it, though he had often pointed it out to her. He had ceased doing that, however; there was no sense in giving up a good card; angry as it made him, it was a sign useful to know. His nerves had grown so accustomed to it that when he heard the sound he automatically asked himself, Now what?

Another sign of strain was Ethel's habit of answering

a question with a question, so that when he asked What's the matter? she invariably answered What? as if she hadn't heard. Perhaps it gave her time to think—she didn't know how to say what she wanted to say. Even in the thick of a quarrel he always felt sorry for her: she expressed herself so pointlessly, she was never able to hold up her end of the argument, she burst into tears, walked out of the room, or repeated, parrot-like, the things he himself had said. Today there was no telling what was wrong. But his conscience was clear; it was something in Ethel's mind. All he could be sure of was that the boat trip he had been looking forward to was now spoiled for them both.

The small cafeteria was crowded; it was next to impossible to get to the counter. The harassed counterman was having a fine time being put upon by the clamoring crowd. King of the moment, he played favorites, took the orders of the old regulars, and seemed not to hear the demands or pleas of newcomers and unknowns. When he got round to listening to Grandin he merely turned to him, raised his eyebrows and closed his eyes, as if to say, Well who do you think *you* are? "One ham, one cheese, and two cokes, please," Grandin said. The counterman turned away with a wearied expression which said, You *may* get them before we arrive in Nantucket; and then again . . .

Waiting for the order to be filled, Grandin shifted in the pressing crowd and glanced about at the passengers behind him. Farther back, barely inside the room, was the big soldier he had noticed on the train, the one who had offered him his seat. Grandin caught his eye and signaled over the heads of the crowd to ask what it was he wanted;

he could save him the trouble of fighting his way through to the counter. The tanned face lit up; he called out in a loud stage whisper, "One ham, one cheese, two cokes." Grandin was curiously pleased; and as he engaged the attention of the snooty counterman and doubled the order, it occurred to him—and again he was pleased by the thought—that the young man had already found a girl.

When he emerged into the open space of the lower deck, the soldier, all smiles, was waiting for him, his money in his hand. He seemed almost unreasonably delighted and grateful; the small kindness scarcely merited such effusive thanks. Grandin pushed the money aside and said, "Forget it." The soldier took the tray with the sandwiches and cokes in one hand, and with the other he clasped Grandin's arm in an impulsive friendly gesture.

"Come over here a minute, sir. I want you to meet my wife."

There was no reason why he should not have been prepared for this, but Grandin could only be surprised. The soldier, gripping his arm familiarly, led him to a chair at the foot of the stairway. Here sat a dreamy-eyed young woman, rather colorless, yet extremely beautiful. The young man said, "Billie, I want you to meet— I mean, this is my wife, sir: Mrs. Hauman."

Grandin bowed and was about to say how-do-you-do when the girl got up from her chair and exclaimed: "Why Mr. Grandin—hello!"

He was dumbfounded then to discover that the girl had been one of his students in the semester just ended. "Of course," he said, anxious to recover his error, "you are Miss—you were Miss—"

"Cowles," she said, and smiled. "I'm not surprised. You never could remember my name in class, could you, the whole year . . ."

It was worse than that. Try as he did to make the name register, she had never made any impression on him whatever, except to this effect: she was the one student in the entire class whose name he had never been able to bring to mind. Luckily, the fact that he had again forgotten seemed lost on her husband, for whom Miss Cowles must have been The Only Girl In The World.

The soldier was joyous that his wife and this man should have known each other as student and professor. At once he busied himself to find another chair and suggested that they sit down and eat their sandwiches together. His eager hospitality gave the occasion the festive air of a party, a mood that Grandin was reluctant to break up by explaining that his wife was waiting on the upper deck. With some misgivings (he remembered Miss Cowles only too well now), he invited the Haumans instead to join him and Ethel. They accepted with such alacrity that he could only be surprised again, this time because of their willingness to spend the voyage across in company with a pair of strangers. For strangers they were, regardless of the fact that he and Miss Cowles (or Mrs. Hauman) had spent a good part of that year facing each other over a classroom desk.

Going up the stairway it occurred to him that he had made a serious mistake. Not only would the presence of these young people prove to be a long and tiresome bore, but also Ethel was certain to suspect a motive: he was taking refuge in the company of strangers in order to avoid or put off the issue of their quarrel. If she thought such a thing, he was hardly to blame; heaven knew he had tried hard enough to bring it out, whatever it was.

Soon they were eating their sandwiches on the windy upper deck, sitting back in their chairs and maintaining the appearance of a group of friends enjoying themselves. Hauman alone did not sit back. With his big hands clasped together and his elbows on his knees, he sat on the edge of the small folding chair, which miraculously did not collapse under him, and leaned forward eagerly into the group.

"Well, Miss Cowles"—Grandin had made an effort to remember the name—"I didn't know you were a married woman."

"Please say Billie," she said, and then added, "I wasn't. Cliff and I were only married yesterday."

"Oh," Ethel said, "so this is a honeymoon. Congratulations, Mr. Hauman!"

"Thank you, ma'am."

"In fact," Billie went on, "Cliff is the reason why I guess I didn't pay much attention in class the last few months. I guess I even missed whole lectures, didn't I?"

"I—yes, I believe there were a few times I was obliged to mark you absent. . . ."

But she was paying no attention. She smiled artificially at the Grandins, just as artificially at her husband, and desperately tried to keep herself together and her large white hat from being blown away. A strong breeze blew in from the sea and tore at everything loose it could find. The dying corsage on her white-silk frock swung back and forth; she clutched at it to prevent its being ripped from her dress. Her hair blew about her eyes so that she was obliged to keep her fingers to her forehead in order to see. The full skirt whipped about her knees, adding a tiny fluttering tremolo to the general noise of the wind.

Ethel kept up an amiable conversation with the Haumans. Under the circumstances, Grandin marveled at his wife's ability to do this; the more so because she had no gift for small talk. Though inwardly troubled by he knew not what, she was yet able to maintain the social conventions as if nothing was the matter. With him, Ethel was a poor dissembler, unable to mask her feelings; to strangers, even to friends, she presented a front that revealed nothing of herself. Further, she showed an interest in the Haumans which he knew, in view of their quarrel, she could not really feel, except for the irresistible fact that they were honeymooners. He was grateful to her for this; it absolved him from the responsibility of taking part, for he soon discovered that he had no grounds for conversation with them.

Billie was as pretty as a picture; an apt description, since it said everything about her that was to be said. Her husband was painfully polite, seemingly without character or mind, and so awkward on the edge of the small camp chair that it made Grandin uncomfortable to look at him. He was truly a giant, six-feet-two or -three, and heavily built: enormous shoulders, large head, blond curling hair, blue eyes—the athlete, the American idol, uninteresting. The face was handsome, but curiously without anything in it, besides radiant health, to hold one's interest. The only features not in keeping with the magazine-cover type were the blond curls, which were a little too long at the back of the neck, and the incongruous way his baby mouth turned up at the corners, so that Hauman resembled a cross between a Bacchus and a Cupid by Rubens.

As Grandin was dismissing this unsuitable notion, he heard Ethel ask what was the meaning of the little silver bars on his shirt collar; and for the first time, he noticed these bars himself.

"That's my rank, ma'am," Hauman said. The tone was almost apologetic.

"Cliff's a captain," Billie volunteered, "in the Marines."

This announcement was little short of astonishing to John Grandin, but Hauman seemed uncomfortable about the whole business. He was extraordinarily attentive and eager to please, but as soon as attention was turned on himself he seemed to withdraw.

"I don't blame you for not knowing," Billie said. "Cliff has the most beautiful uniforms but he never wears them, not even the Marines' emblem—and none of those stunning service ribbons. He says he doesn't have to when he's on leave. I get so mad. All he ever wears is shirt and pants. I wish you could see his hats. He has the most thrilling hats."

"Caps," he said.

"Don't you wear a cap?" Ethel asked.

"This, ma'am." He pulled from his pocket a plain overseas cap, marked like his collar with double silver bars; like everything about him, it was immaculately clean and fresh.

"Are you on furlough, Captain?"

"No, ma'am. Sick list."

"He doesn't look very sick, does he?" Billie said.

"I should think not. For a few weeks?"

Somewhat sheepishly, Captain Hauman admitted he had been on the sick list for over half a year.

It came out then that he had been on Guadalcanal from the first landing, went through the worst of it under the earliest and worst conditions, had been wounded last December, flown out by ambulance plane when he was well enough to be moved, and then returned by ship to San Diego, where he had spent a long recuperation. The nature of the injuries, how he had got them and where, under what conditions, he didn't say—his modesty amounted almost to a phobia—but he was now almost entirely fit again, he said; and certainly he looked it. He returned home to Bridgeport only a week ago and yesterday married Billie Cowles, whom he had known slightly in high school, gone with later, and looked forward to coming back to throughout all of Guadalcanal. He had been an enlisted marine since the month he was graduated in 1941 from Syracuse University—where, Grandin suspected, he had most certainly been a football hero. Since that time he had risen in two years to the rank of captain at the age of twenty-four. To Grandin, who was so often struck by the maturity of the young, this seemed an early age indeed. It spoke of Hauman's qualities as a soldier and a leader—as a young man fitted for today. In the presence of this marine captain almost half his age, John Grandin began to feel, strangely, the younger of the two.

It was ironical now to recall the young paratrooper who had sat all day in the smoker entertaining the men with stories of his training at a Georgia camp, while Hauman, who could have held them enthralled, had not opened his mouth; but Grandin found his mind turning to other things. He wondered ruefully what he had written —or not written—in his last letter to Maine. . . .

Plied by Ethel with polite questions, Hauman began to reveal a good deal about his background. As he himself seemed to emphasize, he was definitely up-from-the-ranks. It wasn't entirely Grandin's fault that he had got the impression Hauman didn't belong on a luxury train. By his manner, he insisted he was from a working-class family; that he and his wife should have had reservations on the Pullman was because of their honeymoon. Further, the suspicion about the football hero was correct; he had won a scholarship at Syracuse on the strength of his athletic talents and physique. During his four years, however, he had declined the easy life that went with such a scholarship, preferring instead to earn his room and board by waiting on table, wrapping bundles before dawn for one of the city's newspapers, tending furnaces. In high school he had worked as a soda jerker and at the same time kept house for his widowed father. "My daddy's a carpenter. He's a wonderful man," he said. "I'm first-generation American, because my daddy's a Hollander."

A couple came by. The man peered frowningly at the foursome and then smiled and saluted, a most amiable and friendly smile. It was the Howards. As they passed on, Mrs. Howard was heard to say: "I never saw so many dogs and children in my life, my god."

While her husband talked, Billie Hauman seemed indifferent, even bored. She listened with a vague smile, and though her eyes constantly sought her husband's, it was clear that her mind was not on him. She was languor-ous, indolent, all but drowsy; which was hardly to be wondered at if last night had been her wedding night. It turned out that this was what she was thinking of.

"We had such a lovely wedding," she said to Ethel, with a sigh very like homesickness. "The bridesmaids wore yellow. Weren't they nice, Cliff? Didn't you think Marion looked just darling?" Her smile was more lazy and lan-guorous than ever, her eyes half closed. "Queer to think of it now. Just last month I had my room done over at home. And now I'm going to move out. Really it looks awful nice, doesn't it Cliff. I just love it. . . ."

"Seems funny to be sitting on a steamer like this," Hauman said, "without plane cover or protection. Not a plane in sight."

"Really, that's all they can talk about," Billie said. "They all the time have to talk about the war."

"Well gee, Billie honey, there is a war on."

"Still, other people have other things to talk about, occasionally."

Hauman smiled pleasantly. "Billie seems to think the war is something that's happening on the front page of the papers and nowhere else. I almost think she doesn't be-lieve it."

"I be*lieve* it all right. Why wouldn't I, with you in uniform, and wounded—maybe even going back one of these days. But honestly," she said to Ethel, "Cliff follows the war like my brothers and dad follow sports. He knows who all the generals are on all the fronts, in Africa and Alaska and I don't know where-all."

"Are you going back?" Ethel asked.

"Yes, ma'am, you bet I am. Just as soon as I can."

"When will that be?"

"Well, I'm not sure, ma'am. But as soon as this honeymoon's over, I report in Brooklyn for another physical. They'll check me over to see if I can get back in. Oh, I can, all right. They don't think so, but I'm just as good as anyone else."

"You do look it," Ethel said; and her husband could not but agree. He believed he had never seen such a strikingly fit physical specimen in his life.

"Cliff could get an honorable discharge just like that," Billie said. "But he won't take it. Sometimes I think—well . . ."

"Now honey," he said, and he smiled charmingly at Ethel. "Billie doesn't mean it, ma'am, but just to tease me she says I think more of the Marine Corps than I do of her. She doesn't seem to realize—well, that—"

"That what," Billie challenged. "You see? He can't explain it himself."

"Well gee, what can a fellow do?" He touched Grandin's sleeve. "That's a nice jacket, sir, if you don't mind my saying so. My daddy would look nice in that. Wouldn't he, Billie?" He fingered the tweed. "My daddy loves nice jackets."

"Do you know something, Mrs. Grandin? All the time Cliff was in San Diego in the hospital, he never once let me go out there to see him. And he was there since last December."

"Billie could never get it through her head, ma'am, why I didn't want her hanging around San Diego. What would she do out there, with no friends, and me in the hospital? San Diego is no place for a young girl." The childish mouth broke into a winning smile. "Anyhow, I came home to you, didn't I—Mrs. Hauman?"

Billie turned away with a blush. "Did you know there's going to be a full moon, Mrs. Grandin? I looked it up."

"Yes, we heard."

"In fact that's why we chose this time for our honeymoon, isn't it Cliff? On account of the full moon. . . ."

X

THE STEAMER moved slowly away from the pier at Oak Bluffs; the deck began to throb again as it started the last lap of the sail to Nantucket.

Though most of the passengers had moved to the rail or gone below, John and Ethel Grandin still kept to their chairs against the wall of the closed saloon. When the engines died down, indicating the boat was approaching Martha's Vineyard, the Haumans had risen to their feet. "We're going to look," Billie said, holding her hat with both hands, and Hauman had called back over his shoulder, "We'll be right back, sir," as though he thought the Grandins might miss them or even worry. Grandin wanted to go with them; he wanted to see what the island looked like and watch the passengers getting off. But Ethel had made no move. Under the circumstances, he thought it best to stay with her.

After a while he said, "It's a long time since I've seen

anyone so polite. I must say I like it." Then he added,
"Isn't it odd the way he speaks of 'my daddy'?"

"Yes."

Taking this for encouragement, he went on. "Not dad
or pop, like our kids. And always *my* daddy."

But that was all. In a moment he tried again. "Curious that I had forgotten her. But I don't believe I ever
heard the sound of her voice till today. She never recited."

"She's a remarkably pretty girl." Her tone as she
uttered these words was as if she had said, She's thirty-five
if she's a day.

Good lord, he thought, can she possibly think I'm
interested in Miss Cowles—a professor-and-student infatuation? But no, that would be too preposterous. Ethel
knew better than to believe such a thing; just as he, to do
her justice, knew better than to believe she had.

"All right, Ethel."

"Hm?"

"I said all right. Let's get it over with."

As if in preparation for what was to come, she opened
her bag and took out a Kleenex. "Well, there isn't much
to say." Her voice was strained and tight; this was costing
almost more effort than she could manage. "Except that
I've had a lot of time to think of things, this past week."

"What on earth can you possibly mean by that?"

"Well, that's all."

"Now look—" he said; but his heart was sinking fast.
"You're just tired."

"I certainly am . . ."

He watched her blinking to keep back the tears.
There wasn't, as Ethel had said, much to say; certainly,

now, everything had been said. But if he left it at that, he was lost.

"How long do you expect to keep this up?"

"I'm not keeping anything up," she said.

"How long is this supposed to go on, then?"

"I don't know . . ."

"Very well! If you won't tell me what's on your mind, I can't do anything about it. I'm no clairvoyant, you know." There was no answer. "Do you want me to take the next boat back?"

"I don't care what you do."

"You can't mean that," he said.

"Why can't I?"

"I've called your bluff before and you know what always happens."

"What happens?"

"You collapse in tears, or come running after me begging me to come back—"

"John, not now! I— Please . . ."

"Why not now? Why wait, why prolong it? *I* want to know what the trouble *is!*"

"I— Please, John." The tears came. "Give me your handkerchief . . ."

"You've got your Kleenex."

His impulse was to get up and go. He had to be by himself, take a walk around the deck, clear his mind. His chest was hot; though his mouth was tight shut, he could hear himself breathing; his hands trembled as he lighted a cigarette. With an effort he waited for the Haumans to return.

They sauntered across the deck after the boat was

well underway. Hauman held his wife's chair while she sat down.

"Mrs. Grandin," she said, "you've been crying."

"Crying? No. . . . No, I guess it's just the wind."

Grandin stood up. "I think I'll take a look around the boat. Will you excuse me, Ethel?"

"Certainly, John."

Hauman half rose to his feet. "Shall I come with you, sir?"

"No, thanks." Walking off, he was aware of the expression on Hauman's face as he had registered the rebuff and sat back again; uncertain, almost hurt. Perhaps he had been rude. In any case, he couldn't worry about that now. He had other things to occupy his mind.

If Ethel was trying to drive him away, very well, he would be driven. If she was out to ruin the holiday for them both, he would help in that ruin. He knew who would suffer over it most in the end. He found he did not mind the strain as much as he had thought he would. Quarreling was, in itself, action of a kind, communication, even rapport; it involved them intensely with one another, so that, much as they stood apart, neither one was quite wholly alone—as they were, for example, during the indifferent silent evenings when he read in his study and she read in bed. Now, the long silences were passionate with feeling on both sides. Sooner or later there would be silence of a different kind, and embraces, and bed; and the atmosphere would be cleared.

He found himself a place at the rail, forward. With the racing wind streaming past his ears, all sound of the panting laboring steamer was drowned out behind him;

no voices reached him whatever; he heard only the loud churning wash of the prow and the plaintive cries of sea gulls.

He drew her letter from the book in his pocket, the letter which had arrived that morning. What did it say? What could it have said, beyond the few practical details he wouldn't have thought of? It was a letter from a wife who loved her husband; it said: "John darling, Up early because of the boys. Will they ever sleep late I wonder? Mama isn't used to it but she'll learn. Had a note from Hammacher Schlemmer saying they had shipped my package on the 22nd. They must have overlooked it before and only got to it after I wrote them. Which is too bad. I told them very firmly that I *needed* it. Mama is crocheting me a bedspread for my birthday but I doubt if it will be done in time. Drove into Old Orchard and bought some khaki shorts for the boys with belts that look like cartridge belts only they're stuffed with wooden pegs. They loved them. Wanted to get myself a giddy beach costume but nothing doing in Old Orchard. Your letter was nice, as always. I read some of it to the boys. They knew I was skipping but I said they wouldn't understand the omitted parts. Which is true enough. But it was so nice, John darling. Be sure to straighten up. Empty all ash trays, they smell otherwise. The check arrived. Your mail comes in, I find, on the 5:35, so we all three go over. Deposited the check immediately by mail and paid Johnson the insurance. Which pays us up for another year. After the boys finish breakfast they skoot out and we don't see them again till noon," and so on.

Like most of her letters, it could safely have been

written to any sympathetic friend; it was aloof, discreet, unrevealing. Ethel found it difficult to speak of love; what she felt deeply was left unsaid—he remembered phoning a few days ago, earlier than usual, and after she had recognized his voice, hearing her say (as if to a casual acquaintance): "We're just sitting down to supper." It didn't matter that it was long-distance, and her husband. Yet, after his first moment of astonishment and exasperation, it didn't matter that she had spoken that way, either, or wrote the kind of letters she did; he knew she couldn't have given voice to her feelings in the presence of her parents, and she had an inbred distrust of the written word. It had been like that ever since he had first known her; that's the way she was; and why should he now want her different from the woman who had attracted him at the beginning—what right had he to expect the impossible, the uncharacteristic? If her letters as a girl in love had been the same during that summer when she had put passion behind her and gone abroad To Decide—(*This afternoon went off on another tour, to Stoke Poges church, pronounced Stoke Pógees, where Thomas Grey wrote the elegy. A lovely old church with a hole in the wall back of the altar, a squint hole where lepers watched the services. The yew tree under which he is reputed to have written the elegy is a beautiful but brittle old tree, at least a thousand years old, according to the vicar who was in the church and told us many things. Which revived my faith in the guide, who had already told us the same. Wm Penn's sons and grandsons are also buried there. Love, Ethel*)—if, that is, this was the girl he had loved and these were the kind of letters he had pored over with the irrational ex-

citement of the lover—why should he expect, now, outbursts of love which would never be forthcoming, which
were not in her power to produce, the very absence of
which, indeed, he loved her for? He knew—*he* didn't need
to be told—and what were words anyhow? Her noncom-
mittal letter then had shown him so plainly the lonely
girl of twenty-four standing in the English churchyard
among the tourists, gazing dutifully at the yew tree because she had paid good money to do just that, but day-
dreaming of the husband with whom, arm in arm, she
might someday stand on this very spot again; and later, in
the dingy hotel room, taking up the pretentiously crested
stationery and resolutely putting all marriage nonsense
aside (how could it be else but nonsense since it hadn't
happened yet?) in order faithfully to describe the church,
the hole in the altar wall, the vicar, the yew tree, anything
but her emotions. So it was still. In the domestic accents
of this morning's letter, which he now folded and put back
in the book, love rang from every syllable—at least to the
man who had kept the letter because it was written by the
woman he knew so well and could never get along without, the woman whom habit or custom sometimes dulled
or obscured, the woman who loved him.

His cheeks grew stiff in the cold wind. He turned his
back to the rail and held onto his hat. His tie blew out
from under his buttoned vest and flapped noisily at his
chin.

What made him angriest of all was his own anger.
He had not meant to carry it so far. Ethel's simple statement that she had been "thinking things over" had told
him all too plainly what the matter was; and though he

would have been a fool to admit he understood, he had
been even more of a fool to let temper carry him away.
His heart had been touched by her helplessness far more
than by her tears, and his pity became anger. The anger
itself, he knew, was a kind of defense.

He'd better return. The Haumans might get ideas in
their heads; Billie had already seen too much as it was.
There was nothing he could do about it for the present
but go back. He would not bring it up again; the next
move was Ethel's. Till that came about, he'd try from now
on to forget it and enjoy himself, or at least be nice to the
Haumans. It wasn't their fault that he and Ethel had had
a falling out. He remembered Hauman's look of surprise
as if he felt he had been rebuked.

Ethel did not look up when he returned. Hauman
sat on the edge of his chair as before; his habit seemed to
be to sit only on the edge of chairs. Billie was hanging onto
herself in a dozen places, her white skirt blowing free
from her grasp, her corsage swinging in the wind. Grandin
was reminded of Swann's Odette, whose idea of country
clothes was a taffeta dress.

"You missed it," she said brightly as he sat down.
"Cliff's chair broke under him and dumped him on the
floor."

Noticing how Hauman blushed, Grandin changed the
subject. "This must be quite a change for you, Captain,
after Guadalcanal and the hospital."

"Yes, sir. It is, sir."

"I suppose you've come in actual combat with the
Japs?"

"Yes, sir, I have, quite a few times."

"Are they—well, as hell-bent on self-destruction as we read about?"

For a moment, Hauman seemed to be thrown off by the careless phrase—(did he actually regard it as "profane"?)—but he recovered himself. "They don't give a darn what happens to them, sir, if that's what you mean. Not a darn. They never let themselves be taken alive, if you understand me." He gave a laugh so hearty and good natured that Grandin had to think back on what had been said in order to understand; for to him, there seemed no connection whatever between the laugh and its cause. "I suppose you read in the papers that the Marines don't take many prisoners? Well, that's more our fault than it is theirs!" He laughed again.

"I often wonder," Grandin said, "how you fellows stand it."

"You people back home, sir, you read too many books. Most of the boys don't mind it any more than a Boy Scout hike." Pleased that he had at last caught the interest of the man whom he regarded as his wife's professor, he moved restlessly on the edge of his chair and leaned forward enthusiastically. "Say," he went on, "you've read these stories about how the Japs put up a white flag, sir? Then we advance, thinking the rascals have surrendered. But when we get within range, they shoot us down like— You've read stories like that, sir?"

Inwardly, Grandin shuddered. "We have indeed."

Pleased, the Captain gave a short sharp laugh. "Heck, that's nothing. We do the same thing ourselves!"

The shudder had been premature. Looking into that boyish smiling face, which spoke so amiably, so cheerfully, of bloodshed, a chill went down Grandin's spine. Involuntarily he exchanged a glance with Ethel.

Hauman caught the fleeting alarm and hurried on, gleefully, to reassure them. "We have to, sir. If we hadn't done it, I wouldn't be sitting here right now. There aren't any rules out there—can't be. Why heck, those rascals wouldn't stop at anything—anything! So we give them as good as we get." The charming smile seemed all the more disarming for being, under the circumstance, so ill timed. "A lot better too, if you ask me!"

"Cliff and I are going to rent bicycles and really get some exercise," Billie said, "aren't we, Cliff?"

"Sure are," he said, and his smile warmed them all. "Got to work off some of this excess fat I've been piling on, lying around for so many months doing nothing."

Grandin looked at the shoulders and the broad chest; and the fact that the seams of the shirt were strained almost to bursting seemed to have little to do with fat. His whole body looked solid muscle as he strained forward on his chair. He seemed to be unable to give enough of himself to them or to Billie, as if he lived under a kind of apprehension lest they should feel he wasn't attentive enough or appreciative of their company.

He puzzled about this attitude. It did not necessarily spring from inferiority, he decided. On the contrary, he could see that Hauman had a stronge sense of the fitness of things and of himself. It was discipline, perhaps, which had produced the habit of respect for seniors, the immaculate neatness of dress, the soldierly attention, the courtesy, the desire to please and fit in. Training of this kind could well erase all differences of background. He took pride in discipline; it was the ideal of the day, better than breeding or brains. Grandin also wondered whether discipline was responsible for the innocent language with which Hauman expressed himself, or whether his choice of words sprang from a mind so clean it could almost seem inane. There was no telling; his very naturalness gave no clue to his nature. One could only be sure of two things: he loved his father; and though very possibly he did not truly love his wife (since he would never really know or understand her), it was touching to see that one of the genuine delights of his life was that she was called Billie. . . .

"I guess we'll be getting there soon now," the Captain said. "Have you enjoyed the trip, sir?"

"Very much. Are we there?"

"The island looks about five miles off. We're just passing some lighthouse."

"Oh dear," Billie said, "hadn't we better go downstairs and get our things?"

"Plenty of time, honey. But still, if the Grandins will excuse us—?"

Anxious to put a better face on his share of the afternoon, Grandin said, "I'm told there's a very fine beach at Sconset. If you should care to try it, I hope you'll feel free to use our room to dress in." He had spoken out of politeness, merely, a politeness which had been generally contagious that afternoon.

And out of no more than this same politeness, Hauman replied as they moved away, "Thank you, sir, we sure will, it's very kind of you I'm sure. . . ."

Automatically the Grandins turned to watch them go.

At the top of the stairway to the lower deck, Captain Hauman looked back for a moment; he sought their glance; and over the heads of many passengers still seated about the promenade deck he sent them a smile of farewell, a smile of pure radiance, youth, and health, which left Grandin gazing at the spot for a full moment after the Haumans had gone below.

He turned to his wife. "I'm tired. It may or may not be the sea air," he added, "but it's a long time since I've felt so old." Yet old as he felt, he also felt, unaccountably, a curious boyishness, a feeling of being again in his earliest teens.

Ethel, gathering her things together, said nothing.

On the pier, behind a fencelike gate, a mob of people in summer dress waited for the passengers to disembark. They stood silent but with a fixed collective smile and hands tentatively raised to wave at the first sign of a familiar face. It was as if the entire island had turned out to welcome the arrival of some illustrious personage. As the first passengers streamed off the boat, relieving the press on the stairway, Ethel and John Grandin went below.

Inching along toward the gangplank, he looked away from the island and out toward the farther horizon beyond. The sky was a pale white-green, so remote that it looked like the static backdrop of a stage setting seen through the wrong end of a pair of opera glasses. Gulls flew and cried against the sky but no stir of life could be seen along the horizon. He was reminded of a dream he had had when a child, a beautiful meaningless dream he had never forgotten because of its pictorial beauty, which he had been able to see ever since in his mind's eye and memory, and which was so much like this distant seascape now. . . . Shoulder to shoulder with ten thousand others he had stood on the top of a cliff rising out of the sea. It was a small rocklike island, high and flat, without beach or shore, rising straight out of the ocean. They stood in silence as if awaiting some portentous event or revelation, packed close together to the very edge of the cliff, their feet half buried in the long dry cliff grasses, while overhead birds wheeled and screamed in the late afternoon air and a cool wind blew in from the sea, across the island, and out to sea again. All around, to the farthest point on the horizon, stretched that remote panorama of white-green and lemon-yellow sky, with far-distant thunderheads piled up on the edge of the sea like rocks. . . .

A vast rickety omnibus with a high wide body quaked gently at the entrance to the pier. It was marked SIAS-CONSET.

Except for the broad back seat, the bus was already filled. They moved to the rear and sat down, and found themselves seated next to the Howards. Mr. Howard introduced the ladies; and then, as the bus began to shudder violently, he rubbed his hands together and said, "This looks like it's going to be fun!" The bus moved off through the town.

Somewhere, from some tower, a clock struck.

"Eight o'clock, my god," Mrs. Howard said. "I wonder if we'll get anything to eat."

Mr. Howard leaned forward. "Any idea how late they serve dinner at Dune House?"

"The folder said eight-thirty."

"Hear that, Mama? We'll just get in under the wire."

"*May*be," she said.

It was getting too dark for them to form any clear impression of Nantucket village; they'd have to wait till another visit, in the daytime—and no doubt they'd be making several trips into town before their holiday was over. As the bus bumbled out upon the rising highway leading to Sconset the night air began to thicken, and not merely with the rapidly descending dark. A white fog moved over the moors; they passed in and out of it as through horizontal layers of transparent veils.

"Look, Bill—fog," Mrs. Howard said.

"Nice!"

"Nice hell. We didn't come here to spend our vacation in a fog."

"Now Mama, maybe it's only tonight."

"We hope. I want to see that full moon this week."

The ride across the island was like a kind of long gently sloping roller-coaster, up and down sudden little hills and valleys. The straining bus seemed to travel at reckless speed. Finally it rolled down a slope and came to an explosive stop in front of a drugstore. From the front seat, the driver yelled:

"Si-as-conset!"

XI

THE ROOM WAS PERFECT. It was a large corner room with a good bath, fronting the sea and also facing south over the dark moors toward Tom Nevershead. But wide strips of black tape had been fastened securely around the shades, and the shades themselves were pulled down to the sash.

"The blackout," Ethel said.

"I'd forgotten."

"I'd like to get into something different."

"No time, Ethel. I told the desk we'd be right down. It's late."

"You go hold the table, I'll only be a minute."

Left to herself, she stood staring into the mirror of the bureau, though this was no time to be dallying. But she dreaded going downstairs, dreaded what might happen later. She did not see herself in the glass and she was not thinking of herself. She was thinking of her husband.

It wasn't fair to spoil his vacation. He had needed it for so long, the rest and change; and perhaps that's all he did need—perhaps, even, everything might be different from now on, from right now, beginning tonight. And yet—how long could she sustain herself on expectation alone?

She loved him—oh, there was no question that she didn't love him; but how long could she go on loving a man who wasn't there? True, he had tried to pay a certain amount of attention to her on the boat, at first, tried to patch up a quarrel which he had sensed at once was in the air, but that had been mere politeness, habit, and pride. It made things easier for him if outwardly everything looked all right. That was all he really wanted: the *semblance* of order and harmony. Provided the outward appearances of husband-and-wifely unity were kept up, basic troubles could be ignored as if they didn't exist, ignored forever and ever till they finally didn't matter any more. He could do that; but she couldn't.

While the boat waited at Oak Bluffs, he had given her her opportunity to speak; and she had failed. The moment having come, she found herself fumbling help- lessly, and somehow the advantage had passed from her to him: as always, he became the one who did the attack- ing, not she. Why was it always like that? Her emotion and her love were truly too deep for words, while he— he could carry on glibly, devastatingly, through any im- passe that came up between them, unanswerable and al- ways victorious. Her misery had been so keen that she had found herself longing for the Haumans to return, the Haumans for whom she did not give a damn; when they did return, it had been more of a relief to her than they or he could possibly have known. A strange reversal had taken place, for which no one was responsible but herself. *She* was the one who was putting it off, thrusting it far into the background, taking refuge in the company of strangers. This, somehow, was the crowning humiliation; far from bringing the matter into the open and facing it, out of cowardice she was helping her husband to cover it up.

She turned her back on the dresser and looked at the room through tear-filled eyes. She looked at the beds. She would take the one farthest from the door, he the nearest, as they always did—and that would be that. But the idea of undressing in his presence (her husband of ten years!) and getting into bed, with him in the other bed in the same room, saying good night and going to sleep—she couldn't do it. Yet she knew she would. She knew that when he took her in his arms as he was certain to do tonight, all her resolution would melt away and the moment would pass forever. For another month, or six months, or for the rest of their lives, they would carry on the pretense as they had been carrying it for so long now, and the moment might never rise again. Perhaps in time it wouldn't matter—somehow this seemed the most dreadful thought of all.

She bent down, unsnapped one of her bags, and took out a green wool dress. She had packed well; it showed scarcely a wrinkle. She stepped out of her skirt, slipped off her jacket and blouse, and pulled the dress over her head. She fixed her hair at the mirror and put on some lipstick.

Had he known what she was talking about or trying to say? Of course he had; he always did. Is that why he had risen so sharply, so instantaneously to the attack? But as she thought it over, she realized she hadn't been talking about anything: she had said nothing, the blame was hers, not his, that nothing had been resolved. Nothing would be resolved; love tied her hands, love and pity for her husband, who, for all his facility in argument, was as much at sea as she was. If she really wanted to reach him, might it not be better to wait a while longer, do nothing whatever about it now, let him make love to her if he wanted to and so carry their marriage through another few weeks? It was a pointless question; she knew she would be unable to decide what to do in any case.

Love is of man's life a thing apart; it is a woman's whole existence. . . . Thus the poet. But it could be her degradation, too. Having so much to give him, getting so little in return, whatever happiness she had now consisted merely in being thankful for small favors. Were small favors worth it; did they really give her anything; was loving him—just loving in itself—enough? If it came to that, her love was big enough to sustain them both; but she had to know, had to *feel* even if he never said a word, that her love was at least wanted and needed.

She turned back to the glass, gave a last look at her hair, and fastened a plain gold chain around her neck. She wished it were longer, wished it hung lower in a longer oval, so that it didn't make her face look so round. She looked at the effect in the mirror, and then, staring at her reflection, again lost herself in her thoughts.

XII

THE DINING ROOM was large, bare, unattractive, with thin pillars upholding a sagging ceiling. It reminded him of some dim Sunday-school room out of his childhood: he could see the pillars festooned with holly and tinsel, hear each tinny note of the flat pitch-black piano. . . . Now through the room from the hall came the tinkling notes of *Beautiful Dreamer* which was being played on a harp in the parlor beyond the lobby. Down at one end of the long room were the Howards, chatting busily together; and a few tables away sat a yellow-haired young man and his mother. Ethel appeared in the doorway, looked in uncertainly, and then found their table. As she came across the room he admired her walk: it was straight, confident, cool, the walk of a young woman.

"You look very nice," he said.

"Thank you."

"I like that dress." He unfolded his napkin. "There seems to be some kind of recital going on, a harp."

"Yes."

"After dinner would you care to go in, for a while, and listen?"

"Not tonight."

The wide still room continued to evoke its associations out of the past; he had only to close his eyes to feel himself back in the Boys' Carving and Weaving Class that met on Friday nights. It was the second time in the past hour that he had had intimations of childhood. First there had been the memory of the childhood dream that had sprung unbidden to his mind as they were leaving the steamer; now, the sense of being in the old Sunday-school room. What brought these images up? he wondered. The pending showdown with Ethel—his feeling of being on trial, so to speak—which inevitably reduced him to something less than adult status? Or was it, possibly, the influence of the Marine captain still, in whose presence he had experienced stirrings of an old adolescence?

A middle-aged woman with heavy black eyebrows and lavender hair, wearing beach pajamas, sandals, and long drop-earrings, came forward and introduced herself as Miss Fly, the hostess. She launched at once into a long one-sided conversation, with an incessant running fire of comment as if she had an anxiety that she would be interrupted—which, it turned out, was the case; for Miss

Fly was deaf as a post and lived in fear of being found out.

". . . I'm sorry but I guess you folks are going to get a more or less cold dinner tonight on account of it's so late and we're short of help anyway. We like to close the dining room at eight-thirty but still we can't very well do you good people out of your dinner just because the boat was late, now can we? In normal times we kept the dining room open till nine but then of course we had more help. Like old Mrs. Westermeier was saying only this noon—and I want you folks to meet her, she's a real person—good servants don't grow on trees any more or even any servants for that matter. We can't get any help nowadays you know in any way shape or form except these high school kids. C'est la vie of course. Well let's hope it won't last forever . . ."

"I can't believe it," he said, as Miss Fly moved away. "Amazing. . . ."

They dispensed with the soup out of consideration for the help and the lateness of the hour. While waiting for the high school girl to bring the meat course, Grandin looked at the young man near by with his mother. He wore a sky-blue linen jacket with large white bone buttons, over a red-and-white striped basque shirt. His elbows were on the table and his long fingers interlaced on a level with his chin. Even from this distance the fingernails gleamed and glinted brightly in the reflected light, as if they had been enameled with some garish lacquer.

"I don't hear the sea at all," Grandin said.

"I guess it's some distance away . . ."

"Besides, they've got the windows closed. I suppose because of the bugs."

"Yes . . ."

". . . Wasn't it funny the way he blushed when I said 'hell-bent'?"

"Who? Oh. I didn't notice . . ."

As they had done on similar occasions, they made conversation. He wondered why they bothered. Pride, perhaps; they would have felt silly indeed sitting in silence opposite one another in that vast quiet room, the more so because laughter and lively talk came continually from the Howards' corner, Miss Fly slowly circled their table at a discreet distance but always with one eye on their progress with the meal, and the yellow-haired young man bent upon them a fixed if abstracted gaze. To finish their dinner without speaking would have been to declare publicly: we've had, are having, or are about to have, a quarrel.

"I wonder how Hauman was wounded. He didn't say."

"I suppose he never does."

"Oh, I don't know. He was willing enough to talk about himself once he got started." Then he added: "Odd how he seems to feel guilty for being out of the war. A real guilt. He of all people."

"Imagine."

". . . You haven't told me a thing about the boys." She hadn't said anything about his book, either, but for some reason he couldn't speak of it now.

"I suppose they're having a good time."

"I miss them. Don't you?"

"No, not really . . ."

"Oh, by the way! I had the damnedest experience the other day. I was on top of a bus, alone, there was no one else upstairs at all, when four young fliers came up and sat down several seats behind me. Their uniforms were a lightish blue, I think they were Canadians; anyhow they weren't Americans. You can't imagine how young they were—just kids—hardly looked as if they shaved. You could tell they were in a fine mood and were out to have a good time—really do the town. I sat there thinking about them, wondering where they'd be six months from now, or even three, or even if they'd still be alive, and I was hoping like anything that they'd have the best time in New York they'd ever had anywhere. Suddenly I heard one of them say, 'How do you like that civilian uniform up there?' I turned around, thinking someone else must have come up on top of the bus, and discovered they meant me. I was being baited. Me, forty-four years old! But that's not the point, of course. The point is—well, I felt awfully sorry about the whole thing; I kept wishing it hadn't happened, or that I hadn't heard them say it . . ."

"I know . . ."

XIII

WHATEVER IT WAS, the thing had gone on for so long, now, that apparently it could be postponed indefinitely or even eventually dropped. It had often happened that way before. He felt no urge to inquire any further and

Ethel herself seemed disposed to forget it. But as they were unpacking in the bedroom later, she began to clear her throat again in little nervous rasps and he saw that she was tense. Suddenly she said, "John, I want to talk to you," and her eyes filled with tears.

He sat down on the edge of the bed. Unconsciously— by some instinctive reversion to an old habit, perhaps— he folded his hands meekly in his lap, as if expecting a scolding from his mother or teacher. Ethel was in a wicker chair by the bureau. They faced one another in the harsh glare of the unshaded light bulb in the ceiling. She breathed hard, thinking it out first; and though she looked directly at him, he knew she was afraid.

He was willing to have it out, whatever it was, but for her sake he would rather have put it off. He felt sorry for her; she expressed herself so inadequately at these times, always found she had nothing to say after all, and came off so badly in the end. With all his heart he wanted at that moment to take her in his arms.

"Just a moment, Ethel, before you begin."

"*I* want to do the talking!"

"I want you to. But I also want you to remember . . ." He hesitated.

"What?"

"Well, never mind."

"You're just trying to throw me off!"

"I'm not. I merely want you to be careful. You're not only spoiling my fun, but you'll spoil your own as well."

"Fun!" she said. "Do you think this is any fun for me?"

"That's exactly what I'm saying, of course. Now, what's on your mind?"

She glared at him in silence. Then she began again. "This week at home I've thought a lot about us. A lot! And—well . . ."

"Well?"

She blurted it out in one breath: "I'm tired of this life I'm leading!"

"Go on."

"What have I got ahead?"

"What has anybody got," he said, "except what they make for themselves?"

"Oh, shit!"

He got up. He was so angry he couldn't speak. He walked to the window to look out in order to calm himself, but the shade was down for the blackout. In the sudden stillness of the room he could hear, from the parlor directly below, the *plink-plunking* of the harp. He was outraged that she should have chosen one of the two or three words which, for some forgotten reason, he was squeamish about and in fact couldn't bring himself to say. Still more, he was shocked; not because of the word, now, but because a woman of Ethel's fastidiousness should, in anger, automatically revert to vulgarity. It was something he had noticed often before, but each time it took him completely by surprise. After a moment he returned to the bed, sat down again, and said quietly:

"What I fail to see is why you pick a time like this—"

"No, that's something you wouldn't be able to see!"

"Why couldn't you wait till later—till we got back

to New York? Why should you want to spoil our whole vacation? Would you mind telling me that, please?"

"No I wouldn't mind! I'll tell you exactly! That's exactly what I want to tell you!"

"You needn't shout."

"It's a— It isn't easy to explain—"

"I suppose," he said recklessly, "it's a moral question."

Her look was filled with hate. "I see you know very well what I'm trying to say."

"Then say it."

"You're right! Make fun of it, if you like, but it is a moral question. And I'm not coming to bed with you tonight.—That's what you've been banking on for the past month, isn't it?"

"Well, hardly. Not on your not coming to bed with me, that is."

She ignored this and went on with a rush. "For the past month you've been telling yourself, 'I'll make it up to her when we get to Sconset.' Isn't that true? Isn't it? Well, this time it won't work! What do you think I am, anyway? Someone to go to bed with just when *you* happen to feel like it, maybe half a dozen times a year? What about me? How do you think *I* feel night after night? Don't you suppose I have feelings?"

His stomach went weak because of all that was happening. Bitterly he was reminded of what he had been thinking on the train: how he genuinely meant to alter his habits, how he planned to move back to her room, how he wanted to be a better husband. . . . But to speak of it now—no, it was most certainly not the moment. What he said was:

"Lower your voice, please."

"Night after night I lie in bed wondering what to do about it—"

Desperately in need of recapturing the initiative, he cut in quickly: "Not for long," he said sarcastically. "You always fall asleep in five minutes. With the light on."

But she had not heard. "I've finally come to my senses about a few things! You're not going to put me in that position again, do you hear? Never meaning anything to you, never knowing whether you want me, never— If you knew the humiliation of getting fixed, and—and then later having to unfix myself because nothing happened! The times I've gotten ready and—"

"Ethel, good Christ!"

"—And I've only gotten ready then because you'd been extra nice at dinner and paid a lot of attention to me and I thought maybe this was going to be the time—"

"Stop! We've had enough of this!"

"I hate it just as much as you do, John Grandin, I hate every bit of it! It isn't easy for a woman to admit these things. This isn't the kind of vacation I'd planned, any more than you did. But it had to happen. All week I've been dreading it, because I knew you'd expect to go to bed with me tonight—because you thought *I'd* expect it —and it was something I couldn't do. Not this time! Not tonight I couldn't! . . . Don't think I don't want to. I do. But if I weakened and went to bed with you and forgot everything I've been telling myself this past week, we'd be right back where we were before—exactly no-where!"

"Ethel! There are people in the next room!"

"Do you want to know something? Every time I menstruate I always manage to tell you in some way or other. Not that *you'd* ever know, but I always drop some hint by saying I have a backache or cramps or just plain having the curse. And do you know why I do that? I don't do it just to relieve your mind of the obligation of coming to bed with me those few nights—"

"Be careful!"

"—No, that isn't why I do it. I do it for myself! I do it because then I don't have to lie in bed alone and know that you're sitting in your study feeling sorry for me, thinking maybe you ought to do something about it, wondering if I'm expecting you, and would I mind it too much if you put it off one more—"

"For God's sake, *Ethel!*"

"I— John, I—" She burst into sobs and ran from the room.

For some moments he heard the water running in the bathroom; she would be applying a cold towel to her eyes. He sat on the bed, unable to move, unstrung. After what seemed many minutes, she came back in and went to the bureau.

Watching her blowing her nose at the mirror, his mind went back several years to the time when, dining in a restaurant, she had suddenly got up from the table and walked out, crying audibly as she went and making a holy show of herself, leaving him in the most public humiliation to finish the meal alone. When he got home he had found her in bed with a bar of chocolate reading a mystery story. It had been their most serious quarrel, but for the life of him he couldn't remember what it was about. . . .

"It's no good," she said, wiping her eyes, "I always cry. . . ."

"Then why do you start anything in the first place," he thundered, seeing it was safely over. "You only get the worst of it!"

"Yes, I do," she said, "I always get the worst of it—whether we're quarreling or not . . ."

He stood up. "Look," he said sharply. "Do you love me or don't you?"

"I don't know. . . ."

"Then all right!"

He slammed the door and went out.

MIDDLE

T HE SUN WAS FLOODING THE ROOM when John Grandin awoke. He glanced at his watch and saw it was nine-thirty. The lateness of the hour surprised him; ordinarily he was a poor sleeper and woke soon after daylight. He could not remember when he had slept so late or so well; he hadn't opened his eyes once during the night. It must be the sea air. He reached for a cigarette and looked across at Ethel's bed. She was not there.

He raised up on his elbow to see if she had left a note, but there was no message on the night table between their beds nor on her pillow. Perhaps she had stuck it in the bathroom mirror. She must have risen early, dressed quietly so as not to disturb him, and gone down to breakfast. If he hurried he would probably find her still at the table, or on the veranda enjoying the morning sun, knitting, working a crossword puzzle, or chatting with one or another of the guests; possibly in the creaking swing. At the thought of the swing, the full recollection of all that had happened last night came over him. He was suddenly in no mood to hurry.

Of course she had not left a note; not today. He lay back on the pillow and closed his eyes.

He could almost be ashamed of himself that he had slept so well. By rights, he should have tossed and turned the whole night through, wakeful and distressed. Instead he had slept as if he hadn't a worry in his head. Perhaps the very violence of the quarrel had cleared the atmosphere more than he knew, and brought out into the open at last something which had been suppressed too long, ridding him momentarily of a tormenting guilt which had been keeping him awake far into every night. He was reminded of a colleague who, almost every time they conversed, spoke lingeringly, all but fondly, of his insomnia, complaining insistently that he was never able to sleep; and how he had thought: "Who is it you don't want to sleep with?"—Was it possible to have an instinctive insight into the troubles of another, and so little about one's own?

After he had slammed the door he had gone downstairs. As he strode through the small lobby, avoiding all eyes and looking neither to right nor to left, his own final words still rang in his ears—*Then all right!*—and he wondered what under the sun they were supposed to have meant. At the moment there had been no doubt; they were inevitable and right, flung out without premeditation. Now they struck him as meaningless except as they marked *finis,* a signing off, to the whole painful futile session. Without these words (or some others equally

pointless and unprovocative, from which bitterer recrim-
inations could not spring) it might have gone on till the
last shred of decency had been stripped from them both
and they were reduced to mere skeletons of hate, unable
further to draw blood.

He had opened the screen door and bumped into a
tight canvas frame stretched from the ceiling of the porch
to the floor, serving as a blackout to the lighted lobby
within. He stepped around this and found himself a chair
somewhere along the veranda in the dark.

Through the windows at his back came the tinkling
notes of the harp. They rippled to an abrupt high finish,
which was immediately followed by a patting of fingertips
and the buzz of released talk. A few feet from his chair a
swing creaked slowly back and forth; he saw the glow of
two cigarettes, going lighter and darker at intervals.

A couple was sitting nearby—young or old, he could
not tell; but from the unbroken silence maintained between them, they were obviously in full understanding
or rapport if not actually in embrace.

He was cold in his stomach. The ordeal had left him
almost physically ill. It was no time to go over in his mind
all that had been said, weigh the justice or injustice of
Ethel's grievances, or plan his defense should they arise
again. All he wanted was to sit in the night air and allow
this sickness of self (if it would) to pass away. Besides, in
view of his long neglect, her complaints were not unjusti-
fied. He could almost be surprised they had not risen
before. What did surprise him was that the attack had
been voluble, articulate, and complete. For once she had
not been at a loss for words. It was the first time in their

married life that he had been left without a rag of self-respect.

There was a strong hint of fog in the dark, a dampness brushing his cheeks and forehead. Somewhere, but as if far off, he heard the sea—not the wash of it as it rose and fell, but only the intermittent dull pound as the breakers struck the beach.

He wondered what Ethel was doing upstairs, in the room just above his head; probably putting her things away, hanging her clothes in the closet, settling down for the holiday. He must be careful not to let anger get the better of him, as it had so often before, when he returned to the room and found her doing her nails at the dressing table or in bed reading a magazine as if nothing had happened. These outbursts always left him shaken and weak for hours after; but for her, they acted as a kind of purge. Almost immediately she was herself again; the more violent the quarrel, it seemed, the more quickly she recovered. Delivered of her burden, she had already begun to feel better before he left the room.

There was a stir in the swing, as if one of them had shifted to a more comfortable or possibly even a more advantageous position. He felt almost certain that some kind of love-making was afoot; but in view of all that had just happened, it seemed vanity, vanity, all vanity. Then, except for the harp, there was silence again—a meaningful silence, but how could it seem anything but inane. . . . Whoever they were, they must certainly have heard the racket overhead.

He supposed the thing to do was to go upstairs, say he was sorry, say she was right, say he understood, and tell her the decisions he had come to on the train. Or say nothing at all: take her in his arms, hold her, lie with her in her bed. But he couldn't have done it if his life had depended on it. Not now; not while this thing was fresh in both their minds. Ethel's accusations had been too much of a demand that he prove her wrong. Aware that she would be questioning his every move, he'd be utterly unable to make love to her now.

The reasons for the completeness of the attack must have been because Ethel had had a week to think it over. Violent though they were, her vituperations sprang less from the emotion of the moment than from cold calculation or malice aforethought. She had had plenty of time to marshal her points in a fair semblance of order, and once started, had run through them rapidly to their shattering climax. Half a dozen times he might have stopped her by some facetious, ironic, or cruel remark; but after a moment or two of protest he had found himself spellbound, both repelled and fascinated by the naked way she was exposing them both, shouting details which normally she could not have been induced to mention. Unbidden, an advertising slogan slid into his mind: Nature in the raw is seldom mild.

Did women never tire? Did they want one man forever and ever, and him all the time? Why was it that love didn't sift down to a comfortable level in their lives, as it did with men, one with work, play, sleep, and the other rewards of normal existence? Early or late, there was always the conflict. Men brought to marriage a full awakened appetite, to which in some cases their wives were passive for so long that the period when their separate natures

corresponded was short indeed. This period had come
about when his passion was at its peak and hers was
beginning to awaken to a matching intensity. Looking
back on this, he thought of it ruefully as the happiest time
of his life, the completest, the best. But even the best loses
something of its delight when it lasts too long. In any
case, it hadn't lasted. His passion had slackened while hers
increased. What had it turned into, on his part? A love
more real in its way than the other, though needing less
expression? Or was less than the best, nothing?

But this was casuistry. In all honesty he felt the justice
of what had happened and was completely undone by it,
unable to see any possible way out of a dilemma which
had been so plainly stated at last. He faced the inevitable
and dreadful fact that whatever he did from now on would
be wrong. His every move and motive would henceforth
be suspect.

"Shall we go up, Mama?" a man's voice asked with
quiet urgency from the swing.

"Any time, darling," answered a sleepy contented
woman.

Appalled to discover who was sitting so near him in
the dark, John Grandin was on his feet in an instant; a
second or two later he had not only quitted the porch but
traversed the little lighted lobby and gained the second
floor.

He stood for a long moment outside the bedroom
door, in the corridor, composing himself. The raffia-like
matting at his feet, scuffed up, spoke of his hasty exit half
an hour ago. He straightened it with his foot. There was

no sound from within. At length he opened the door. The
room was dark.

He felt his way in, found the edge of the bed where
he had sat before, and undressed, dropping his clothes
noiselessly to the floor. He hadn't unpacked his pajamas
but to hell with that now. He pulled back the covers of his
bed and got in. The sheets were cool and comforting to
his body. He lay on his back, his palms under his head.
The room was stuffy. As his eyes grew accustomed to the
dark he saw that the shades had not been pulled up.

He stepped out of bed, tiptoed to the windows, and
raised the shades. There was a real fog in the night air
now; he felt it drift in through the screens. He came back
and got into bed again. He listened for Ethel but there
was no sound. Her breathing was quiet and she did not
stir.

This was hardly the kind of first-night they had been
planning for their holiday. Perhaps it was just as well.
Without their having realized it till now, their marriage
had passed into a new phase. It was well that they think
of what it meant—of what they were and what they had—
before they made any attempt to reach one another again.
With a constantly sinking heart he knew full well that the
quarrel had not been a thing of the moment. Almost, the
fact that he had not been coming to bed with her had
little to do with it. He could only ask himself pointless
unanswerable questions: Why did she want him so much?
Did she think she was losing him? Or, since a man wants
to be wanted, why didn't this, if nothing else, bring him
more often to her bed?

He wondered how many other husbands genuinely

loved their wives, yet had grown tired of the marriage duties (how shameful to human dignity that the thing they could hardly wait to get married for had at last become a duty!), enjoyed them physically as much as ever when it occurred to them to seek their beds, yet looked forward to the day when passion would no longer be expected and they would be free to love their wives without reminding themselves—or being reminded by silences or reproach—that weeks had passed and it was "time to do something about it again . . ."

A small flare lit up the dark ceiling. Ethel was lighting a cigarette. The flare went out. He turned his head on the pillow. He could see the tip of her nose each time she took a puff. He watched the tiny pink-yellow glow fading and fading.

He watched it to the end. He heard her stir on the pillow as she reached for the ash tray and put out the cigarette. He heard her settle back again.

After a moment or two more, he got up, crossed the small space that separated them, and sat down on her bed.

He put his hands on her shoulders. She stiffened.

"Ethel," he said.

She stirred. He thought she was moving to make room. He got in beside her.

"No," she said. "No."

He waited there, neither in the bed nor out. He reached to find her hand. She pulled away.

"No."

He lay down against her and was still. She did not move. He placed his arm across her body and drew her

close to him. Without a sound she released herself from
his embrace and got out of bed.

Against the dim squares of the open windows he saw
her go to the wicker chair by the bureau and sit down.
He stayed where he was, uncovered by the quilt she had
thrown back, feeling chilly as the night breeze blew over
him. In a moment she arose, came to the bed table to get
her cigarettes, and returned to the chair. From time to
time he heard the wicker creaking.

He went back to his bed. He did not know how long
she had sat up. As far as he remembered, she was still
sitting there when he fell asleep. . . .

II

John Grandin looked at his watch again. It was nearly
ten o'clock. He still didn't feel like breakfast, but the best
of the morning would soon be over if he didn't get up.
Besides, to lie there till noon would have been a tacit
acknowledgment of failure if not guilt. Best to get up and
act as if nothing had happened. As he stepped from bed,
his feet tangled with the clothing he had dropped on the
floor the night before.

He went to the window to see what the place was like
and discovered, in daylight, the relation of Dune House
to the sea. The hotel fronted a bluff, with a road along
the edge. Below, a barren expanse of sand stretched like
a vast arid prairie between the bluff and the beach, half
a mile away. Far down on the shore a few large umbrellas
had been set up, tilted at an angle against the sun; he

could see two or three early figures lying about in the spots of shade. Though the sun was high and the day warm, a faint white mist hung over the sand, so faint as to leave him unsure whether it was mist at all or the glare of sun and sea.

An old lady coming along the drive stared up at him with a fixed stare and he moved quickly back from the window. He opened a suitcase, got out his shaving things, and his clothes for the day.

While shaving at the bathroom mirror, it suddenly occurred to him that if he hadn't got into Ethel's bed without his pajamas on, last night might have been a different story. He was angry to think that perhaps she thought he had planned it that way, as bait or lure or some such silly thing. That's what came of quarreling; it made him self-conscious about his every thought. Nothing he did afterward was right; everything had to be weighed carefully for its possible effect or non-effect; each innocent move could be misconstrued. Double meanings would be rife, now, for days to come.

He opened the medicine chest and put away his shaving things. The small mirrored door caught the reflection of a figure on the grass outside. He looked out the window. On the rear lawn of the expensive-looking cottage next door, a young girl with red hair lay on her back, sunbathing, partially covered with a white towel. Near by, on the grass, was a small heap of white clothing and a pair of sun glasses with white rims. The towel lay across her middle, fully exposing her full thighs, nearly exposing her breasts. She lay not more than a hundred feet away from him. Naked himself, he stood looking down at her almost naked figure. Because he did not know her—because she was someone he had never seen before and might never see again—a small excitement began to gather in his chest, sinking slowly down to his loins; and he yielded to the common daydream. He would like to walk across that wonderful lawn in his bare feet, drop down beside her, draw the towel slowly away, fold himself round her, and there in the hot sun, with neither of them knowing who the other was, take her and give himself up in one and the same act. A hundred people might look on; but if one word was spoken between the two of them, all would have been destroyed.

Not reluctantly (because nothing could come of this but further discomfort) he turned away. He went back to the bedroom, feeling both foolish and set up. Perhaps there was something in the air of this place, an indolence or sensuality to be aware of from the sun . . . .

Dressed, he discarded the yellow sleeveless sweater he had been about to put on in favor of another, because whenever he wore the yellow one Ethel invariably said, "I've always loved that yellow sweater." There it was again: if he wore it this morning, Ethel was sure to give him a look—he had chosen it purposely, he was trying to win her back—and she would have been resentful.

He felt self-conscious entering the dining room alone; it seemed to him an admission that something was wrong, almost a confirmation of a rumor probably afloat already. Besides the Howards, who had been sitting in the porch swing, had anyone heard the row? Surely in a place like this, where voices carried through walls or windows, no secret could be kept for long. Owing to the very nature of the place—the idleness of the guests (fallow ground for gossip), plus that natural interest in other people's business which was the very essence of a summer hotel—someone was already talking, probably.

Ethel was not here. He must breakfast alone and pretend that all was well. The deaf hostess with the lavender hair, her left hand absently fingering one of her earrings, circulated in the center of the room, straightening folded napkins that had already been straightened, turning clean glasses upside down, gradually approaching his table and preparing her monologue as she came.

". . . Good morning Mr. Grandin and isn't this a fine morning. My you must have slept late, your wife was in hours ago. Well not hours but— Oh and she said she'd be going down to the drugstore this morning I suppose in case you wanted to know where she was . . ."

"Did Mrs. Grandin ask you to tell me that?"

"Mmm? Why I believe you're going to have a very nice day but then this time of year is always wonderful anyway. Of course we do have a little fog at night and sometimes it doesn't go away in the morning as early as some of us would like it to but as I tell the high school girls we can't have everything, don't you agree? My you look summery but then that's what you're here for isn't it. Well I'll go find a girl to get you some breakfast if there's one still on duty but you never can tell these days . . ."

It wasn't like Ethel to confide her plans to a stranger. Amused at this oblique way of communicating with him, he was yet relieved that she had taken the trouble to do so. —He wondered if it meant anything; that is, if it promised well for their day.

A girl came with the orange juice. He ordered his breakfast and looked about the room.

With the shades half drawn, the dining room was pleasantly dark, but beneath the shades could be seen the white glare of the morning. The cool semidarkness gave an attractive sub-marine effect to the bare room; looking outdoors, it was as if one looked up through brighter and brighter layers of water to where the sun shone, in all its ultimate brightness, somewhere far above.

The only other guests present were the yellow-haired young man and his mother. Except for a slight difference in the cut of their garments, they were dressed exactly alike in beach pajamas of green shantung, and green sandals. She was reading him a letter. He sat very straight at the table; and when they left the room together, he walked so erect that he seemed to be leaning over backward. They had not exchanged greetings with him, though once he had caught the young man's glance and nodded good morning.

III

THE ONE BUSY SPOT in all Sconset, the only hive of activity in the place, seemed to be the drugstore. Ethel Grandin sat on a bench at the bus stop across from the store and watched the people go in and out. There were, of course, ten women to every man; with very few exceptions, each male was either under eighteen or well over forty. Those who came between—half a dozen at the most, during an entire hour—were in uniform.

It was a full white day, so white with a morning glare that the sky was not blue at all, though there was not a cloud to be seen. The day was not yet warm; a kind of early morning coolness still lingered on the air; but by noon or even by eleven, this coolness was sure to be gone. The beach would be blazing, the day hot and enervating like the tropics.

She had yet to get postcards; but inasmuch as she had forgotten them in Woods Hole and again when they landed at Nantucket, it didn't seem to matter too much. After Boston the chain had been broken; further cards could wait awhile.—She now remembered, also, that she had forgotten to telephone home last night, letting her mother know they had arrived. That could wait too, till tonight; she would try to call early enough so she could speak to the boys.

Far more important than cards or phone calls was the problem of the holiday: how to save it or, failing that, how to get through it. When the dreadful moment was met, something deep inside her had risen up at last and taken the stand for her, willy-nilly: it was as if she had had no part in it, almost no say in the matter. To apologize or backtrack, now, was impossible. The step was taken; it had to lead where it would, and she to follow.

And yet she was bitterly aware of how completely she had cut off her husband, certainly without intending to do so. She had gone to such lengths that he had been left with nothing. She had not wanted to spare him; yet she had not wanted to tie him hand and foot, either, or reduce him to such a zero status that whatever move he might make from now on would be inacceptable as husband or lover, almost even as friend. It had all been necessary, last night; but now, more than ever before in their lives, they must find some way of getting together again. He was alone and she was alone; they must face this fact, and seek an opening for a return to one another. With all her heart she wanted to put her arms around him and say, "Look, John. . . . John. . . ."—but from there she could think no further. She did not know what she had to say to him; in plain fact, she had nothing to say, really; but how else were they to reach one another again? He would not be coming to her bed, nor could she blame him for that; and it was utterly impossible for her to go to his, and thus invalidate the truth of what she had been trying to tell him last night.

Ethel Grandin was no nearer knowing this morning what she would do than when she had sat for so long in the wicker chair, waiting for him to go back to his bed. Even when he did go, she must have sat there for another half hour or even an hour longer, long after the harp recital was finished in the parlor below, the hotel quiet for the night, her cigarettes gone, and her husband asleep. During that period she had thought literally nothing; she was shaken and frightened because of what had happened, yet somehow curiously relieved at last.

The one moment when she had been at all afraid of weakening was when he first got into her bed and she felt at once that he had no pajamas on. Stiff in his pleading embrace she still resisted, though her heart went out in pity for his nakedness. He seemed at that moment more pathetic than ever. It hadn't been his fault; not more than half a dozen times in ten years had he done such a thing.

It had long been part of his tact and consideration that he never took it for granted beforehand that she would let him make love to her, so that whenever he came to her bed it was always with his pajamas on, both jacket and pants; if he took them off at all, it was only after their love-making had begun. Last night he had had no pajamas to put on or take off because he hadn't unpacked. When she heard him undress in the dark, in fact, and get into his bed—when she lay there in the dark herself and thought of him lying naked between the cold sheets of the unfamiliar bed—she wished she had thought to lay out his pajamas for him before he came back upstairs.

From the little square where she sat, irregular lanes wound away toward the back alleys of Sconset, toward the moors, or the beach. Along these lanes could be seen incredibly small cottages of the salt-box variety, high and tiny, packed so intimately close together that one could scarcely have walked between them, unpainted or else weather-beaten to a harmonious uniform hue that was not color at all, and every one of them all but smothered in rambler roses which were fast fading from their bright original pink (for the season was getting on and the sun was strong now) to a pink-white. Many of them had quaint but quite useless picket fences hemming in their infinitesimal yards, useless because knee-high; into the parlor of most of them one could have stepped directly from the street in a single step. It was all picturesque, charming, and self-conscious, exactly as one expected to find it, so that pictorially Sconset held no surprise whatever to anyone who had ever seen picture postcards of Nantucket, Martha's Vineyard, or the Cape.

After her husband had left last evening, she had unpacked and got into bed. When he returned he must have
supposed she was already asleep; either that or he pretended to think so. Perhaps he was afraid that if he put
the light on, the thing would start up again. But there was
nothing more to be said: he could have turned on the light
and read all night, or tried to talk it all out with her, and
she would not have had another word to say. She would
certainly not bring it up again today; no more would he;
but what was going to happen when they met again? They
couldn't just go on in stony silence for two whole weeks.

One of the reasons why they had chosen Sconset was
because they knew no one here; now, for the first time, she
wished they did. If ever they needed the company of
friends or someone to pass the time with, it was now.
Could there be anything in the Howards? she wondered.
From their twenty minutes in the bus together, he seemed
amiable enough, but there was something about Mrs.
Howard that disconcerted her and discouraged an intimate
exchange. She did not especially care for women, to begin with, particularly women her own age, so many of
whom were too sophisticated for her, unsimple, or dis-
honest. Happily married women, those in full possession
of their husbands (as Mrs. Howard seemed to be), put
Ethel Grandin off her ease, made her self-conscious, unwilling to compete socially or take part. She was much
more comfortable in the company of older women, who
thought her an ideal young matron full of sound sense
and thus did not really know her at all, or women younger
than herself who looked up to her as an experienced wife
and mother or talked freely and at length only of them-

selves and their problems, thus exempting her from social effort. This preference to stay aloof was not snobbishness; it was partly her New England upbringing, partly her lack of confidence in herself as a wife. Had her marriage been completely happy, even blindly so—or even had she been one of those wives who feel superior to or contemptuous of their husbands—she would have been able freely to enter into whatever relationships came up, casual or intimate. As it was, besides the friends of her husband, she had no close friend whatever of her own, and there was small chance of her making any.

It had not been fair to light that cigarette last night and so let him know she was still awake; this was the kind of feminine trick she deplored and so seldom indulged in. She had known what it would lead to when she did it. Woman-like, she had been unable to resist the temptation to tell him, in this way, that she hadn't fallen asleep as if nothing had happened, she was still firm, she had not forgotten. She had wanted to make him feel it still, in short. When, her cigarette finished, he had got out of his bed and come over to hers, it was no more than she expected; indeed, what else could he have done? Had he ignored the trick she would have despised him, and despised herself even more—therein lay the risk. In any case, he did feel it: his tone of voice as he whispered "Ethel" was as lonely as any she had ever heard. But what else could she have done, either? She would never have forgiven herself had she stayed in bed after he got in beside her; all that had gone before and all she had said would have been made ridiculous and cheap. No matter how badly she wanted him, last night had been one time when nothing in her life was more important at that moment than to say "No"—how few times lately had it been given her (oh, humiliating!) to say it? The shameful part of these many past weeks was that she had not even been allowed to deny him; for all he knew, she was ready and willing night after night on end. She had been, too—up till now.

A flock of young girls went sailing by on bicycles, wheeling recklessly about the square, narrowly missing pedestrians whom they ignored as if they did not exist (not because they were pedestrians but because they were old and thus didn't count), and carrying on, with petulant shrill cries, an un-understandable conversation among themselves which had no apparent logic or sequence whatever. The questions shouted back and forth seemed to have been put for the edification of anyone who overheard, without expectation of answer; but at one point one of them called out querulously, "Oh dear, isn't it time to go to the beach" and another answered, "Have you lost your mind Jimmy, are you absolutely wacky, why it isn't even ten-*thirty*."

When she had got up in the sunlighted room she had not dared to stay there looking at him, innocently asleep in the bed next to hers. How many mornings in the past, when he had stayed in her bed till morning, had she delighted to wake early and look at him before he awoke, study him in sleep beside her, so unconscious of them both or of where he was. Then she loved him so that it took all her self-control, all her consideration and thought of him, not to bend over and kiss him, or wake him and hold him again. This morning, for all his forty-four years, he had seemed again like a man much younger, giving

himself intensely to sleep: he lay on his right side partly
turned away from her, one knee bent and one leg thrust
straight down, the left wrist and hand dangling loosely
over the side, the other under his head so that his cheek
was cushioned in his palm; his thick sandy hair was disarranged more attractively than he could ever consciously
have arranged it. She had never got used to him physically,
never overcome the attraction of his physical person, perhaps because he had been hers only, the only man she had
ever had or wanted. Because he was asleep, she could look
at him with the eyes of memory, though the night before
was not forgotten. But she did not look long, lest he wake
and spoil her reverie by at once becoming a stranger.

Why had she picked a time like this for a showdown,
a time when he could have been her lover for two weeks?
But he himself had known the answer to the question even
as he asked it: because he expected to be that lover—
expected that it was expected of him. He knew; which was
why, reckless, he had dared her with mockery, saying such
an outrageous and true thing as "I suppose it's a moral
question." In preference to a holiday of love or at least of
love-making (long delayed, intended merely as a stopgap
for another month or few months), she had pulled ruin
down upon them both. Neither of them, now, could ever
undo last night. Well, out of that ruin they would build,
or part; there could be no half measures from now on, no
evasions, pretenses, or falling back on cowardly custom. If
he wanted her, she was his to take, but not as he had halfheartedly tried to do last night. Let him pull himself out
of his apathy first, emerge from the strange murk in which
she had lost sight of the man she loved; let him declare

himself and show his love as if they were just beginning. Once she was assured that she still counted as his wife, she would be only too willing to meet him halfway and try again. But she had to know—from inside herself and from him, not from his just saying it—that he wanted her. And in that there could be no make-believe.

Of course the problem had not been solved at all, or even faced; it had been stated merely. But since the first step toward the solution of any problem is to state it, perhaps there was hope. Or was there something else back of it; did a problem exist beyond the issue, always personal for her, of their marriage? She did not know; she only knew now where she stood in the matter, and had so expressed herself. How it was with her husband—that would be for him to say.

It was time to go to the beach. She preferred to go alone; she wanted to lie in the sun and not think about it any more: not think of anything. She got up from the bench and crossed the square to the drugstore to get some sun-tan oil and cards for Alan and Ted, dodging bicycles as she went.

IV

HE DID NOT FIND HER in the lobby, in their room again, nor on the long veranda. He looked along the porch to see where he had sat last night in the dark, and at the memory of who had been sitting in the porch swing, directly under their open window, he was reluctant to run into the Howards this morning. The drugstore, he remembered, was where the bus had come in. He stepped off the porch and started down the hot road that led along the bluff.

A young girl in white shorts, white halter, and white-rimmed sun glasses came tearing around the bend on a bicycle; he had to step quickly aside to escape being run down. Her red curls streamed out from under a white jockey cap and she had passed by before he recognized her as the girl he had seen sun-bathing on the grass. He turned to look back but he knew her now, and she was no longer the creature of allure she had seemed to be from the bathroom window; her behind, tight in sharkskin, was like a fat white heart upside down on the bicycle seat.

The drugstore was crowded with young girls in various stages of undress. They were buying postcards, magazines, sodas, cigarettes, bathing accessories, Kleenex, sun glasses, sun-tan oil.

Ethel stood at the drug counter, looking hardly older than the young women in backless dirndls and boys' trunks; certainly looking smarter. She wore a straight plain dress of blue chambray with a tan belt. He was so uncertain of his welcome that he almost turned to leave.

She glanced up, then bent to open her purse. "Here's a pencil and some cards," she said. "Will you write something on them for the boys, please?"

He leaned on the glass counter for a desk and addressed the cards. But when he had got the names down, he could think of nothing to say. On this summer island—in this drugstore, surrounded by so much youth—his sons seemed very far away. *Dear Alan, he finally wrote, I saw a terrific submarine from the train and thought of you. Have a fine time but be sure to help your grandparents as*

much as you can. . . . Dear Ted, This would be a won-
derful place for you boys so we'll all try to make it to-
gether next year. Remind me to tell you of the submarine.
He signed the cards *Love, Dad,* sensing keenly the inadequacy of those words, and of his own feelings. . . .

Ethel had made her purchases. "I'm going back," she
said.

"Yes, I want to put my shorts on and get into the
sun."

"I bought some sun-tan oil. The beach looked
blazing."

"Ethel—"

"Yes?"

"Let's go off by ourselves and just lie around . . ."

"We'll see."

He dropped the cards into a mailing slot and they
stepped into the hot square outside.

The noisy bus from Nantucket joggled in; it came to
a gasping stop at the curb. The wide door next to the
driver's seat swung open.

"Ethel," he said under his breath, "look who's here."

V

". . . You DID SAY that if we came out we might use your
room. Anyway, we took you at your word," Billie went on.
"Cliff has our bathing suits, see?" and she pointed to the
fat roll of towel under her husband's arm. The Captain
beamed on them both, as if they were the only two people

in the world he wanted to see at that moment—and doubtless they were.

"We're glad you did," Ethel said. "John and I don't know anyone here and it's nice to have someone."

"Yes, that's what we thought. For us too, I mean. Why, you can't imagine how lonesome we've been in Nantucket . . ."

As they started up the bluff road, Hauman swung an impulsive arm around Grandin's shoulder and gave him a kind of hug. "How are you, John?"

This familiarity took him so completely by surprise Grandin could only laugh, nonplused. The Captain's boundless delight at seeing them again was puzzling. Standing in the door of the bus, looking incredibly handsome, healthy, clean and young, his face had lighted up with pleasure even before he caught sight of them; when he did so, he gave the impression that he and Billie had expected to be met all along. His hearty handshake and beaming smile all but said, Have you been waiting long?

Billie wore a shiny white silk dress. Hauman was dressed as before in khaki shirt, trousers, and GI boots, his service cap stuck in his canvas belt. His spirits were irresistible; it would have been stuffy to hold oneself aloof from such good-natured if unreasonable affection. He was apparently the kind of young man to whom a second meeting was the equivalent of a long friendship. All his diffidence of yesterday was gone. His politeness and his almost archaic niceness of speech persisted—there were the words rascal, heck, darn and so on—but the new confidence he had seemed to find in himself on seeing the Grandins again told them that from now on the party was in his hands.

He took Grandin's arm and led him ahead as if he had something intimate to confide. But the move turned out to have sprung from nothing more than his native assumption (which Grandin was to notice increasingly) that men should be with men, women with women. Ethel and Billie followed along behind.

Hauman talked effusively of their rooming house in Nantucket, the funny place they had found for breakfast with the wonderful doughnuts, the Children's Beach near their street, the Whaling Museum they had already been through (the first admissions that morning), the Yacht Club. He turned continually as he walked along, not to assure himself that he was being listened to but to note what response he was getting. Though it was all senseless, Grandin couldn't help but be pleased. It was a long while since anyone had paid him such flattering attention.

Mr. Howard was sitting on the veranda alone. He frowned on the party, then sprang to his feet as Grandin introduced the Haumans. "Glad to meet you, Captain," he said, noticing at once the double silver bars. Grandin lingered behind a moment while Hauman shepherded the women inside. He wanted to find out if the Howards had been aware of the quarrel; perhaps Mr. Howard's attitude this morning would tell him.

"Why don't you come down to the beach with us?"

"Maybe later, thanks," Mr. Howard said. "Right now I'm trying to get used to the fact that I'll probably be a bachelor most of the morning. On a day like this, too!"

"All the more reason for coming with us, then." But since this didn't seem to be the answer Mr. Howard was expecting, he added: "Is Mrs. Howard a late sleeper?"

"She never gets up," Mr. Howard said, almost with pride. "I don't expect to lay eyes on her till noon, if then."

When he opened the door to the bedroom he found Hauman alone, pulling off his shirt.

"Hi, John!"

"Where are the women?"

"Oh, they're in the bathroom. I thought you and I could dress here, and Mrs. Grandin and Billie in there."

It did seem an odd procedure; the custom generally, in Grandin's experience, was that husband and wife dressed and undressed together. For a moment he wondered what it was it reminded him of. Then he remembered. It was like schooldays, like dates in his youth, like a college houseparty, when the men dressed together in one room and the girls in another, with jokes, as often as not, over the partition or through the door, and mock threats of entering before the girls were ready, to their delighted screams of protest.

But Hauman was too busy for joking or perhaps the women were farthest from his mind. He was out of his clothes in no time, but careful to leave them in a neatly folded pile on the chair. Out of a kind of furtive curiosity, Grandin could not keep from stealing a glance or two at the exposed and splendid physique. It was heroic: Hercules, Hector, a younger Odysseus, seen as they were never seen in the storybooks, and made modern by the startling whiteness of the hips above and below the tan. While he did not display himself exhibitionistically, Hauman nevertheless stalked about in the nude as if he were alone, apparently completely unconscious that his was a figure to be looked at. In the act of pulling on his khaki shorts, which were like old basketball trunks, he discovered something out the window.

"What's that down there, John, few miles along the beach?" He strapped his waist in tight with the canvas belt. "Looks like Nissen huts to me."

Grandin stepped to the window. Hauman put a hand on his shoulder and they looked out.

Three or four tubular convex structures spread themselves in the sand, very near to the shore, some distance off, They looked like dark silos which had been split down the middle and the two halves laid horizontally on the ground. Smoke rose from several small chimneys.

"Must be a Coast Guard station," Hauman said. He bent down and picked up his boots. "Better wear my boondockers to the beach. Looks like a long walk."

"It is, rather, but I've noticed there's a broad path half the way, and the rest is sand."

"I'll wear 'em anyway. Anything I hate is to walk barefooted in a lot of sand.—You should see us out at the 'Canal, John. We run around naked, most of the time, but nobody'd think of going without their boondockers."

He stepped into one of his shoes and then leaned on the small dressing table while he pulled on the other. There was a sharp cracking sound, followed by the brittle smash of glass.

"*Clifford Hau*man," Billie called from the bathroom, "what have you broken *now!*"

"Nothing, honey," he answered plaintively, "now never mind, everything's all right." He turned to Grandin and ducked his head guiltily. "Sorry, sir. Look what I've done."

The leg of the dressing table had given way under his weight and the small shaded lamp had tipped over, breaking the bulb.

"It's nothing, forget it."

"I'll be glad to pay for it, sir."

"Nonsense."

"Well, gee." He smiled. "You're darn nice about it, John."

From the bathroom Billie called: "Can we come out?"

"Come ahead, honey," Hauman said, "we're ready."

Billie found the damage at once. "Clifford, *honestly!*" She faced the Grandins with a gasp of exasperation, her hands on her hips. "Isn't it the limit, he's always *breaking* things! Everything he touches or handles gets broken before he's through with it. Like that chair yesterday. And then he borrowed my father's car the other night, a big heavy Buick mind you—"

"Well gee, Billie, I didn't do it on purpose, did I? It's just an old light bulb," he added.

"Light bulb nothing—look at that dressing table, Clifford Hauman!" Then, as if suddenly remembering that this was the first time her professor was seeing her in a bathing suit, she assumed her sleepy smile and sauntered across the room to admire a calendar.

She wore an ultrafeminine bathing dress of white satin lastex with a short pleated skirt and bare midriff. It had probably been made especially for her by a dressmaker and, as Billie well knew, it strikingly set off her figure and beauty. In the crude phrase, she was built for comfort, the comfort of a man. He could see how it would be delightful and exciting to go to bed with her, but only if she were interested in him as well—or, better, if she were someone he had never met.

Ethel wore espadrilles, a black woolen bathing suit (it fitted her tight, without ruffle or frill, and made her figure look straight and firm, almost hipless, like a girl in her teens), and a long yellow *peignoir* of toweling which they had bought in Paris seven or eight years ago. For her cigarettes, comb, sun-tan oil and other trifles needed at the beach, she carried the rubber-lined canvas bag they had used to carry diapers in when Alan was a baby.

"Mrs. Grandin," Hauman said, "I'm going to call you Ethel if you don't mind. Do you mind?"

"I wish you would, Cliff."

He felt better. Now they were all friends. Assured that this was so, he took Grandin's arm. "Okay, John, let's go."

In the hall Billie could be heard confiding some news to Ethel which, from the intensity of her usually languid voice, should have been exciting. "Do you know what we heard at the diner in Nantucket? We heard that Toni Lansing was here in Sconset! Wouldn't it be thrilling to run into her?"

"Who's Tony Lansing?" Grandin asked.

"Imagine, Mrs. Grandin," Billie said, " 'who's Toni Lansing'! Aren't men the limit?"

Hauman rose to his defense. "Well, I didn't know myself," he said. "It seems she's some movie star. Billie knows them all. You'd think from the name it was a man. But boy"—he gave a short laugh and lowered his voice— "I saw her in a movie once and Toni Lansing's no man."

Mr. Howard saluted from his chair on the veranda. "Sadie's down after all," he announced happily. "Latest report is she's in the dining room now having her tenth cup of coffee. I expect we'll be joining you in no time."

Across the road from the hotel, set in a profusion of rosebushes prodigally abloom, a substantial wooden staircase led in two easy flights to the sandy waste below, where the wooden path to the beach began.

"Isn't that a *dread*ful name," Billie said. "Sadie!"

VI

THE SMOOTH SLOPING beach had been raked clean by the lifeguard. From the shade of their umbrellas, a dozen or more persons looked up at the party arriving. No one was in the surf; all lay stretched out in the baking sand, indolent; but an expression of curiosity came into their lazy looks. John Grandin knew that his morning would be spent in the same fashion, quiet in the sand. The surf looked much too strong to attempt today, the pounding breakers too high and rough.

Ethel spread her robe and towel, opened her bag to get out the sun-tan oil, and arranged herself for the morning. Her husband wondered who among these people had heard the shouting in the bedroom last night; and if they had, what were they thinking? He nodded again to the yellow-haired young man and his mother lying in the sand fifty feet away but received no answering nod of recognition. Affecting a nonchalance he was far from feeling, he took out a cigarette.

Hauman reached down to light it for him. Then as if hearing the breakers for the first time, he dropped his towel and raced for the surf. It was amazing to see a figure of such bulk move with such speed and ease. He plunged headlong into a gray-green roller and Billie followed. A moment later they emerged, laughing and coughing; and for the next half hour they pulled each other about in the surf, swam far out to ride in with the breakers, or stood in the black sand and allowed the water to slide around their ankles.

The lifeguard approached and introduced himself. "My name is Pete, sir. Would you like an umbrella and some back rests for your party?" He explained the rates by day or week.

Four back rests were engaged for the day and a large sunshade for two weeks. Pete hauled them from a shack and set them up in the spot the Grandins had chosen. He was very young; he was tanned the color of molasses and looked strong enough, but he had the figure of a child, not at all what one expected in a life-guard. When he bent down to adjust the sunshade, a blond fuzz could be seen on his upper lip and along the jawbone. . . . The war, it's the war, there's a war on, don't you know there's a war. . . . His chore done, he retired to his perch nearby and resumed his duty of scanning the sea and the surf. But the Haumans were so far from needing his or any help that he might have taken the morning off. No one else was going to be in the water at all.

The mother and son lay on an enormous striped towel like a carpet; their green beach pajamas had been

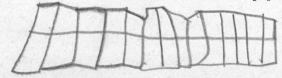

replaced by identical light-green bathing suits. He was the only man on the beach who did not wear shorts.

With everyone else, Ethel and John Grandin watched the two bathers. Though nothing had been said, it had been a relief to them both when the Haumans had shown up. Her cordial welcome at the bus stop had not been mere politeness.

"You'd better ask them for lunch," she said.

"If you like."

The Haumans stood at the edge of the surf with ruffles of white water around their ankles, looking out to sea. His legs were planted wide and firm in the sliding sand, his head thrown slightly back. As he had intimated on the boat, he was faintly inclined to fat, but the excess weight interfered not at all with the noble proportions of his build; it seemed rather to add to the heroic physique, as though he were some giant figure out of mythology come down to show these mortals what a Homeric god looked like. Billie leaned toward him, one knee bent in toward the other and the relaxed foot to the rear, in the accepted pose (consciously or not) of the fashion model or movie star. Her short white skirt flipped and snapped about her wide hips.

"Who's that, my god," a woman's voice murmured over Grandin's head. Mr. and Mrs. Howard were joining them. "No slouch, he," she added; "but he looks dangerously like that old Michelin-tire man."

"Now Mama, don't go making fun."

"I'm not making fun. Quite the reverse. Who is he?"

"A Marine captain we met on the steamer," Ethel

explained. "It happened that his wife had been a student
of my husband's."

"Is that she? Lovely girl."

"Mm-*mmm*!" Bill Howard made a humming sound
deep in the back of his throat, a cross between a grunt
and a groan.

"Striking pair. Too bad about those rubber tires,
though. And lord, his arms and shoulders—they look positively blown up!" Mrs. Howard laughed at her own notion. "I'll bet if you stuck a pin in him, you'd hear the
wheezing sigh of his collapse all the way to Woods Hole."

"Always belittlin'," Mr. Howard said.

"Belittlin' my foot. I wish you were half as good."

If the Howards had any inkling of last night's quarrel, they gave no sign of it. John Grandin felt vastly
relieved.

"We hear there's a movie star in the vicinity," Mrs.
Howard said. "Toni Lansing or somebody."

"Boy, Toni Lansing! Just tell me where," Bill Howard said.

The Marine Captain was roughhousing at the edge
of the surf. He scooped Billie up in his arms and flung
her about while she screamed in panic. He turned hand-
springs along the sand, then a long series of cartwheels.
Grandin got the impression, though he couldn't have
said why, that Hauman was doing this neither for his
own pleasure nor for Billie's—that his heart was not in
it, in short. He raced back, ducked low, and tackled Billie's legs, but it seemed make-believe, somehow. She stood
still, crouching, and screeched. The whole beach had heard
and was watching, fascinated. Finally they ran up from

the surf and began vigorously to dry one another with
their towels.

Ethel introduced them to Mrs. Howard. Grandin noticed how she took them in, coldly, objectively, but interested. She glanced at her husband and raised her
eyebrows in a cynical yet admiring expression. Bill Howard made a move to give up his place in the shade of the
umbrella but they insisted on remaining in the sun. They
knelt in the sand and took turns applying sun-tan oil to
each other's backs.

Before he settled himself to rest, the Captain bent
forward, took up a match folder, and lighted the cigarette
that Grandin had just put into his mouth. Grandin was
amused by these manners (which could hardly be called
manners, however, when they ignored the women entirely) but they made him feel old. His own students,
who had cause to seek his favors for a dozen reasons,
never deferred to him to this extent.

"Were you folks on the boat John and I came over
on?" Hauman asked of the Howards.

"We were."

"Funny we didn't see you."

"You just weren't paying attention to anyone but that
beautiful wife of yours. We saw you."

John Grandin wondered again where or how the
Captain had been wounded. From the story of his long
hospitalization and the fact that he was still on the sick
list, the injuries must have been damaging indeed; yet
there seemed to be no outward sign of them whatever.
Considering the strenuous athletics in the sand, he was
in the best of health. But as Hauman turned his face to

the sun, he saw for the first time a thin scar that ran from the left ear down along the jawline to the chin; it was well healed, and must have required the best of surgical skill to leave so fine a scar. Only at the base of the chin, just underneath, reposed a small knot or lump of scar tissue. He wanted to ask about it, but he felt sure that Hauman would be embarrassed in the presence of the Howards; time enough later in the day when they were alone.

Billie was talking to Ethel in low tones; there was an oddly wistful note in her voice. ". . . You've no idea how homesick I've been for that room ever since we left, isn't it silly? Dad gave me the money to do it over only last month. It's right next to Mother's room but I have my own bath. We didn't dream then that Cliff would be back so soon or—or that I'd be a married woman. The whole room is done in a real baby blue and it's adorable. The dressing table has a mirrored top, of course, and on the tables I have the dearest little mirrored cigarette boxes. I don't smoke but most of my girl friends do, and anyway they're darling. The lamps next to my bed and the chaise have blue bows. On the bed, lined up against the bolster, are my dolls. I can't wait to see it again. And you know? It's an awful thing to say but I hate to give it up. . . ."

"I don't see that you'll have to," Ethel said. "You and Cliff won't be able to take a house together for some time."

"Oh yes, we're going to find a house just as soon as we get back."

"But I thought Cliff was to report for duty again?"

"That's just his talk. Wouldn't it be silly when he can get compensation and all, for the rest of his life?"

Bill Howard roused himself (and roused them all) with a loud exaggerated yawn. "Going in swimming, Sadie?"

"Certainly not."

"Good, that let's me out." He looked about restlessly. "Well, I don't know about you-all, but I-all am going off and find that Toni Lansing. Mm-*mmm*! If she's anywhere in Sconset, she must be along the beach taking the sun—and probably disappointed as all hell because nobody comes to find her. Want to join me, anyone?"

"I do," Billie said.

"Okay, if my old lady doesn't object. Or your old man."

"My old man," Billie said. "Funny, I never thought of him that way."

As Grandin watched them go, his eye was caught by another figure trudging in lonely fashion through the sand a few hundred feet back from the beach, about midway between the sea and the bluff. It was a man in white, walking parallel to the beach, and he appeared to be plodding doggedly, leaning slightly forward, as if he had come a long way and still had far to go. "Pete," he called out, "who's that?"

"The Coast Guard," Pete said. "He just passed along here behind us, few minutes ago. They patrol the island day and night. See that black post where he's stopping at now? There's a time clock there and he punches it every hour. Oh, you'll see him—or one of the others—going by here good many times a day."

"Lonely job, I should imagine."

"Not nearly so lonely as at night," Pete said. "Still, they have a police dog for company, then. I suppose you know that since the war, civilians aren't allowed on the beach at night?"

"I didn't, no."

"It's something to keep in mind. After dark, nobody can come within five hundred yards of the beach. If they do and get caught, there's an awful fine. But the fine's nothing compared to what those dogs'll do to you."

"Is that the Coast Guard station far down the beach?"

"Yeah, down near Tom Nevershead. Good many men live there."

"Well, that takes care of that," Mrs. Howard said. "Bill and I planned to spend the evening on the beach, come the night of the full moon. Really, they ought to tell you these things in the catalogue."

Grandin watched the figure of the Coast Guard disappearing slowly over the reaches of sand, his white uniform like a tiny diminishing spark of light. It was a melancholy job, to say the least, that patrol; and the fact that the coast guardsman's duties brought him so many times a day past the sun bathers enjoying their leisure couldn't have made the job any easier to take.

Mr. Howard and Billie came hurrying back. They ran stamping into the group, both of them breathless.

"We saw her," Billie gasped, "we saw her! She's sitting down there just like—why, just like you and I!"

"No!" mocked Sarah Howard.

"Mighty worth looking at though, Mama."

"She's all in white," Billie went on rapturously;

the fact that she herself was all in white seemed to have escaped her. "White suit and sandals and white jockey cap—even white sun glasses!"

"How could anybody have white sun glasses?" Hauman said.

"I mean the rims, as you very well know. And she has the loveliest red hair, real fiery red! I wonder if it's real . . ."

Hauman got to his feet. His shorts were so tight that the belt seemed to cut into his flesh. "What do you say, John, shall we take a look too?"

"I don't mind," Grandin said, getting up. "Want to come, Ethel?"

"No thanks."

"I'll come," Billie said; "I know just where she is."

"We'll find her, you stay here with Ethel and the others," Hauman said. He took Grandin's arm and they started off.

Alone with Hauman, Grandin felt self-conscious; he sensed within himself the feelings of a small boy again, a boy who looked up in hero worship to the other. This became the more unreasonable when he reflected that *he* was the one looked up to, by Hauman. The responsibility that this put upon him in their relationship was something he would rather not have had.

"Cliff," he said, "do you ever think of not coming back?"

"Why gee, I hope we do, often! Billie and I love it here."

"I meant from the South Pacific, or wherever you're going. After all, a good many of them don't came back."

"Oh. Well, that's something you always think of as happening to the other guy, I guess."

The beach was hard, smooth and hot under their feet; to the left, the water slid up and back on the wet dark sand.

"You know something? I heard the Major say once that if he named ten guys to go out on a raid and knew in advance that nine of 'em wouldn't be coming back— and told 'em so, too—there isn't one of them but what would go. Of course they might look at each other in a funny way, because each one would be thinking they were the one that was coming back and it was tough on the other guys, but they'd all of them go." Then he added, "I don't know what it's like in the Army, but that's the way it is with the Marines." He laughed. "Gee, I wouldn't dare say that in front of Billie. She'd think I was bragging, and anyway she doesn't like to hear about the war. But darn it, it's true."

"What about yourself, Cliff? Doesn't the thought of death—"

"Thought of death!" He laughed heartily. "Nobody has thoughts of death, don't you know that, John? That's just something in people's mind—not real at all. Anyway you don't have time, you're much too busy. Why, the way they keep you jumping out there, you never give it a thought."

"Not even when someone you know is shot down? Your—well, your buddy, say?" The word made him feel awkward, but he felt it was the one which Hauman would understand.

"That's just tough luck. But you can't stop and think

about it every time. That wouldn't get you anywheres. Besides, if you'd seen as much death as I have— Gee, maybe that sounds like bragging again."

"I suppose it's a matter of—getting used to it."

"Why say!" Hauman placed a broad hand on his shoulder. "When you see those big bulldozers come grinding along and push 'em all into one big trench, you begin to think life doesn't amount to very much, or death either. Nobody can take time to bury the bodies with shovels in the old-fashioned way, in the right kind of grave, and all that."

"The enemy dead?"

"Oh, our own too! You can't beat those bulldozers, they do the job on the double. A guy sits up top steering —I've done it myself—with nothing on but a helmet and a pair of shorts and boondockers. It's pretty hot work; those engines give out a lot of heat when they got a big load to shove around.—Look, I'll bet that's her now, though Billie didn't say anything about the officer."

In the sand some fifty feet back sat the young girl in white whom Grandin had seen twice now, and a young naval officer in a dark-blue uniform and white cap. They did not talk as they watched Grandin and Hauman go by.

It would have been silly not to turn frankly and look at her; it was what they had come down here for and she must have known it. Grandin saw that their curiosity was not unwelcome. From under the visor of the white jockey cap she returned a gaze as frank as theirs, and her amused smile was a good enough substitute for hello.

"Well, I guess that's that, John. Let's go back."

Grandin felt that for dignity's sake it might look better if they went on a short distance farther; but in view of the girl's smile and her frank acceptance of their frank curiosity, he took Hauman's suggestion and they turned back at once.

"Didn't we tell you, wasn't it worth it?" Bill Howard asked, in a fairly accurate imitation of Billie's excitement.

"Oh I don't know," Hauman said, "she's got to go some to beat Billie."

"Why Clifford Hauman, thank you very *much*."

"Mighty nice husband you've got there," Sarah Howard said, "in more ways than one. If you know what I mean."

"Never mind, Sadie."

"By the way, Captain," she went on.

He came to polite attention at once. "Yes, ma'am?"

"Your wife has been telling us you're on the sick list."

"Yes, ma'am, I am."

"Well? Come come, tell us about those wounds. I'll show you mine if you'll show me yours," and she roared with laughter.

"Really, Mama, cut it out."

Hauman's embarrassment was painful to see. "I guess there isn't much to tell, ma'am. I'm not a hero, if that's what you mean. I was wounded, yes, but—well . . ." And now, as if eager to get it over with at last, he told the shameful story almost in one breath. "I was leading a few of my men through a path in the jungle when we were ambushed. It was my own darn fault. I knew the Japs were there but I made a wrong mistake and took the wrong path. Anyway, those rascals jumped us and I don't remember anything then till I woke up in a hospital tent and they told me it was sixteen days later. Eight of the other fellows were dead, they told me, but one other guy and myself came out of it all right."

"All right, yes," Billie snorted, "with ten broken ribs, all his teeth rammed down his throat, his whole face cut open to his jaw, a fractured skull and concussion of the brain—if you call that all right! He laid there in the jungle for two whole days before they found him, didn't you, Cliff?"

"That's what they tell me but I don't know, honey, I don't remember."

"Are those store teeth you're wearing?" Mrs. Howard asked.

"Yes ma'am," and he smiled obligingly to show them.

"What about the fractured skull?" Bill Howard said.

"I think it's all right, sir. I get dizzy once in a while and I don't have any nerves working in the left side of my face, but that's something that won't show up in the examination."

"What do you mean?"

"Oh, Cliff thinks he's going to get back into the service," Billie said.

"I sure am, and I'm going to pass that examination, too! *They* can't tell I don't feel anything in my face."

Sarah Howard folded her arms and looked at him appraisingly. "I think you're a fine boy and all that," she said, "and one of the most beautiful I ever saw. But I also think you're a damned fool."

Hauman blushed, but one couldn't have said whether

it was because of the extravagant compliment or the word
"damn." "Well," he said uncomfortably, "I guess it depends on how you feel about these things, ma'am. I mean
I've been there. And those fellows— Well, I don't know
how to explain it, but I guess that's where I belong."

"Did you enjoy it as much as all that?"

"Enjoy it? I don't know, ma'am, I never thought
of it that way. But I know one thing! I sure miss it, and
the fellows . . ."

VII

As THE SUN ROSE higher in the sky and the day grew
hotter, conversation diminished. The distance shimmered
and danced in the heat waves that rose from the sand.
There was an indolence in the air that seemed more
sensual than lazy; it acted as a soporific upon them all.
The sea pounded not thirty feet away, but unnoticed,
forgotten, scarcely part of the scene. People lay about in
a kind of unconscious languorous communion, as if the
beach were an enormous bed. Some were prone, hugging
the sand in luxurious exhaustion; others had fallen into
uninhibited attitudes which, paradoxically, they would
never have assumed in public had they been fully clothed.
Along the hot sand blew the heavy sickish-sweet odor of
sun-tan oil.

". . . Those curls of his," Billie was saying in a whisper, scarcely audible; "I keep telling him he's got to get
a haircut. They do when they're on duty; it's a strict rule.
But you know what? I think he really likes them. He

doesn't want to have them cut off. Isn't it the limit? I know that's it, but he won't admit it . . ."

If Hauman had heard, he didn't show it by the slightest move. He was stretched full length, his arms and legs spread wide, giving himself to the sun. The tawny curls trembled lightly in the breeze, his chest rose and fell in a steady slow rhythm. Below the ribs the body sloped sharply to the hollow of his stomach, so that the shorts, so tight when he stood up, lay loosely about his waist. The blue eyes stared into the sky. John Grandin wondered what he was thinking, but he was reluctant to disturb that repose, which seemed, except for the heaving ribs, deathlike. He could not say why he admired him so; it was like one's feeling for the very young, whom one takes pleasure in merely to look at or watch, without expectation of return, without thought of any exchange at all, intellectual or emotional. . . . But now a different picture presented itself to his mind, called up by what morbid intuition he would never know: a picture of Hauman in battle dress, gaitered, helmeted, strapped about with cartridge belts, a tommy gun grasped in his outstretched hand, lying (as he here lay) on a beach, but sprawled face down, with the first small waves of the incoming tide washing gently around him. . . .

Did the intensity of his emotion reach across to the other? If so, Hauman did his best speedily to reassure him that all would be well. As if they had been at that moment in some secret communication, he turned his head on the sand and regarded Grandin with a grave smile —a smile which his good nature (or vanity or youth or eagerness to please) could not long keep from turning into a broad grin.

Undone, John Grandin felt himself slipping into a peculiar morass of emotion, unprecedented in his experience: sadness, desire for he knew not what, admiration, and a foolish wish that it might be he who was to die instead. . . .

VIII

"I HATE TO BREAK this up," Bill Howard said, "but ain't it time for lunch?"

A good half of the sun bathers had gone. Pete had left the umbrellas standing, against their possible return later.

"I could lie here all day," Mrs. Howard murmured from the sand, "and just die."

"Mustn't die on an empty stomach, Sadie. Come along." He picked up their towels and his robe and headed for the path to the bluff.

"I don't mind about lunch," his wife said as she started after him, "but god, I *am* interested in washing off this sickening *smell*."

"They're comical, aren't they," Hauman said.

"We're expecting you to stay to lunch with us," Ethel said.

"But that's not fair. In the first place—"

"In the first place, our lunches are already paid for at the hotel," Grandin said. "Please don't disappoint us."

"Well I'm sure we thank you very kindly. What do you say, Cliff, do you think it's right we should accept?"

It was and they did. They gathered up their things and began the long trek back, single file through the sand, Billie leading, Grandin bringing up the rear. At the foot of the stairway to the bluff, Hauman made a discovery.

"Look, a shower bath."

"Oh, good! Where?"

"Not for you, honey, it says MEN."

On a small platform, with a bench in front, were two open stall showers, screened by rosebushes climbing a trellis; they were marked, as Hauman had said, for the use of men only.

"That's a rotten shame," Billie said. "After salt bathing I feel just gritty all over."

"There's a shower in the bathroom," Ethel said.

"We'll be up in a jiffy, honey, you run on."

The women went up the stairs and Hauman stepped into one of the stalls; a moment later his damp shorts fell with a smack on the floor outside.

"Hey," he called out, "what am I thinking of? I can't take a shower, I haven't anything to put on afterwards."

"You can wear my robe," Grandin said, "I'll forego the bath till later." He slipped off his red-cotton robe, laid it on the bench, and sat on one of the lower steps of the stairway to wait. He lighted a cigarette; this was one time when he could get away with it by himself, without having Hauman spring to light it for him.

Hauman could be heard inside the stall sloshing vig-

orously about. From the sounds that came forth, it was
as if some obstreperous pony were being hosed down.
Suddenly he broke into song—rather tunelessly, though
the tune and the words were recognizable enough.

"... From the halls of Mon-tuh-zoo-*oo*muh, to the
shores-of Trippo-leee ..."

Abruptly the song broke off as suddenly as it had
begun. For some reason he had changed his mind.

Grandin wondered why. He guessed that Hauman
had become self-conscious of being overheard and had
cut himself short rather than risk Grandin's thinking he
was trying to create an effect. Musing on whether or not
this might be so, a whole series of pictures opened out
in his imagination, in which, possibly, neophytes and
cadets in boot camp, too suddenly proud of the Corps
and anxious to show off, had been slapped down by marines of superior rank and longer service for indiscrimi-
nately slinging the sacred hymn about. Hauman had been
one of these, and may well have been so slapped down.
He was a captain now and could afford to sing the hymn
where and when he pleased; but perhaps the old discipline persisted and he remembered well. Perhaps, too, he
himself regarded the hymn as something sacred, to be
sung in company with other marines and then only on
proper occasions. ...

The water was turned off. He was silent inside the
stall. Then his voice came over the partition. "John—"

"Yes?"

"Mind if I ask you something?"

"Not at all, Cliff."

"Tell me." He sounded grave. "Are you happily married?"

"Am I?" Grandin had to adjust himself to the unexpectedness of the question. He did not for a moment think Hauman had been perceptive enough to gather that he and Ethel had had a quarrel; he knew there was something quite different back of it. Indeed, the question had been almost a rhetorical one. "Why, yes," he answered at last; "very, I should say." He pondered—not the question itself but what had made Hauman bring it up. "Why do you ask?"

"Oh"—the answer was offhand, matter-of-fact—"no reason, specially."

"Did you think we weren't?"

"No, not for a second, honest. I was thinking of something else. Somebody else's marriage, I mean. Fellow I know."

He stepped from the shower, sat down on the wooden bench, and began to dry himself. As Grandin watched, he began to be oppressed by a melancholy uneasiness. Hauman's question had provoked a few questions of his own. He felt an overmastering compulsion to inquire of things he had no right to inquire about: questions concerning that secret life sitting over there on the bench which he would never really know or reach, which was mysterious, alien, and remote from his own, and which would one day die. With inward despair, he checked himself, unsatisfied, because what he wanted to know would have been so unseemly to ask. . . . And in another moment he heard himself saying: "The thing I've been thinking is: you and Billie can't very well afford to have children

at this point—can you? I mean of course if you're going
back into the service."

"Well, I don't know, John; I guess it wouldn't be so
good."

"What about children, Cliff?"

"What about them, John?"

"I don't wish to interfere, but— Does Billie—or do
you— That is, would you care to have me suggest—"

"Oh, I see. Well, don't worry about it, John, it's all
taken care of."

He was rebuked; yet the prying inquisitiveness remained. He could not say why he felt such a consuming
curiosity about Cliff Hauman, a curiosity about so many
different things relating to him. He thought he had detected in Hauman's playful attentiveness to Billie, his
frolicking with her as though she were the world's ideal
playmate, a suppressed impatience; and he wondered what
was the cause of it or even if it were true. When Hauman
had asked if he was happily married and then said he
was referring to "somebody else's marriage," he had not
been very subtle. Perhaps for the first time in his life
he had made the discovery that the future was something
to think of, a looming prospect soon to become an actuality. Had he begun to regard himself as a husband—
did he like the idea, or not like it? Or was the reverse
of this true: was he beginning to think that his date with
Billie was lasting a little too long? For it was as a "date"
that he seemed to consider their holiday and honeymoon,
a date that would soon be over, enabling him to get back
to the fellows. When he did get back he would tell them
all about it, though revealing none of those details which

most counted—which John Grandin, for example, would most like to have known: which, indeed, he felt an increasing, a dangerous desire to ask about. These Hauman would not relate, because, as his buddies well knew, love was the same everywhere and women all alike.

Love—or how to take care of oneself in love—Hauman understood. ("Don't worry about it, John, it's all taken care of.") Grandin would not soon forget that rebuke. The reply, as well as Hauman's attitude during the whole nervous but brief discussion, had been so matter-of-fact that he felt humiliated—and oddly, too, a little proud of Cliff, gratified that he had terminated the discussion then and there and so helped him out. For now he realized with a genuine shock that he had introduced the subject of contraceptives all but deviously in an unconscious hope that Hauman would talk about his sexuality. He bitterly regretted his intrusion; yet in a way, he was glad: it was a warning to him. The rebuke had been timely and welcome; from now on it was up to him to see that such a thing did not come up again.

Hauman threw the red-cotton robe around his shoulder (it was, of course, much too small), tied the sash, picked up his towel, and turned to Grandin with a smile.

"Okay, John? Shall we go?"

IX

IN PANTS AND BRA, Billie Hauman stood before the mirror, doing her face. Ethel Grandin, dressed, watched her from the wicker chair. She did not really hear the aimless chatter. She was thinking: Billie's such a pretty girl, too bad she doesn't have a better figure. Neither malice nor envy prompted this thought. Billie's was the classic soft womanly figure so well represented in art, the curvy form which artists loved to paint but which had been scorned by women of her generation. It was not at all the mold of the modern girl, the kind of figure she herself had aspired to and achieved. Billie's lushness may well have been the natural complement to the hard upright body of the male, but in Ethel Grandin's eyes the hips were too wide, the waist too narrow, the thighs thick, too soft, even rather fatty.

"Oh I'm so tired," Billie was saying. "That water just *en*ervates me."

"You can take a nap after lunch, if you like."

"Funny how that word sounds different than what it means. 'Enervate' ought to mean pep you up, give you energy or something." Billie was adapting herself to the wife of the college professor she could not lose sight of in Mrs. Grandin. "There's a lot of words like that when you come to think of it. I wrote them down in a notebook once. Just for fun; you know how you do those things. I remember one of them was 'meretricious.' It ought to mean 'meritorious' or something of merit, like. But it means just the opposite. Look," she said, pointing out the window, "there goes that Coast Guard man again. Wouldn't you think he'd get sick and tired of the same old walk all the time?" She drew in her lips and pressed them tight together to rub the lipstick in. "They're certainly not breaking their necks, are they? I'm starved." She moved away from the bureau, picked up her white dress, and slipped it over her head. Then she began to work on her hair. "Goodness, the way he thrashed around this morning, isn't it the limit? I don't know how he does it after all he's been through."

"You mean Guadalcanal?"

"I was thinking of the hospital and all those months he was so sick. There was a long time when they thought he wasn't going to live. But he comes up very fast out of anything like that. I remember once in high school he broke a few ribs in a football game and a couple of days later he was right back in school. A couple of days!"

"Have you known him long, Billie?"

"Cliff?" She gave the name a high-pitched inflection that seemed to say it was nothing to have known Cliff long, millions of people had known him a long time, and who was he to know anyway? "Dear yes. Why I guess I've known Cliff, why, at least eight years."

"You've gone together all that time?"

"Oh my no. I didn't run around with Cliff in high school. I knew who he was but I didn't go with him. I couldn't. Lots of girls did but *I* couldn't."

"Why not?"

"Well you see, Cliff was always kind of a—well, not a tough, but he isn't very well bred, you know. Nice girls didn't go with him. I remember once I gave him a date in junior year and all my girl friends just lit into me. They said I simply couldn't go out with a boy like that and I guess they were right—then."

"Perhaps they were jealous." With difficulty, Ethel Grandin made the appropriate remarks, though her mind was not on this conversation at all.

"Of Cliff? No no. Not at all. Any one of them could have had Cliff any time they liked—he was dying to go with nice girls like us—but we'd have been talked about." She opened wide the fingers of one hand, laid them on her hair, and drew them slowly together again to preserve her wave. "But I will say this for him. The first time he took me out he behaved like a perfect gentleman. He didn't even try to kiss me. I told the girls and they all thought I was lying."

"Then I should think," Ethel said, "that would have made it all right for you to 'go' with him."

"Well no, because you see there was always his—Well, it isn't very nice of me, but I know you won't repeat it: there was his family. They live in the wrong part of town, he and his father. His father's a carpenter or plumber or something—an immigrant, of course. The Haumans aren't very much, you know. I suppose you've noticed."

"Your mother didn't approve?"

"Mother didn't know he existed. *I* didn't approve." She gazed into the mirror with a dreamy expression. "Funny how those things change . . ."

Automatically Ethel replied: "They must have or you wouldn't have married him."

"Sometimes I'm so crazy about him I can't stand it. All last month I was; all last year. And other times I could just— But I suppose that's life."

Her hair set, she moved to one of the beds and half leaned, half lay alongside the footboard. She fixed the older woman with an unseeing gaze and Ethel Grandin grew self-conscious. She knew she was in for a session of self-revelation and she felt herself both ill equipped and unwilling to take part in it. Why did women always have to do these things, what gave them the right always to be airing their feelings? Had they no pride—had they no respect for their husbands? Love was a thing intimate and exclusive, one of those fundamentals which one did not discuss because, universal though it may be, it was personal even more. Her ten years of marriage had little to do with Billie or indeed with anyone else. What was true of herself could not be true for another, or have any meaning or interest for an outsider. Thus she had believed; not because her experience was special but because it was personal, private, and her own. "Mine is different," she had always thought—forgetting that in this world nobody's experience is unique.

This reticence sprang less from her natural disinclination to talk about herself than from loyalty to her husband; she could not have discussed the smallest aspect of their relationship if her life depended on it. Had her marriage been ideally happy or, on the other hand, miserably barren and loveless, she would never have mentioned it to another living soul. It was simply not in her to communicate her feelings about herself, still less about her husband. To have done so would have been a violation of love: it would have cheapened him, made him common property, removed him to the outer world of other men where (as her husband) he did not belong.

"Funny about Cliff," Billie said dreamily, but with a kind of impatience, too. "It almost doesn't seem to matter whether he's around or not. I loved him just as much when he was out in the Pacific as I do now that

we're married, and maybe I even got just as much out
of it. This week he's been different than I've ever known
him. When he comes to bed, I almost wonder whether
it's him at all, or even me. Still I guess it's Cliff all right.
I just sort of wait till it's over and he can come back
to me. The last two nights I kept thinking, oh dear, if
only he'd go away so I could dream about him like I
used to. But of course I don't want him to go away either.
I love to have him around so I can just look at him.
Don't you think he's wonderful looking? But when he's
close to me, like when he makes love, I can't *see* him . . ."

No, Ethel Grandin did not think he was wonderful
looking. In uniform, yes, perhaps. But she couldn't forget
the impression she had got as she walked behind Cliff
through the sand, returning from the beach. By compar-
ison to the trimness and compactness of her husband's
physique, which spoke breeding, tact, and gentleness in
his every move, Cliff seemed almost a creature to beware
of. His feet turned in when he walked, like an aborigine's,
and the ponderous half-closed fists at the ends of his long
arms swung monkey-like at his sides. How a girl could
have fallen in love with such a man, whose physical attraction lay only in being massive, was beyond her.

". . . At our wedding, in his dress whites," Billie
was saying, "he was the most stunning thing you ever
saw. The very same girls who warned me against him
a few years ago were simply carried away. At the reception everybody decided he'd turned out all right after all.
A captain in the Marine Corps *is* different, you know—
not something to be sneezed at, I mean. To see him at
the reception you'd never think he came from Haag

Street." She examined her wedding ring absently, and then added: "Of course he doesn't have his uniform on *all* the time. I mean there are times—" She stopped, and looked at Ethel with childlike directness. "Is this not nice to talk about, Mrs. Grandin?"

"Why do you ask, Billie? Do you think I don't approve?"

"I mean about his coming to bed with me. But that's what marriage is, I guess. Isn't it?"

"Partly."

"At least it's what *they* want." In a smaller voice, intimate now as if thinking aloud, she went on: "He's the best fellow I ever had—to dance with, go out with, all those things. When he comes to call for me, and when I first see him standing in the door, you can't imagine. And out somewhere, or coming home, when he puts his arms around me and pulls me up against his chest, I just die. But later, all that goes. He seems to turn into a different person. I don't even know whether it's me he enjoys, or just—himself. For all he knows, I might be just *any*body. He doesn't even know I'm there."

"Of course he does. He wants you."

"Anybody can want—that."

"But it's you, Billie. He married you, didn't he?"

"I suppose so. But what we've had the last two nights we could have had anyway, without being married at all. He'd have been just the same if I'd been any other girl. Marriage doesn't seem to have anything to do with it—Cliff doesn't know what marriage means!"

"These things take time, Billie."

"Not for Cliff they don't."

"I didn't mean Cliff, I was thinking of you. With the right man, love and love-making become all one, after a while."

"But he becomes such a stranger to me! He just plows ahead like I was—dirt. . . ."

"Maybe he'll always be a stranger to you. That sometimes happens. Men and women aren't alike. They never can be."

"Tell me," Billie said, "is Mr. Grandin a good husband?"

Ethel drew a pack of Camels from her pocket. "Toss me those matches on the night table, will you please? Thanks." She lighted her cigarette. "It takes an awful lot of love, Billie, to keep a marriage going. An awful lot, all you've got. That's something you'll have to remember —for years."

Billie gazed absently about the room. Then she said: "Which bed is yours, Mrs. Grandin?"

"By the window."

"Why do you have twin beds?"

"We always have had."

"Even at the beginning? Even the first few months?"

"I'm afraid I don't remember. . . ."

"But that's awful."

"Awful? I don't think so. We don't love each other any less for"—it was hard to say it—"for sleeping alone."

"But if you have a quarrel or anything, sleeping in the same bed makes it just that much easier to get together again."

"There are other ways," Ethel said, and heard the awful ambiguity.

"I want to be with Cliff all night long. Or I will want to when he calms down. I just love lying beside him. It's beautiful then, and I feel wonderful. You know?"

Ethel Grandin could not reply.

"You've really been married ten years?" Billie asked.

"Does that seem so long? If you're in love, it isn't long enough."

"I suppose it gets easier," Billie said. "I guess the first few weeks are difficult for any girl. Were they with you? Did you find him hard to get used to at first?"

Much as she would have liked to help Billie, Ethel Grandin could say nothing. She remembered things she could never have spoken of in the wide world.

"I'm sorry," Billie said. "Excuse me if you mind this. I've—I only want something to hang onto."

"Hang onto your love. You did say you loved him?"

"Cliff? How could I help it!" She sighed with a real impatience. "Here they come now, I hear them in the hall," she announced. "About time, too. Who do they think we are, I'd like to know. . . ."

X

THE DINING ROOM gazed with frank appreciation at the handsome Marine captain and his beautiful wife. Forewarned by Ethel, Miss Fly had given them a table near an open window so that the visitors could admire the view. She beamed at the Grandins and their guests, then proudly surveyed the surrounding tables to see whether other guests had taken note, as if she were directly re-

sponsible for giving the diners this added treat. Two or
three nodded by way of acknowledging her coup. The yellow-haired young man, his shoulders hunched so high
they almost touched his ear lobes, stared at the Grandin
party, lost in unfathomable reverie.

"Gee, it's nice being out here in Sconset," Hauman
said, as if they had just arrived. His three cocktails, which
he had downed at a gulp as being in the nature of lady-
like drinks, were taking effect. "Isn't it nice being out
here, Billie honey? I wish we lived at Dune House too.
Why don't we? I love a big dining room like this, don't
you? Gee you ought to have seen my daddy's face when
he saw our mess hall down at Parris Island. But that
room wasn't as big as this, I'll bet. I don't think it was
nearly as big as this. Well, maybe. Say, I better order.
Have you ordered, Billie honey? Oh excuse me! I'm forgetting! You first, Ethel."

A moment later, Grandin saw Hauman frowning over
his soup, his brow furrowed in thought.

"What are you worried about, Cliff?"

"Me? I'm not worried about anything! Nothing in
the world. I'm not worried at all. Look, there's Mr. and
Mrs. Howard down to the other end of the room." He
angled for their glance, shifting his big frame back and
forth, and waved. "Gee, they're comical people, aren't
they? Aren't they nice people, Billie?" He put his spoon
down and frowned again. Then it came out. "Look,
John," he said, hitching in his chair as if to emphasize
the seriousness of the matter, "I want to know your honest
opinion. But honest, you know what I mean? I want you
to tell me the truth, even if it hurts our feelings. Promise?"

"I will if I can," Grandin said uneasily. "What is it?"

"Now listen. Tell us what's your honest opinion of Billie's chances as a writer. You've read her compositions and stuff. Now I mean, I've always said I'd never stand in the way of my wife's career and I mean it. If she wants to become a writer, why then she should. Don't you think so?"

"I'm afraid," Grandin said, "it isn't quite as easy as that—just wanting to." It was his first knowledge that Billie "wrote," something which he himself, having too much respect for the five or six great novels of the world, wouldn't dream of attempting. He strove to avoid his wife's eyes, and the eyes of the Haumans still more; he began for the first time to regret the whole happy day. But Billie herself took the problem out of his hands by announcing, importantly:

"You mustn't hurry these things, Cliff. They take time. Besides, I haven't definitely made up my mind yet whether I want to be an author or a chemist."

Hauman's enthusiasm was deflated. "Well gee, honey, I didn't think there'd be any harm in asking, as long as we've got your professor right here. It's a chance in a million to find out, isn't it, if you're on the right track?"

But Billie's attention had been caught by something in the room. "Look at that over there, will you." Her undisguised nod indicated the young man sitting with his mother, fixing their party with fascinated concentration. "Did you ever see anything like that one?" Her smile was unabashed contempt. "Blindfolded you could tell he's 4-F —and why."

Hauman followed her nod, then immediately brought

his glance back again. "Gee this potato salad is good,
though. Sometime you ought to try the potato salad I
make. My daddy loves it—says it's the best he ever ate."

His tact had been so swift that it was not tact at all.
Far from diverting attention from what Billie had pointed
out, he had unconsciously emphasized it; though he did
manage to get the subject changed and the allusion (which
for some reason he had found so inept) forgotten or passed
over.

Crude though her remark had been, Billie was at
least honest to her instincts; but her husband was embarrassed. The reason was not flattering. Young people did
not mention such things in the presence of their elders.
It was one more example of the age difference between
them, one more reminder that Grandin was old enough
to be his father. Or did Hauman's refusal to acknowledge
what indeed was obvious to them all spring from his natural decency and clean speech? Again and again he had
observed the Captain's avoidance of the least off-color
word. It was not prudery or priggishness; on the other
hand, maybe it was just that. In any case, he could not
but admire that healthy clean-mindedness which automatically forced Hauman to change the subject, when
almost any other man of Grandin's acquaintance would,
in like circumstance, have given instant utterance to the
obvious and the vulgar.

XI

JOHN GRANDIN awoke from a nap. The sun was low; it was late afternoon. He had been sleeping since the Haumans left at three. ("We've had a wonderful time, John, it's been swell, it really has, honestly I mean it.") He had slept hard, so hard that now he felt out of sorts, dull, not rested. It was after six o'clock. Ethel was not in the room. As he sat up and tried to shake himself fully awake, she came in.

"I've been unconscious practically the whole afternoon," he said. "Can't say I feel better for it, either."

"Put some cold water on your face."

"Yes . . ."

He pulled off his shirt and went into the bathroom. He filled the washbowl, then splashed water over his eyes and forehead. Observing his face in the glass, he didn't know when he had seen himself looking so tired, so much in need of sleep. The nap had done him no good, the cold water did not refresh him. He felt a pressure back of his eyes like a headache: the cocktails before lunch, perhaps, or too much exposure to the sun.

A couple of drinks before dinner helped some, but dinner itself was a dismal affair. Both he and Ethel felt strangely let down; the Haumans had taken a great deal out of their day. They now felt disinclined to talk and did not bother to do so; tonight, for some reason, it didn't matter. Toward the finish, their meal was enlivened by the appearance at their table of the yellow-haired young man.

His mother had gone through to the lobby but he stopped to greet the Grandins cordially and to introduce himself. His name was Arne Eklund, he confided; his parents were Scandinavians; his father had died when Arne was four years old.

He stood at the table in an attitude of self-conscious grace. In spite of the disconcerting glitter of his appearance, he was an amiable young man, well mannered, interesting, and at last friendly. For some reason of his own he explained that he was not in the service because he was sole support of his mother and two sisters; it developed further that he was a well-known decorator from Chicago.

"I create interiors—for people on the North Shore with too much money and no taste," he said good-humoredly; and something in his attitude seemed to indicate that he was mocking himself as well as the rich. "By the by," he added, "I couldn't help noticing your guests this noon. I should love to have met them. I thought the girl a ravishing creature."

"I don't see why that can't be arranged," Grandin said; "that is, if they come to Sconset again."

"Oh, you're not old friends?"

He explained the circumstance of their knowing the Haumans, and Mr. Eklund took his leave.

"It's time to put in a call for home," Ethel said.

"Yes." He changed a bill at the desk and went to the telephone booth. He turned the crank in the side of the box and gave the number and town. He heard the operators, with identical voices, at Woods Hole, Boston, Old Orchard; it seemed strange being connected with the mainland again. Then he heard his mother-in-law's voice. "Just a moment, Mother," he said. "Call the boys, will you? Here's Ethel." He beckoned through the glass door, and quitted the booth.

Ethel emerged. "Didn't you want to talk?"

"There was nothing to say, specially. Everything all right? Are they well—having a good time?"

"Mama says Ted was in the water for three hours. I suppose that's all right, though," she added uncertainly.

He dawdled in the bathroom. For a moment or two he considered shaving tonight so he wouldn't have to shave in the morning; then decided against it because it would throw his schedule all off and he'd have to be shaving nights instead of mornings from now on unless he skipped a day to get back to the morning routine again; then realized that the question had not been serious for a moment: he was unconsciously planning or trying any dodge to stall off what awaited him when he faced Ethel alone in the bedroom.

He couldn't have another row tonight. On the other hand, he couldn't ignore the issue as if it didn't exist, either. He loved Ethel; he had missed her keenly all day; he longed to get back to her again. He did not dare hope that they would end up in bed together tonight and certainly he wouldn't try to; not after last night. But something had to be said or done to re-establish him as her husband. Ten years didn't count for nothing. There had been so much between them; they were not, and never had been, strangers. He leaned on the washbowl and gazed unseeingly into the mirror, asking himself for courage.

When he came from the bathroom in his pajamas, Ethel was in bed reading a magazine.

Almost before he had time to think, he found himself saying what he had not meant to say at all. "What about it, Ethel? Don't you think you've carried this on long enough?"

She regarded him for a full moment over the edge of the magazine. Then she said: "I'm terribly sorry about last night, John, terribly. But I—I—"

"You don't need to be sorry."

"But I want you to remember something. I love you, John. I always have loved you and always will."

"Isn't it a little late for all this?"

"Why?"

"You told me what you thought of me. I'd feel like a fool or hypocrite or pretender if I tried to make myself out as something more than the complete nothing you've made of me . . ."

Sometime in the night he awoke. At once he was wide awake, and he was instantly aware that there would be little possibility of sleeping, now, for who knew how long? He was in for a spell of sleeplessness which would be profitless, possibly disturbing, and certainly damaging to his well-being tomorrow. He blamed it on the nap of the afternoon.

Again he noticed that the shades had not been lifted. He got out of bed and raised them on the ocean side. He leaned on the window sill, his nose to the screen. There was no sound but the faint wash of the sea. Far along the beach to the left, over the dark bluffs, could be seen the intermittent sudden spark of Sankaty Light; it flashed red, then dim, then glaringly white like a diamond, as it revolved ceaselessly in the night. Foolish to maintain such a rigid blackout, he thought, yet allow the lighthouse to throw its beam farther out to sea than any bedroom lamp could hope to penetrate. Directly opposite was the beach where they had lain that morning in the sun: thinking of this, he could almost smell the sensual heavy odor of sun-tan oil. He glanced toward the Coast Guard station near Tom Nevershead; it was dark there, but somewhere in that lonely reach of sand the coast guardsman and his dog kept their hourly patrol. He breathed the air. There was no fog. It promised well for the full moon due two nights later.

He wanted to read or perhaps write a letter, in an effort to make himself drowsy again. Unwilling to disturb Ethel's sleep by using the bed light, he went to the dressing table. He sat down and flipped the switch of the lamp under the mirror. To his surprise it did not go on. Then he remembered. ("He's always *break*ing things!") He must get the lamp fixed or replaced in the morning, though possibly all it needed was a new bulb. He went back to his bed and lay a long while thinking over that day.

. . . If any human attribute exercised over him a charm more potent than the charm of youthful well-being, he did not know what it was; his imagination could not transcend the resplendent young manhood of Cliff Hauman or the physical fact of him. . . . *Youth large, lusty, loving—youth full of grace, force, fascination.* . . . Too

long shut away from the livelier pursuits of the young,
confined too exclusively to the classroom and study, he
had forgotten the pull of the athletic ideal, that pull
which drew thousands upon thousands to the basketball
courts, the football games, the swimming matches, the
track meets, the fights. Add good looks to this ideal and
John Grandin found himself, in Hauman's overpowering
presence, an unprotesting captive, taking delight in merely
being an onlooker. Did the holiday have something to
do with it, the sea and the sun and the weather? Or was
it the power of the uniform, which, though discarded, had
made itself felt even on the beach? (He could see it still
—the skivvy shirt, the stiff pants, the shirt with the silver
bars on the collar—neatly folded on the chair over there
by the bureau.) For every thousand who cheered on the
athlete with passionate cries, ten thousand others backed
the soldier with love; and indeed, regardless of the splen-
dor of Hauman's physique, he was somehow not nearly
so compelling a figure in bathing trunks as he had been
when clothed from chin to foot in the cheapest khaki.
At the beach he was just another well-built young man,
a little on the big side, so that Sarah Howard's crack
about the Michelin-tire man, for all its exaggeration, had
had some basis in fact. In uniform, Hauman presented a
different personality altogether. Composed though he had
become since their first meeting, he was yet charged with
some inner tension which tactlessly cried out his relief
that any day now he would be off; and the poignancy
of the figure lay in one's certainty that he would not
be leaving his heart behind with Billie or anyone, but
would take, instead, the hearts of all who knew him—of

those, indeed, who had barely met him. . . . How often
had John Grandin encountered on a bus, a street corner,
or merely in a photograph, some uniformed youth for
whom he had felt instantly a personal concern, an actual
anxiety for his welfare. Because it took him each time
unawares, he was always unprepared for this unreasonable response. Now he had time to adjust himself to the
reaction, examine it, question it. In the person of Cliff
Hauman on the beach that morning (not Hauman at
all, but a vivid symbol, an abstract larger than life), the
once-fleeting concern became an active emotion, neither
ephemeral nor momentary; and remembering the way the
guests had watched with pleasure his antics in the sand
—a soldier, clearly, from the dog tag around his neck and
the GI boots upright in the sand—he sensed that the
whole beach had begun to fall a little in love with
Cliff. . . .

But why the need to concern oneself with the welfare of the soldier? The disorders of war had beset those
left behind. The calm poised faces of traveling or returned servicemen made him wonder why he should feel
or have felt in the past an anxiety for them. Young men
back from the fronts, their chests beribboned with the
decorations of battle, showed a composure—a dignity,
reserve, and freedom from strain—that could not be found
on the faces of clerks traveling to and from their offices.

The war photographs which had been drawing his
melancholy attention for so many months—what were
they but a nostalgia for youth? He envied the solidarity,
fraternity and fellowship of servicemen (which they themselves would scarcely be aware of till it was a thing of

the past) and felt keenly his forty-four years. The thousand pictures of GIs at chow, the young fliers strapping on their parachutes as they ran for the bombers tuning up in the gray dawn, the helmeted half-naked leathernecks grinning for the camera at the wheel of bulldozers, the packed waving soldiers crowding the rail of the transport and all of them smiling as if they were setting forth on some wonderful holiday, the marines holding their guns aloft as they jumped down the landing platforms or sprawled or crouched on the furious beach—these were today's tokens of romance, pored over by millions, vicariously experienced by men and women alike. His desire to be part of it was not diminished one whit by reminding himself that the aim of it all was death.

A night breeze had sprung up and the window shade flapped; it brought him back to where he was. Suddenly it seemed to him a preposterous irony that he should be lying here, so near to Ethel's bed and to her, indulging in fantasies as remote from their marriage as the poles from each other. He could almost think: It's a good thing Ethel doesn't know what I'm thinking; for he had become completely oblivious, for the moment, to the issues which had been raised the night before. He was ashamed that his mind could have wandered so far afield. With an effort (for, like an adolescent daydream, the other had been a pleasant indulgence), he brought himself back to Ethel, to marriage, to earth.

Had his will left him entirely? Was he to do nothing about it? Why under the sun didn't he take matters in his own hands and settle the thing himself? There was good reason why he didn't, and it was not a comforting thought, no pleasant thing to face alone with himself here in the night. What Ethel had brought out in this very bedroom only twenty-four hours ago was all too true. Had there been a shade of feminine casuistry in her diatribe, had it been in the least specious or unfounded, he would have risen at once to his own defense, refused to take it, and slammed home a point or two of his own. In short, he would have got mad. That she was the one who was mad, and that he was in the position of hanging around till she had made up her mind what to "do about it," emphasized only too clearly where the guilt lay, the guilt of neglect.

He did not believe she would go so far as to ask for a divorce or even a separation. Far worse, they would probably let it ride eventually and go on with a loveless marriage for the children's sake, for habit's sake, or out of sheer inertia or inability to find a substitute. But it was not a loveless marriage—it never had been: never would be, no matter how many brutal sessions they put themselves through in the future. He loved Ethel Cameron; and if he was not in love with her as he once had been, he needed her still, wanted no one else, and would make love to her again when he found his confidence restored as a husband. Many men would not wait for that; if he were half the man he had been, he would move over to her bed this minute. But that was not true; half the man he had been or indeed any man at all would never have made a move in her direction, after the shattering accusations of last night. No man could make love to a suspicious woman; to have done so would have been to make him feel lonelier and more base than any charge in this unhappy world which she might yet bring down upon his head.

He looked over at her bed. There was no flare on the ceiling tonight, no lighted cigarette, no smoking in the dark to show him she was still awake. She was asleep; he could see the outlines of her figure. At once the image of the angry woman vanished and in its place he saw the girl he had loved and married. As a bride she had been the world's freshest and most delightful creature; if he was to have nothing in his life again, he had had that, and he would never forget it. How much of that love could they recapture? None, probably; but he loved her still, she loved him, and if they hung onto that, it might be fortification enough for age and middle age which lay just ahead of them.—In spite of the presence of youth all that day, John Grandin was still unable to think of himself, at forty-four, as middle-aged.

What had happened seemed all the sadder, somehow, because of the bride and bridegroom who had yesterday entered their lives, if only fleetingly. He was never merely sentimental about marriage, but it did seem a shame that the Haumans had been in on it at all, even though they were probably unaware of the chilling atmosphere of a relationship so unlike their own. They were in love, and consequently saw no one but themselves . . . And again he lost himself in reverie about the Marine captain and his bride . . .

. . . As he thought of Billie and Cliff on the beach that morning—of what a vivid sight they had made and what pleasure it had given him—he couldn't help wondering again when, and on what beachhead, that splendid body of Cliff's would lie rotting, and how soon Billie would console herself with children or another man or her own mother. What would Billie remember of Cliff; was she at all aware of what she had now and what she might lose? And having lost it, what would it mean to her? Would it mean more to her, for example, than her own grief, or the fact that she was a Marine captain's widow and her dead husband a hero—something her girl friends would always be conscious of and point out? Would this small neighborhood-fame take the place of her love—take the place of Cliff, too, in time?

But this was idle romantic speculation. Nothing mattered but that Cliff would, in all probability, die. He was the hero headed for the fulfillment of death, which was as it should be: Grandin's childhood hero out of literature and mythology. In simple artistic justice he would not have arrested that inevitable course or have it otherwise; and yet, in Cliff's brief transit, he wanted to take something out of that life before it passed from sight forever. What that something could be, he had no idea; for clearly Cliff had nothing for him or anyone.

These and other fantasies, aimless now, were to be given direction, if not purpose, when the Haumans moved into Dune House the next afternoon.

XII

THE HEAVING BREAST of the sea was like a billowy bed, pulling him down to ineffable luxurious sleep. In spite of the struggle to keep afloat, and the danger, he felt a longing to go far out—far, farther, past any possibility of return. His wonderful battle with the buffeting rollers, and the sensual falling sensation they constantly provided, seemed to him the only intoxication he had had in many months, the only good losing of himself. . . . *You sea! I resign myself to you also—I guess what you mean.* . . .

He was swimming alone; and that, somehow, added to the lulling exquisite pleasure. He was the more at one with the sea because no one was beside him; the solid shore counted for nothing, nor did anyone on it. He gave himself up to the sea, as if he and it were in lusty intimate communion, and allowed himself to be drawn on and on. . . . *Sea of the brine of life! sea of unshovell'd yet always-ready graves.* . . .

He plunged through the sharp stinging crest of a breaker and swept down and up the long downward swell to the top again; momentarily he rode high there, then dropped into the green deep trough as the wave he had quitted rolled on toward the beach and the next one reared up. Actually, there was little swimming he could do; it was a matter mostly of staying afloat and riding the waves, which drew him out farther and farther. When he turned to go back, he felt beneath him the strong seaward pull even more; during the last fifty feet he had to work fast to overcome it. Reaching the crest of the final onrushing breaker, he was yanked rapidly landward and cast up on the beach in a thundering crash of water and pebbles. Amid the boil of the hissing swirling surf, John Grandin got to his feet.

Ethel lay in the sand under the umbrella. It was early; besides Pete the lifeguard, they and the Eklunds were the only guests who had yet come down from the hotel.

As he finished drying himself, Arne Eklund left his sunshade and came across the sand with a magazine. He knelt between them, then sat back on his heels, his body perfectly erect, as if the figure itself (far more than the face and eyes) was the instrument to express superiority. His hands rested lightly on his thighs, only the fingertips touching; the highly lacquered nails glistened in the sunlight.

"Your friends aren't coming out today?" His voice had a strangely singing quality; it had, too, a perverse good humor, as if any moment he would go into a broad burlesque of himself and thus satisfy them all.

"They must have other plans. As a matter of fact, we know very little about them except that they're on their honeymoon."

"How exciting! But oh, I do hope we'll be seeing them again," Mr. Eklund said, "they're such a *very* striking couple." He pushed the magazine toward Ethel; it was a popular illustrated weekly of the cheaper variety. "Perhaps you'd like to look at this, Mrs. Grandin; Mother and I've finished with it."

"Why, thank you."

"Oh, by the by!" He drew back the magazine and opened it. "Let me show you something. Look, see this?"

He pointed to the photograph of a Navy flier in helmet and goggles strapped above his forehead. The face was that of a boy in his earliest twenties, possibly even his late teens, with calm clear eyes and the kind of plain American good looks that were so much more attractive, because more typical, than mere handsomeness. The boy looked like anybody; but from what followed it was clear that he was somebody indeed.

"Listen to this," Mr. Eklund said peremptorily; "it says: 'Flight Lieutenant Harold L. Manku— Mankie—' Well, I can't pronounce it, it's something Polish with about a million syllables, but *any*way: 'One of the greatest dive-bomber pilots the Navy ever had, Skipper Whatever-the-name-is was noted for his brilliant skill and daring. Although he ran up a big score of Jap battlewagons, cruisers, and even a carrier, he had a yen to sink a Jap destroyer just to round out the record. At last his big chance came in the Solomons and he dove on the leader of a tin-can flotilla. After his bomb struck the water alongside, he calmly radioed, "My flaps won't close." As he headed for his carrier, Jap zeros ganged up on him and the Skipper's SBD plunged into the sea.' "

He turned the magazine so they could see the picture better. He gazed intently at Ethel. "Isn't it tragic? Isn't it?" he said insistently. "So young, and so attractive." With a dismayed yet oddly challenging expression, looking Ethel straight in the eye, he held out the photograph—held it a shade too long (John Grandin realized this almost with a shock), as if to make sure that the erotic thought had registered.

Disgust and a sharp hot anger rose up in him. He felt an impulse to turn savagely and say: "Look here, Eklund —if people dislike you and your kind, it's your own damned fault!" He said nothing, of course; but he was immeasurably relieved, as if some smothering pressure had been lifted, when Eklund moved away to rejoin his mother in the sand. . . .

After lunch John Grandin took off his shirt and slacks and lay down on the bed for a nap. Ethel had been getting ready to go for a walk through the back lanes of Sconset but at the last minute, to his increasing apprehension, she changed her mind. She sat in the wicker chair, lighted a cigarette, and said:

"I think we've had quite enough unpleasantness for the time being and I honestly believe you feel as badly about it as I do. So let's try and drop it. Incidentally, I wish you'd get that light fixed."

"I'll speak about it, this very day."

"But I thought you'd like to know something," she went on. "When we leave here I planned, as you know, to get the boys in Maine and come back to New York for the rest of the summer. That was so you wouldn't be alone."

"Well?"

"But now I think"—she looked away from him—"I'm not coming back."

He sat up. For some reason he felt foolish in his shorts and undershirt; it almost seemed indelicate, as if a strange woman were in the room. "What do you mean?" he said.

"What do you think I meant?"

"For God's sake stop parroting me! What do you *mean*, I asked."

She flushed. Then she lifted up her head, looked him squarely in the eye, exhaled a faint cloud of gray-blue smoke, and said: "I mean, of course, I'm going to stay at Mama's."

"For how long, please?"

"What difference does it make to you?"

"I asked how long! I have a right to expect an answer."

She took a drag on her cigarette. "It depends."

"On what? That's no answer."

"On a lot of things. I think I'll stay with the family until I—until I know."

"I see," he said. "Do you think you'll 'know' by the time the boys' school opens?"

"They could go to school in Maine, if it came to that."

"Oh no they couldn't. That's one thing I insist on!"

"Well," she said, "I need a few weeks to think it over."

The conversation had an almost farcical quality, a nervous wordy banter, but at least it didn't lead them into those dangerous bypaths (bound to come eventually) of insult and outrage which shattered them both—which, however fundamental they might be, were yet filled with hazard. Another session or two like the one they had been through the other night would have carried them past the breaking point, not only the breaking point of their marriage but of their native individualities and self-respect. Each realized this and strove to maintain the brittle equilibrium; for the only deviation possible from the present norm of strain could be nothing but the passion of love-making or the passion of the blow.

"Just what are you going to think over?" he said.

"I don't know. . . ."

"Not much to work on, is it?"

"Plenty." For the first time during the discussion, her look was spirited and meaningful.

"Then I'm to be a bachelor for the rest of the summer, is that it? While you," he added, "fiddle around and —decide my fate."

"The children's," she said quietly; "not yours."

He got up and drew on his red-cotton dressing gown. He noticed how one of the shoulder seams was split; that was Cliff. "I suppose it's as sensible an arrangement as any," he said. "At least it will give you and the boys a pleasant summer."

"And you."

"Now what's that supposed to mean?"

"I'm sure you know better than I do."

He hesitated a moment; then: "You needn't have said that, Ethel. If you're hinting at something dark, you know better. I'm not a cheater and never have been."

"I only meant," she said, "you'll be better off alone. You don't want us."

"I will not have you thinking for me! I know what I want, even if you don't think so."

"Your dressing gown is ripped," she said.

"I know that."

"I've got a needle and thread, if you'll give it to me."

He did not answer. He lay down on the bed again, propped himself against the pillows in a half-sitting position, and picked up the *Herald Tribune* and a pencil. He glanced at the date; but because he had lost all track of time he could not tell whether it was yesterday's paper or

today's. He did not want to read the news. He turned at
once to the crossword puzzle on the next-to-the-last page.
He knew this was a snub to Ethel if not actually a cowardly dodge, but he persisted in taking refuge in the paper,
fearful of where the discussion—so far well-mannered
enough, and controlled—might lead. Behind the paper
held between him and her, he could feel that she was re-
garding him from the wicker chair with probably a very
real hate.

As he began to work on the little squares, he was
vaguely aware of a solid mass of several closely printed
columns to the right of the puzzle, which, without looking,
he dimly gathered to be stock-exchange figures or market
reports. Lost in thought over some definition in the
puzzle, his eye finally roamed over these columns, and it
was a full moment before he took in the significance of the
caption printed at the top of the page:

CASUALTIES

(Continued from Page 2)

The long list of names—endlessly long, since this was
only one day out of many days past and to come—was
divided into the three states of the metropolitan neighbor-
hood—New York, New Jersey, Connecticut—and these in
turn were separated by smaller captions reading: *African
Area, Alaskan Area, Pacific Area.* By no act of the imagination could one conceive that each of these names listed
so succinctly in fine print had been a living young man
with an identity of his own; it was equally impossible to
grasp the individual death, the young life somewhere

stopped, the anguish left behind in some fine house, flat, slum or farm at home . . .

> MATYJASIK, Richard, t/4; wife, Mrs. Agnes B. Matyjasik, Binghamton.
> MATZKO, Donald L., pfc; wife, Mrs. Phyllis Matzko, Batavia.
> MATZKOWITZ, Irving J., pvt; wife, Mrs. Rachel Matzkowitz, Brooklyn.
> MCCUE, Charles G., t/sgt; mother, Mrs. Doris McCue, Utica.
> MEADER, Henry W., pvt; mother, Mrs. Dorothy Meader, Palmyra.
> MILLER, Emerson A., pvt; mother, Mrs. Alice E. Miller, Buffalo. . . .

There was a rap on the door. He threw the skirt of his robe around his bare knees and called out: "Come in."

A young boy entered, the lad who served below as porter, doorman, bus boy, and sometimes desk clerk. "Message, sir."

"Thank you, Joe."

The envelope was engraved DUNE HOUSE in the upper left corner and addressed simply: "Mr. Grandin." He ripped it open and read the brief note, written in a painstakingly legible hand; it almost looked as if the writer had resisted an impulse to print the entire message in block letters:

> Dear Johnnie,
>   What do you think! We have moved into Dune House. We are in Room 212. Come on down!
>   Cliff

He read the note again. Then he got off the bed, slipped out of his dressing gown, and began pulling on a clean shirt. He was tying his tie in front of the mirror when Ethel said: "Where are you going?" He handed her the note.

"Do you mean to tell me," she said after a moment, "that you're going down there now, this minute, the very moment they—"

"The very moment they what?"

"Whistle," she said.

"I don't hear any whistle and it isn't 'they' to begin with. The note is from Cliff, if you'll look again. For that matter, is there any reason why I shouldn't?"

She still hadn't answered by the time he left the room.

XIII

"HI, JOHNNIE! You surprised?"

"Rather." He closed the door behind him.

"Well, I'll tell you. We got kind of fed up with Nantucket, if you know what I mean. We'd been everywhere and done everything. So Billie and I decided we'd have more fun out here in Sconset with you and Eth. It'd be company. Billie didn't want to make the change at first on account of the money but gosh, money's no object right now. You don't go on honeymoons every day in the week, isn't that right, Johnnie?"

He was on the floor, on one knee, bent over an open suitcase, but he beamed up at Grandin with childlike pleasure and welcome. He looked immaculate, incredibly

healthy, fresh, and full of good spirits; and he had got a
haircut.

"Where's Billie?"

"Billie? Oh, she's gone out to find a dry cleaner some-
wheres.—What's the matter, Johnnie? Aren't you glad
we came?"

Grandin sat down. "Of course I am, Cliff."

"I just thought for a second, there, you looked kind
of—well, funny."

"I'm surprised, that's all."

"Oh, I knew you'd be surprised! I bet I said twenty
times this morning, gee, won't Johnnie and Eth be
surprised!" His smile was enchanting; John Grandin resisted an impulse to leave.

"I see you got a room all right," he said.

"Sure, no trouble at all. I called up first—said I was
a friend of yours."

"How long will you be staying?"

"That depends on when I hear from Brooklyn. I may
have to report back any day now," he added happily, as
though it meant the promise of everything he wanted in
life. "Did you miss us this morning?"

"Yes." For the first time John Grandin realized he
had missed him indeed.

"We missed you! Gosh, last night and this morning
Billie and I didn't know what to do with ourselves." He
lifted out a pile of shirts and put them away in a bureau
drawer. "Billie's all settled," he said. "Look, she's even got
my picture up already."

On the dresser, in a mirrored glass frame, was a large
photograph of Cliff in dark-blue Marine jacket with a

white cap. The face looked stern and unhappy, self-conscious to the point of pain. It seemed to have no connection whatever with the buoyant good nature which at this moment charged the atmosphere of the dingy bedroom with an almost overpowering vitality.

"I've got some more of those, Johnnie, if you'd want one."

"Thank you, Cliff, but I don't care particularly for photographs of friends. They—age too quickly."

"Yeah, I guess you're right. Well, Billie's got to have something to show the girl friends. You know women."

In the suitcase, on top of a pile of clean skivvy shirts, lay a pale-khaki overseas cap with a pair of silver bars pinned on it. It was very flat; it took up hardly more room than a folded handkerchief. Grandin sat looking down at the cap. It looked almost touchingly neat, fresh, and military; exactly like Cliff. Here was something he did want.

"This vacation's sure done me a lot of good. Isn't Nantucket a wonderful island, Johnnie? Never felt better in my life! Why, I'm going to go through that examination like a breeze. . . ."

All in one passing moment John Grandin wanted it (that was all he did want of Cliff, he thought now), wanted to be able to look at it occasionally by way of remembering Cliff and the holiday—wanted it somewhere at hand when Cliff was far off on the other side of the world and gone forever; and in the same moment he rejected the idea and the thought as being shameless sentimentality, disliked himself acutely for having had the impulse at all—and could not keep from looking at the cap even as he refused it in his mind.

Hauman saw him looking. He reached out for the cap, held it for a moment flat in his palm, and said: "Would you like to have it, Johnnie? I got another."

"What for?"

"Oh"—he shrugged—"souvenir . . ."

"Yes."

"Lots of people like war souvenirs. They're nice to have. Specially later, after it's all over."

John Grandin felt sick at heart. He wanted to say— he felt it impossible to keep from saying—Cliff, I'm very fond of you. The words stuck in his throat, he would never be able to get them out, never in a thousand years; and he was glad that this was so. He folded the cap and thrust it deep into his pocket; and as he did so, he believed he had never felt so foolish in his life.

XIV

When the Grandins came down to dinner, they found Billie and Cliff Hauman seated at their table.

"That Miss Fly put us here," Billie explained, "I suppose because she knew we were friends. I tried to tell her that maybe you'd rather be by yourselves, but it seems she's deaf as a clam."

"Clams aren't deaf," Hauman said; "they're dumb."

"It's ox that are dumb. Or wait, maybe you're right.— What is it that's deaf, Mr. Grandin?"

"Miss Fly."

"Say Johnnie, I forgot to tell you! There's a big party

for servicemen tomorrow night at the Nantucket Yacht
Club. How about going as my guest, Johnnie?"

"He means all of us, of course," Billie said to Ethel.

"But I'm not a serviceman," Grandin said.

"The heck with that. I'm invited and I can bring
anybody I want. The Coast Guard's even going to send a
car out for me. Driver and everything." He grinned.
"That's because I'm a captain."

"What kind of party?"

"Big dance. Do you like to dance, Johnnie?"

"Please say you'll come, Mrs. Grandin," Billie
pleaded. "We'll have a lovely time. Tomorrow night's the
full moon, too. Oh, and Toni Lansing is going to be
there, they say, giving out autographs to the boys. Free.
Goodness, maybe *I'll* even get one!"

"Say, we might ask the Howards too, Billie honey.
What do you think?"

"Well, aren't they maybe a little too old?"

"Indeed? The Howards," Grandin said, "happen to
be at least four years younger than I am."

"Oh dear, I didn't mean— I mean if you think I
thought—"

"I didn't think you thought at all." He turned to her
husband. "I don't see how five civilians can get in on one
uniform, Cliff. We haven't the right: it isn't fair."

"That's my lookout, Johnnie, not yours. Don't you
worry, they'll take it okay. If they invite me, they've got
to take who I bring along."

Though his wife was unspeakably angry with him
(she seemed to have registered his rebuke to Billie more
deeply than anyone), Grandin could see that Ethel wanted

him to say yes. She would have a wonderful time at a party of young people; heaven knew their holiday had been dull enough till now. It was an opportunity not to be missed —their one chance, possibly, of being able to get together again during their stay on the island; but the thought of attending a party for servicemen depressed him intolerably. It was just about the last thing he wanted to do in this world.

The Howards, called to the table as they passed through the dining room, accepted with pleasure. "Will we not!" Sarah Howard said. "At last I'll have a chance to wear a long skirt."

"Goodness," Billie said when the Howards had gone on, "I hope nobody's going to go formal. All I've got is an old blue thing about a thousand years old. Well, you can make it up for me, Cliff, by wearing your full-dress uniform."

"Fat chance. Don't forget I'm on a vacation."

"You're also on your honeymoon, if you'd only realize it, and I think you're being just as mean as you can be. I know you, Clifford Hauman. You'll wear those cheap old khakis that look worse than fatigue clothes even. To a party, too!"

John Grandin was so oppressed by Billie's chatter and by the prospect of the Yacht Club dance—if indeed he did intend to go through with it for Ethel's sake—that he felt he couldn't sit there for the rest of the meal. When the dessert orders were about to be taken, he suddenly stood up. "If you'll excuse me," he said, "I'm going upstairs."

Ethel gave him a distressed and angered look, and

Hauman called after him: "Hey, don't you want your dessert, Johnnie? Or coffee?"

"I don't feel like it, thanks. Excuse me. . . ."

When Ethel came in she stood just inside the bedroom door looking at him with a searching gaze for a long uncomfortable moment. Then she said:

"I think you ought to be ashamed of yourself."

He looked up from the wicker chair, affecting surprise. "For Pete's sake what's the matter with you?"

"What's the matter with you, that's what I'd like to know. You're acting like a ten-year-old child."

"I didn't care for dessert. Is there anything wrong with that?"

"Why did you have to pick on Billie in that shameless way? And if you're objecting because she called the Howards old, you're being pretty silly. Where's your sense of humor? They are old. To a girl Billie's age we're all old."

"I'm not interested in her opinions. Billie's a fool."

"John!" Ethel came across the room. She stood directly over him, her arms folded, looking down at his averted face.

He waited in unbearable silence. Finally he said, as casually as he was able: "If you don't mind I'm going out for a walk."

"I do mind! I want you to go down to the Haumans' room this minute and apologize, or I—I'll—"

"You'll what?"

She stared at him with a kind of fierce searching intensity; but when she spoke, the words were scarcely audible: "I'm beginning to think, John, that I don't know you at all. . . ."

He walked out to the road. Except for a barely perceptible glow along the far horizon of the sea, the night was almost totally black. Behind him he heard the tinkly notes of the harp grow fainter and fainter. He felt the hard surface of the road beneath his feet; it seemed to vibrate regularly to the pound of the surf a good half mile away, though this may only have been because he could also hear the sound as well. He turned his steps in the direction of the resounding beach; but remembering the wartime rule forbidding civilians to come within five hundred yards of the beach at night, he had no intention of going there. Nor did he want to: it was a long and difficult walk, the night was dark, and he was tired, sick with a self-distaste.

He felt with his hand for the rose-covered bower through which one descended the long wooden stairway of the bluff. It might be pleasant to go down the steps and sit at the bottom for a moment. Though it was too dark to tell, there seemed to be no fog; at least he did not feel its dampness blowing across his face. He started down.

Near the bottom was the small landing where he had sat smoking a cigarette while Cliff sloshed about in the shower singing *From the Halls of Montezuma*. All around, along the railings on either side and spreading in unchecked profusion up the slope, were the rambler roses indigenous to the island, fast fading with the season. He could not smell the roses, for they were a variety without scent, nor could he see them; but he had seen them by daylight and he knew they were there. In the harsh glare of noon they looked hard, cold, and pale, as if they were paper, wax, or iron painted.

Over the southeast horizon, out of the dark water

that was literally one of the roads to the South Pacific, a blurred salmon-colored shape arose, which, clearing the edge of the sea, slowly revealed itself as the nearly full moon. Round but for a vague edge, enormous, faintly glowing, it hung low in the eastern sky looking far nearer than it would later look when it had risen high and bright in the zenith. The illusory shapes and shadows of its surface were discernible only to the first casual glance; when he stared at them to search them out, discover their pattern or trace the contours of the legendary face, they vanished.

It was also at this spot, he reflected, where Cliff had said, so diffidently, Are you happily married?

The moon with its worn edge was well over the rim of the sea now, exaggerated in size, overdone, theatrical, red as the red of a flag. The palpable brilliance of its color, looking as if still wet from the brush, didn't last. Rising higher, it began gradually to slide under some unseen far ledge of sky, till only its lower diminishing half glowed hot above the sea. Inevitably this piece too was drawn up under the obscuring layer of cloud or fog, and the moon was gone.

He heard the ceaseless rumble of the beach, muted but still thunderous. He thought of the warm sand where they had lain for so many hours in the sun, possessed by a sensuous luxury which had pleasantly undone them all. He wondered if the gaudy beach umbrellas still stood in the dark; or did Pete put them away each afternoon? Did the tide come up at night to cover that spot, perhaps; or was it farther withdrawn from the familiar shore, to toss restlessly far out beyond where the pebbles began? He

listened intensely, as if with all his senses; it almost seemed
as if he could hear the running pebbles as the surf slid
back and back. . . . He got up from the step and walked
forward into the sand.

He had no intention of going far—not so far that he
would transgress the wartime rule—but suddenly, close at
hand, he heard the savage low snarl of a dog, and the
white uniform of the coast guardsman took shape in the
night.

On a taut leash the coast guardsman held back the
dog, then spoke up sharply: "Who's there!"

John Grandin stepped back. "Sorry, officer, I was
only—" He broke off; the vicious snarling of the dog made
it impossible for him to be heard.

"*Quiet,* Trump!—Who are you?"

"A guest in the hotel. I came down for a moment
because of the moon. . . ."

"Don't you know you're not allowed on the beach at
night?" the coast guardsman said tensely.

"This isn't exactly the beach, is it?"

"That doesn't matter! Get back up on the bluff where
you belong or I shall have to report you!"

"Yes. . . . Well, good night. Sorry . . ." He turned
back toward the stairway.

Reaching the top, he looked down to see if the coast
guardsman and his dog were still there. He thought he
detected a vague blur of whiteness below, but he couldn't
be sure.

When he came into the room, the light between their
beds had been turned off. He started for the lamp beneath
the mirror of the dressing table, then remembered he had

again forgotten to get it fixed. He undressed in the bathroom.

In bed at last, he lay wide awake listening to the night. There was no sound whatever to be heard now, not even the distant wash of the sea; and the hotel itself seemed silent as an empty house. Everyone had gone to bed. Room 212, only a few doors down the hall, must be quiet too by this time. The Haumans had said—rather unnecessarily, he thought—that they were going to bed early. . . .

XV

"I must say I don't know why Mother doesn't send those *wed*ding pictures. She promised! I'm dying to see them."

"We can call her up tonight, Billie honey."

"Oh, you and long-distance. Really, the way he throws money around," Billie said to Ethel. "He never thinks of saving. The times he called me up all the way from San Diego . . ."

"That isn't why I called from San Diego, just to throw money around. Did you think it was?"

"Well, you could have written more often. Letters mean—well, don't they, Mrs. Grandin. They give you something to put your finger on, like. Honestly, I never could remember after we hung up what we'd said at all. Could you, Cliff?"

The day was fine and cloudless, but unbearably, dangerously hot. It was as though—unless one moved fast: swam, ran, played in the sand (but few felt like doing that)—actual danger lay just beyond the shade of the sun umbrella. A heat as stifling as the heat beating down from the sun rose from the beach; all of them lay in a kind of atmosphere of torrid suspense, relieved only occasionally by a coolish breeze blowing from offshore or by a faint spray of sea water from the crest of a breaking wave. Sometimes the crashing surf sent small vaporous clouds along the sand, and tiny rainbows moved with them in the sun.

The Howards lay covered up under a sunshade touching the Grandins'; the two umbrellas formed a little tent for the party of six. Nearby, on the carpetlike towel beside his mother, Mr. Eklund regarded them inquiringly, as if awaiting an invitation to join them. John Grandin avoided his glance.

"When we get back, Johnnie," Hauman said, "you must come up to Bridgeport right away and see us. You'd love my daddy. Wouldn't he, Billie?"

"Sometime," Grandin said. "We'll see."

"My daddy would love to have you as much as we would. He loves company. You'd have a whole room all to yourself, Johnnie, any time you like. You don't need to give us any advance notice, even. I sure hope you'll come out and see us. . . ."

Ethel and Mrs. Howard were to leave on the eleven-thirty bus for Nantucket, where they had appointments at two o'clock with the hairdresser. From the time they had got up that morning, Ethel had seemed to take it for granted that it was all set about the Yacht Club dance, though he had not discussed it further. There was little he could do but agree to go. Much as he dreaded the evening, it would have been an open declaration of trouble if he stayed behind while all the others went to the dance.

Bill Howard sat up. "How about a swim, Sadie?"

"No time. We'll be leaving in a minute."

"Me, I can't stand it any longer. I'm no channel swimmer but I've got to get my money's worth." He began applying sun-tan oil to his arms and shoulders. The odor of the heavy sweet-smelling stuff floated over the group like another kind of heat.

Hauman sprang up. "Here, let me do that for you."

"Much obliged, on account of I can't reach my back."

Hauman poured some oil into the palm of his hand and began spreading it over Bill Howard's back and shoulders. Howard murmured contentedly under the pressure of the broad hands. "Boy, this is service."

The job finished, Hauman moved over to Grandin. "I'll do it for you too, Johnnie."

"No, thanks. I can manage myself."

But Cliff ignored this. "I can do it much easier than you can, Johnnie." He bent down and placed his hands on Grandin's back.

Grandin pulled violently away. "I said I didn't want it!" He was surprised at the sharpness in his voice.

A sudden silence fell upon the little group, as if it were a moment of painful embarrassment to them all. The situation was saved by Bill Howard who, though no one listened to him, said casually:

"Better let him. I knew a guy once who dislocated his shoulder putting sun-tan oil on his back. And jeepers, I do believe it was the same brand as this: Sun-Glo. Though

I don't know; on second thought, I guess it didn't smell so bad. . . ."

Ethel got up, and Sarah Howard followed. "Don't expect us till late afternoon," Mrs. Howard said. "We'll lunch in Nantucket and then maybe do some shopping after the hairdresser's."

"Get yourself done up right, Mama. You're going to have some heavy competition tonight, with Toni Lansing there."

"I'm not worrying. 'Bye, darling." She kissed him, and the two women went off toward the bluff.

John Grandin felt it keenly that Ethel had said no word by way of farewell, but it would have been even more of an admission of strain—a kind of pleading as well —if he had called after her: Good-bye.

When she had gone about a hundred feet, she turned and came part way back, to say: "I left my sun-tan oil for you. Please don't forget it and leave it behind."

He was grateful to her for this attention in the presence of the others; it helped. He had the small sticky bottle at that moment in his hand, his fingers tight around it. The warm moist grit of sand that had gathered upon its surface stuck to his palm; some of it had come off and collected uncomfortably beneath his fingernails. . . .

When, on their way to lunch, they were halfway to the bluff, Grandin realized he had forgotten Ethel's parting words: he had left the sun-tan bottle behind after all, somewhere in the sand. Well, they could buy another for ten cents at the drugstore. . . .

XVI

THE BUCCANEER was a converted frigate anchored at the pier, with chairs and tables set about a broad sloping deck and great canvas awnings stretched overhead between the masts. Waitresses in colonial costumes came up the gangplank from a kitchen housed on the pier, and sea gulls hovered at the edge of the deck, flapping their wings and uttering shrill cries. A crust of bread tossed into the air by one of the tourists brought the great birds in a sudden shrieking flock to the spot; others bobbed gently about on the waves below, waiting for scraps of food to be thrown down. A sharp wind blew across the deck, the paper napkins took to the breeze when the plates that weighted them down were lifted, and occasionally a glass of water was blown over or a vase of flowers strewn about one of the tables.

"I'm so busy hanging onto things," Sarah Howard said, "that I can't keep my mind on my food. Not that it matters," she added; "it's stone cold anyhow."

"The boys would love this place, though. My children, I mean."

"Yes, and all the old ladies who trip about Nantucket—and that vast American public to whom anything quaint is the equivalent of romance."

Ethel Grandin felt rather uncomfortable with the cynical Mrs. Howard; they had little in common, and she wondered how they were going to get through the next hour or two together. She wondered even more when Sarah

Howard suddenly opened up a subject which she herself wouldn't have dreamed of mentioning, had their positions been reversed.

"I hope you won't mind too much if I speak of something that's absolutely none of my business. But Bill and I have both noticed it, we like you and your husband, and —well, naturally we're concerned. I'm talking about the Haumans, of course."

"I'm afraid I don't understand—"

"Let's be frank, then. That Billie is an extraordinarily pretty girl. They don't come any prettier. But just because she's been a student of your husband's, and they seem to be carrying it on even here, doesn't mean anything necessarily."

"Carrying what on?"

"Look, Mrs. Grandin, Bill and I weren't born yesterday and neither were you. Your husband is infatuated with her."

"What makes you think so?"

"Don't you think so yourself?"

"But the Haumans are just married—they're on their honeymoon."

"Do you think that makes her any less attractive to your husband? Men are always titillated to their finger tips in the presence of a young bride. Now I don't mean for one second that she and your husband are actually having an affair, but they've known each other for some time and he's interested in her, and she knows it. It's the only reason Bill and I can think of for their moving in on you like this. Cliff seems to realize it too, or else why would he go to such lengths to be so damned broad-minded about it? He's positively ostentatious in trying to show that it's all right with him, just so nobody else will notice. The way he goes on about Johnnie-and-I-this or Johnnie-and-I-that, as though he and your husband were bosom pals, whereas in reality they haven't the remotest thing in common or even the faintest reason for liking each other. My god, he talks as though you two wives didn't exist. It's pretty obvious."

"That's just his way, perhaps."

"Of course if you mind my butting in, I'll shut up."

"I don't mind, really. I only—"

"As I said, we're concerned because we like you, and I thought it wouldn't do any harm to air the thing, just between you and me. Bill and I are happily married—completely, I think—but even so, there have been several times in the past few years when his eye has been caught by a pretty girl and I've had to pretend I didn't notice. It's the only thing to do. They always come back. These momentary flirtations mean nothing. The boys are beginning to feel their age and they don't like the idea. It helps some if they can sort of make believe they're having one last romance with a young girl before the long freeze sets in for good."

"I appreciate your interest, but—maybe you're imagining all this."

"Maybe I am. I hope so. But Bill and I have noticed you're unhappy and we thought it was because of Billie."

"I— This is difficult to talk about, really. It seems so unfair to John—behind his back . . ."

"To hell with him. Think of yourself first, why don't you? Then maybe he'll think a little more of you and less of Billie. Me, I never for a moment let Bill Howard lose track of the fact that I'm the most wonderful woman he ever met. So I'm a complete fraud, you see, but at least it works. Bill does think so—and will to his dying day. . . ."

XVII

As JOHN GRANDIN was getting into his blue suit just before dinner—the suit would have to take the place of a uniform that evening—he saw from the bedroom window that a fog had begun to gather on the flat sandy waste between the bluff and the sea. It moved along the sand like a low smoke, like vague amorphous vapor as yet unformed into clouds. It was like watching from the rim of a nearly extinct crater the little emanations of steam or gas arise faintly from its depths and float aimlessly about somewhere near the bottom. Yet the fog, unseen, had come from the upper air or from over the sea, drifting unseen toward the flat waste in the late afternoon, to take shape and become visible with the passing of the warm sunlight.

Ethel, her hair freshly set, her mouth touched up with the lipstick she so rarely used, was ready. She wore a long dark-blue dinner gown with short sleeves, silver sandals, and no jewelry. She looked younger than at any time since they had come to the island; her figure was easily a match for the figure of any woman he would be seeing that evening; certainly more than a match for Billie's broad hips and short stature. They went down to dinner early.

They had finished before the Haumans came in. Billie had on a short dress of shiny changeable silk, neither blue nor green, very bouffant and very young. Hauman was dressed as always in khaki; the only concession he seemed to have made to the evening was a clean shirt and an immaculate field scarf.

"We'll be on the veranda," Ethel said.

"I know," Billie said; "you want to watch the moon rise."

"I'm afraid it doesn't come up till much later," Grandin said.

"Goodness, I hope we won't miss it at the dance. It's full tonight. Isn't it thrilling?"

They sat on the porch just outside the half-open window beyond which the Haumans were still at dinner. A heavy mist had gathered on the flats below; it was now almost certain that the evening and the night were to be obscured by a real Nantucket fog.

"I'm sorry, Ethel, but I hate dancing, as you know. However, I'll try it once or twice, if you like."

"It doesn't matter."

He glanced at her, saw again how attractive she looked, and wanted to say something about it. But all he could bring out was: "In any case, I'm glad we decided to go. I'll do my damnedest, Ethel, to see that you have a good time."

"John," she said, "I'm trying to forget that dreadful first night, I truly am. But it would be awful if we forgot it entirely and just let ourselves slip back into the—the nothing we've had for so long. . . ."

"O lord."

"Very well, if you don't want to talk about it."

"I'm afraid I don't," he said, "if that's the way you

feel." Then he added, suddenly very angry: "Jesus Christ, the way women can hang onto these things . . ."

"I'm afraid I'm not hanging onto very much at all. . . ."

Infuriated he turned away and lighted a cigarette. It was a fine start for an evening he hadn't been looking forward to in any case. Through the window at his back he heard the Haumans talking to the Howards, who had stopped at their table. As he took in the conversation, he was almost shaken out of his chair with astonishment.

"Hey, Bill," Hauman said gleefully, "I want you to lay off that pretty boy over there, the fag. *You* can't have him—he's mine!"

Howard laughed, while the women tittered. "The blond with his mother? Now, Cliff, I marked him for my own the first time I saw him, so you're a little late."

"Want to lay any bets about who makes him first?"

Hauman's laugh, then, was so hearty and good-natured that John Grandin was nonplused. Considering Hauman's embarrassment the first time the subject came up, he was totally unprepared for the little exchange. In spite of his own reaction against Arne Eklund on the beach, it seemed to him outrageous and cruel; and bitterly he wished he had not heard it. . . .

The Haumans joined them on the porch. "Say, Johnnie, that's a nice topcoat you've got there." He picked up the coat from the arm of a chair and fingered it admiringly. "My daddy would look nice in a coat like that. He loves good tweeds and things, and so do I. Mind if I try it on?"

It was an English Burberry in the full loose raglan

style, the kind of coat that would fit anyone, even the wide shoulders of Hauman. He had bought it in London many years ago and expected or hoped to have it for the rest of his life, for he was very fond of it.

Hauman put on the topcoat and turned to see the reflection of himself in one of the windows. Standing profile to Grandin, he buttoned it down the front. The sleeves were a good four inches too short, but it fitted his shoulders and back very well. He held his arms straight and admired himself in the glass of the window.

John Grandin looked at the reflection too, and at the figure itself. He had a curious prevision of the future. It wasn't Captain Hauman of the Marine Corps who stood here but a young roughneck in a borrowed topcoat.

Above the reflection of his shoulders, Hauman caught Grandin's glance. He pulled off the coat at once and said no more about it.

The boy from the desk came along the veranda. "There's a car here from the Coast Guard, sir, for Captain Hauman and party."

"My, aren't we grand," Billie said, getting up. "Will you call Mr. and Mrs. Howard, Joe? They're in the dining room."

Suddenly Hauman said: "You go along, Billie, and I'll follow in a few minutes. Something I want to do first —just an idea."

"But how will you get to Nantucket?" she asked querulously.

"Ever hear of a serviceman not being able to pick up a ride? I'll be there soon, but I know you're anxious to see Toni Lansing."

"Clifford Hauman, what are you up to? I want to know!" But he had already gone in. Pleased, she turned to the Grandins. "Now isn't that sweet. I'll bet he's going to get dressed up after all."

The Howards came out and the five of them got into the dark sedan that waited at the steps, with a young man in Coast Guard blues at the wheel. He was very polite and reserved, and greeted them with succinct military formality. Grandin sat in front with him while the others arranged themselves in the back seat. As the car pulled away, they heard the harpist begin her evening recital.

Leaving Sconset behind, the car was soon rolling over the moors toward Nantucket. The night wind was cold and damp with fog.

"I guess we're going to have a real blackout," Grandin said.

"I believe so, sir," the driver replied. "But the fog might lift if the wind changes."

In the back seat he heard Billie and Mrs. Howard talking.

"Is your name really Sarah?"

"Yes."

"Then why do you let him call you Sadie?" Billie asked, almost petulantly.

"Because I love it. I insist on Sadie."

"Why not Sally? That's so much nicer."

"Sally, my god. Makes me sick. Sadie is much more sophisticated. All those names are coming back, didn't you know? Libby and Annie and Maggie and— They're fashionable again."

"I think they're horrid!"

"Why are you called Billie?"

"Well you see, my mother's mother was named Bertha—"

"Oh, my god."

"Well, *I* can't help it."

"You can and did," Sarah Howard said with a laugh. "I guess I can't blame you much for Billie. But Bert would have been much more chic. . . ."

As they reached the outer streets of Nantucket, there were signs that it was to be a gala evening for the island. Many people moved in the direction of the steamer pier; when the car turned the corner by the Whaling Museum and drove on toward the White Elephant, it became apparent that the destination of the crowd, old and young alike, was the Yacht Club. The clubhouse was lighted up festively without regard for the dimout, which apparently had been lifted for that evening.

Groups of townspeople, mainly women and young girls, lined the canopied walk that led into the club, waiting to see Toni Lansing arrive. As the car pulled in under the portico and John Grandin stepped out to assist the women to the curb, the faces of the crowd fell with disappointment; an actual moan of dismay and reproach went up from the women and girls. It was, of course, though on a much smaller scale, a down-East variation of the well-known Hollywood phenomenon—the frenzied "preem" of Sunset Boulevard—transferred for the evening to this small New England island, in tribute to the visiting movie star.

XVIII

JOHN GRANDIN was not alone in his feeling of being an outsider. If other civilians present did not feel themselves unwelcome guests, they did look upon the real guests of the evening with a kind of awe. The hundreds of uniformed young men—heartbreakingly young, most of them —of all ranks and branches of the service and each looking his cleanest and best, were the admiration and envy of all, the very spirit and beauty and life of the evening, while the Nantucket dignitaries at the reception table were anonymous and less than nothing.

The clubhouse had become charged with an atmosphere of youth, an oppressive feeling of young masculinity so real as to be almost tangible, unlike anything John Grandin (or for that matter, any one of them) had been accustomed to in the recent and comfortable past. Evening parties, receptions, dances and other public gatherings of this sort had always largely been given over to the attraction of, and response to, pretty women and girls. Young women in bright dresses set the tone of the evening, and the success or failure of the social occasion depended on the femininity present, its quality, glamour, or charm. Now the reverse was true. The evening was given up to the worship of the male; it was his night. The uniform dominated the scene like a physical lure, it imposed itself on the consciousness of all, and made even the least imaginative respond to its attraction. Something of this feeling seemed to have entered into the behavior of the

young men themselves. The normal shyness characteristic
of youth in the presence of girls and older folk was nonexistent. The boys were too aggressive in their attitude
toward their adoring partners; and what ordinarily would
have been commented on by their elders as arrogance or
actual rudeness was recognized tonight as the natural and
charming play of young men about to go off to war. Under
the influence of the predominant uniform, women and
girls bloomed like flowers, and the citizenry responded
alike with pleasure, with admiration, and with affection.
No one could do enough for the boys.

There was a small flurry at the door and Toni Lansing, in a simple white dress like a tennis frock, came in.
She walked rapidly and with enormous composure to her
place at the reception table, followed by a young naval
officer carrying her light fur-collared coat. She apologized
to the Commander for being late, then ducked under the
table and came up on the other side next to him, as if it
was far too much trouble to go all the way down to the
end and back. She looked up brightly at the boys who,
one and all, stared at her, and she signified humorously,
with an inviting little pantomime which seemed good-
naturedly to burlesque her celebrity, that she was ready
and willing to give out autographs all night long if anyone
should be so foolish as to want one. During the little performance she managed with charming tact to convey the
impression that they would be doing her a favor instead
of the other way around.

Billie Hauman gazed enthralled. Grandin himself
could not but be impressed, though for different reasons.
It was curious to look at that slight figure and realize what

an enormous earning capacity she had, what an extraordinary amount of money she attracted to box offices throughout the country, and what she meant, in romance and glamour, to millions of men and women. Apart from her skill, Toni Lansing had little to do with it. It was an illusion: something that existed only on the screen or in the frustrations of many humdrum lives. . . .

Suddenly all conversations ceased and the entire place came to attention, respectful and grave. It was a full moment before John Grandin realized that the national anthem was being played.

Erect, he waited beside Ethel amid the suddenly quiet crowd of strangers—which now, for some reason, included the Howards and Billie. The strains of *The Star-Spangled Banner* floated down from the raised platform and provided a curious suspension of time, a break in the normal sequence of events, a time out, in which John Grandin felt as alone as if he had been in a vast empty room. In all that strange crowd he knew only his wife, cared only for her, belonged to no one else; side by side with her during the playing of the anthem he felt acutely the poverty, loneliness, and brevity of life, its ineffable transience. He heard her voice, a confident but quiet alto, and he was deeply touched. Out of all the confused people in the whole confused world she was the one he knew; it was urgent (but now!) that they should look at one another, see who they were, and hang onto what they had: life moved so fast! Each single moment was alive, if one was only aware of it, and none more charged with meaning than this. He had lost track of themselves for so long, but it now seemed clear, plain, and immediate that

a man's sole purpose was to look about, to see whom it
was he loved, and to love her. . . . He felt for the hand
beside his own, found her fingers and clasped them in his,
while the voices soared around him. He turned his head
to catch her glance. She was looking straight ahead at the
platform where the band played, her chin slightly raised.
His eye was caught by something just beyond. In the
doorway was Cliff Hauman, standing alone at attention.
From his visored cap to his shoes, his uniform was a resplendent, a breath-taking white.

The shoes were so white that the stuff would surely
rub off at a touch; the stiff twill trousers had been pressed
to razorlike creases. The blouse was emblazoned with gold
buttons straight down to his middle, with area or campaign ribbons studded with stars; and the silver bars of
his rank adorned his shoulders. The dazzling garment
fitted him tight, so that the many gold buttons were somewhat strained; the high collar looked uncomfortably close
beneath his chin. Above the shining patent-leather visor,
just below the wide starched crown of the cap—and on
either side of the high collar of the blouse as well—was the
emblem of the Marine Corps in silver and gold: a replica
of the Western Hemisphere, showing the Americas, super-
posed upon a fouled anchor surmounted by an eagle with
spread wings.

Here again, but more than ever now, was the hero
out of Homer—Hector or Achilles—or Lancelot (far more
than Galahad), Siegfried, Jason of the Argonauts, who had
been his boyhood companions. A thousand times he had
sailed in the windy *Argo* over the wine-dark sea, eaten
with, slept with, fought with and loved with the men of

that manly and various crew. Here was one of them now, the epitome of them all, who in another moment would step forward and call him familiarly "Johnnie."

As he waited for the anthem to end, the expression on his young unself-conscious face was one of strained, almost worried, respect; but the general impression he created was something else again. In his most extravagant flight of vanity or eagerness to please, Cliff Hauman could not have begun to calculate the full effect he had produced. The white made him look even larger than he was; he glowed in the doorway like a figure abstract, luminous, and mythical.

The band came to the finish; with scarcely a pause it broke into a lively dance tune. Hauman stepped forward, and for the moment was lost in the crowd of young men and girls who came to life at once in a swirling mass.

"Here comes Bill Howard," Ethel said. "Will you ask Mrs. Howard to dance with you?"

But when he approached her, Sarah Howard said: "You don't want to dance, you're just being polite. I don't want to, either. Let's sit it out."

From chairs at the side they watched the bouncing frenzied crowd. A young sailor jitterbugged by himself in front of them, while his partner performed the exact same gyrations a couple of feet away; when they came together, it was with the force of a blow. Bill Howard and Ethel passed, their reserve a strange contrast to the modern antics all around them. In the center of the room, his tawny head towering above the others, Cliff Hauman could be seen bobbing happily up and down; Billie, her

eyes shut, nestled against the broad white chest, oblivious
to everyone but her husband.

"Do you know what this reminds me of?" Sarah Howard said. "I can't get it out of my mind:

> " 'There was a sound of revelry by night,
> And Belgium's capital had gathered then
> Her Beauty and her Chivalry, and bright
> The lamps shone o'er fair women and brave men . . .'

I suppose that sounds pretty sophomoric to you," she
added.

"Indeed it doesn't. Do you know how it goes on?"

Sarah Howard gave a small laugh. "I think I do,
though I never thought I'd be quoting Byron at my age:

> " 'A thousand hearts beat happily; and when
> Music arose with its voluptuous swell,
> Soft eyes looked love to eyes which spake again,
> And all went merry as a marriage bell;—
> But hush! hark! a deep sound strikes like a rising
>   knell! . . .' "

"I had forgotten how good that is," Grandin said.
"It does have a mood . . ."

The band had shifted to a new tune, a slow swinging
nostalgic melody like a college song, and in a few moments
the voices of many young men and girls had taken up the
refrain. They listened to the swaying dancers singing as
they danced, moving in a slower tempo now, their heads
together, many of them in public amorous embrace. The

melody was not unlike the *Alma Mater* of Hauman's own university—*Where the vale of Onondaga Meets the eastern sky*—or the *Far above Cayuga's waters With its waves of blue* of Cornell, which was the same; but suddenly, with a mounting disbelief, John Grandin realized what he was hearing. At the same moment Mrs. Howard said:

"My god, did you ever hear anything more comic in your life? Listen!"

> "Let's re-mem-berr Pearl Har-bor
> As we go to meet the foe. . . .
> Let's re-mem-berr Pearl Har-bor
> As we did the Al-a-mo. . . ."

Heads together, lazily smiling, the young men and girls poured forth the song without thought as they moved slowly around the dance floor. It was a simple melody, the kind which, heard once, one knew immediately; it flooded the hall like a football song on the night of a rally before the big game; and like a football song, when sung in unison by a mixed company of young men and women, it was a love song as much as anything else. . . .

> "We will al-ways re-mem-berr
> How they died for lib-ber-ty . . .
> Let's re-mem-berr Pearl Har-borr
> And go on to vic-tor-reee. . . ."

Grandin felt the need to escape the place for a moment or two. "Would you like to step out and get some fresh air?"

"You go," Sarah Howard said; "I wouldn't miss this for worlds."

XIX

HE FOUND HIS WAY to the lawn back of the clubhouse. He crossed the lawn to a concrete breakwater which ran at right angles to the pier. In the half-dark he bumped into a small bench. He lifted the bench, turned it around so that it faced the bay, and sat down in the cool night, his back to the club.

Heavy mist lay over the water, but through the mist could be seen small red and green lights bobbing or swaying back and forth, the night lanterns of boats anchored in the bay. Almost at his feet was the lapping water, washing against the breakwall in soft little slaps. He gazed below, but the water disappeared in the fog a dozen feet away.

From behind came the music of the dance, the shuffle of many feet, laughter, voices; and when the band stopped between numbers, there was loud applause accented by shrill whistles. He was sure the middle-aged matrons, who normally would have been shocked by such vulgarity in the Yacht Club, tonight thought it was delightful.

He had been there perhaps half an hour when suddenly a voice spoke directly behind the bench.

"Is that you, Johnnie?"

Hauman moved around the edge of the bench and sat down. "I was looking for you. Mrs. Howard said maybe you were out here."

"Where's Ethel?"

"Oh, Eth is having a high old time. I just danced with her myself and now some other guy has got her. Lieutenant jg. Personally I wouldn't wipe my feet on a lieutenant but this guy was good-looking as all— Say, Eth is a swell dancer. You better watch out!"

In the half-dark his white uniform was a great blur of white. Grandin saw him reach up and unhook the tight collar.

"Aren't you going to dance, Johnnie?"

"I may."

"Look, isn't this the month for falling stars? Still it wouldn't be any good tonight, with the fog. But this would be a swell place to see them—all that sky. Or maybe it's August. You ought to see the stars out in the Pacific," he went on. "Gee, they're so close it looks like you could knock them out of the sky with a stick. There's something they call the Southern Cross. You ought to see it, Johnnie. If you stare at it hard for a while, it seems to shake, like it had been jarred or something. Of course it isn't really a regular cross but it looks enough like a cross to call it one. My buddy Walt, I must tell you about him sometime, he knew the names of a lot of the big stars and planets, but I never could remember them. Just like in school, I was never any good at languages."

It was little short of infantile prattle; and why it should also have been charming—oppressively charming and touching—John Grandin couldn't discover. He was overpoweringly conscious of the white figure glowing beside him in the dark. It disturbed him profoundly to realize again how the presence of Cliff Hauman, who was almost half his age, should make him feel half of Hauman's, so that he was stirred through and through by a schoolboy worship of the dazzling uniform and the figure in it. It was bizarre, outlandish, out of all precedent with anything that had ever happened in his experience. He was ill equipped to comprehend or control his feeling, unable to determine his dilemma, even to put his finger on it and say it was this, or this.

"Do you believe that falling stars mean somebody has just died, Johnnie? But gee, if that was true, the skies would be just showering with 'em. Specially these days."

Grandin lighted a cigarette and tossed the match into the dark water at their feet, which, for all its small lapping sounds, looked solid, hard, a substantial flooring or roadbed leading off into the night and far far on, under the fog.

"Go on back to the dance, Cliff."

"You coming in too?"

"Soon."

"Yeah, Billie'll be missing me—maybe I better go."

"Yes."

"See you later, Johnnie."

The mysterious tension held. When he had gone, John Grandin was more than ever certain that Cliff Hauman was marked for death. Viewed realistically, his dying could be of little concern or interest. Death in itself didn't matter, it was not even dramatic. What did matter—what was dramatic and passionate—was the intense fact of his present living, his vitality, charm, and enjoyment of life, and the peculiarly refreshing effect he had on everyone he came in contact with. Hauman's imminent death was of no real moment. Grandin was only involved because Cliff Hauman was supremely alive *now*, almost a "classic" example to him of the wanton and extravagant waste that was the pattern of the times.

The fog had settled in so that he could scarcely see the breakwall at his feet. He was chilled and needed his topcoat. He got up and returned to the lighted clubhouse, to find Ethel and go back to Sconset.

He ran into Bill Howard.

"Sadie's been looking for you. She wants to go home."

"I'm ready."

"Then why don't I stay on with Ethel for a while?" Bill Howard said. "Would you mind?"

"Not at all, if she wants to stay," and he meant it.

But Ethel was ready to go too, or at least would not stay without her husband. The four of them made their way to the checkroom and collected their things. They were unwilling to interrupt the Haumans' fun by seeking them out to say good night, which might seem to suggest that they should leave too. From the small group of drivers at the door, the young man who had driven them from Sconset came forward and ushered them to the car in the parking lot.

The ride home was quiet. Grandin offered Ethel his topcoat but she did not want it. The moors were overlaid with a thick mist, very lovely to see in the headlights of the car, very pleasant to ride through. The cool dampness of the night blew in at the windows; it refreshed Grandin's fatigued spirits, causing him to become wider and wider awake as they neared Sconset. In the opposite corner of the dark back seat the Howards were silent, engrossed in one another like a young couple. Up front, the driver kept his eye on the vague but flying ribbon of road, almost ostentatiously oblivious of his passengers.

Except for the unusually loud rumble of the beach, the midnight air of Sconset was soundless. The village had gone to sleep. Dune House was blacked out and quiet. They alighted on the steps of the veranda and the car drove off at once.

"Good night, kids, I'm dead," Sarah Howard said, and she disappeared with her husband into the dark hotel.

John Grandin sat down on the bottom step of the porch; Ethel was just above.

"What are you doing?" she said.

"Nothing. I thought I'd sit here a moment."

"It's too foggy and damp."

"I'm all right."

"John, I want to talk to you."

"Now listen," he said sharply; "I'm not going to move and I'm certainly not coming upstairs if you're going to fight! I'm sick of it!"

"Be quiet, people will hear you!" She came down the steps. "John—what's the matter with you?" she said tensely.

"I don't know what you're talkng about. Do you?"

"I'm not sure . . ."

"If you mind because I didn't ask you to dance, I'm sorry. I couldn't."

"I never thought of it. But you might have asked Billie."

"Why the hell should I have asked Billie? I didn't want to dance with Billie!"

"Cliff asked me!"

Their conversation was carried on in savage whispers, tense and unreal as if they were involved in some dreadful make-believe conspiracy, against no one but themselves.

"What difference does it make to you whether I danced with Billie or not?"

"Oh, it doesn't, I suppose. . . ."

"Then what in Christ's name are we fighting about!"

"I don't know," she said; "I don't know . . ."

He stared into the fog, wanting to be alone.

"You're not yourself, John. That was a stupid performance of yours on the beach this morning! Everybody noticed!"

His anger rose. "What performance?"

"The way you acted about that sun-tan oil! Cliff was only trying to help you."

He was incensed; it seemed impossible to sit there any longer—he had to get away from her. "I didn't need any help!"

"Bill Howard took it. Why couldn't you?"

Hot with rage, he did not trust himself to answer.

"I never saw you so childish. I was ashamed! So was everybody else."

He got up and stepped forward into the road.

"Where are you going!"

"For a walk. . . ."

"But it's midnight! Besides, you can't see your hand before your face!"

"Good night. . . ."

"John! . . ."

XX

IN SPITE OF the density of the atmosphere, the night was not entirely dark. The full moon somewhere above transformed the moving mist into a yellow-white murk, which glowed darker or lighter as the fog settled or rose. Weird though it was, the effect was quieting, like an escape into sleep. The hurrying shifting fog created a magical unreality, in which things near at hand—the veranda of Dune House, the markers indicating the driveway, the arbor of roses at the top of the stairs leading down the bluff—were remote, nonexistent, questionable. He knew where they were and that they were there; but could one be certain? Staring at them, fixing his gaze on where he knew them to be, he saw their shadowy outlines which, even while he traced them with his eye, vanished like the face in the moon the evening before. Was Ethel still waiting on the steps or had she gone up? He alone was the only certainty in the world, the one presence of which he could be sure. He started up the road.

Fine, so long as he kept away from the rose arbor and stairway, he told himself, remembering his encounter with the coast guardsman. The fellow had done his best to act tough, a match for his snarling dog, perhaps; but Grandin suspected the young man had probably been as uncomfortable with him—as surprised and thrown off— as he had been with the other. They had play-acted, automatically carrying out a stern little ritual which had been imposed upon them by the war.

He remembered how the macadam road ran for a couple of thousand feet past Dune House, then turned back into Sconset; but at the turn, another road of soft dirt continued straight along the diminishing bluff toward Tom Nevershead. He took this direction now, to walk as far as the turn.

The silly quarrel had been no more serious than the family fights which are the very life of the comic strips. It was hardly to be taken seriously; it had happened before and would doubtless happen many times again. What was serious, however, was what had happened to them since they had come to the island. What was very serious indeed was the need to discover why the holiday which they had both been counting on to bring them together again should, instead, have blasted them further apart than ever.—Yet he was still possessed by a raging anger. It was intolerable that Ethel should have taunted him about Cliff and the sun-tan oil—so exactly like a woman to attach such unreasonable and exaggerated importance to an episode which had no meaning whatever.

In marriage, a man's chance of happiness—of survival, it almost seemed—depends far more on his knowledge of himself than of his wife. One doesn't mean the trying first year of adjustment which, long enough, has been the concern of comedy. For many men, the realer period comes later, ten, a dozen, or fifteen years, when fatigue has set in. At twenty-some, he knows why he married. At forty he is far from sure. He asks himself: What am I getting out of it; what keeps us going; is it worth it?— To answer such questions, he must be aware not only of the immediate problem or crisis that prompts them, but of his life as a whole.

His feet moved into a soft sandy path; he had reached the bend where the road wound back from the bluff to Sconset village. If he stayed on the macadam he would lose his way; the thing to do was to continue straight along the dirt road which gradually descended as the bluff diminished, and turn back when he got tired. This path would be safer; besides less chance of getting lost, there would also be less danger of being run down by a motor-car in the fog, coming home late from the Yacht Club party.

Half of his childhood had been spent looking forward to the pleasures of adulthood when he would be old enough to take life in his own hands and do something with it; yet how free was a man to do this, how much was the choice ever his? What he had found was surely far different from what he had expected to find. He had always been living in the future, and was still, at the age of forty-four, in the habit of doing so. All of his courtship, as well as the first years of his marriage, had been but a promise of further delights to come. When their first child arrived, no man had been happier or more proud than he; yet reality was not the same as dream. Had that early happiness been illusion, like the dreams of his youth? He was in exactly the same position of which he had charged Ethel only a few months ago, when he had accused her of being unrealistic about marriage; to her, marriage automatically meant happiness. He was living under the same delusion, for that's what it had meant to him; instead of which, marriage was something one had to work at, constantly, continually, daily; never more than now.

His had been a very ordinary boyhood and young manhood, in no way unusual, almost embarrassingly average; his experience, such as it was, could be duplicated or matched by that of thousands of other American youths. Yet sometimes he looked back on those days of unreality as the richest, the most promising period of his life, because it was a time when to *look forward* meant possibilities of happiness undreamed of. What did "looking forward" mean now? Except for watching his sons develop—except for a promotion at the university or recognition because of his book, the chief pleasure of which had been in the doing of it, not because of the way it would be received—it meant a checking off or verification (hardly more imaginative or exciting than a business inventory) of all which common sense or experience had long since told him he could expect from life, no more and no less.

The white opaque night enveloped him pleasantly; yet there was a sinister quality about it, as well, which he could not define. He felt, for one thing, that he was fleeing from the concrete to the nebulous and unreal, possibly the dangerous; he felt, too, as if he were stumbling along over quicksands which gave underfoot and threatened to engulf him or pull him down out of sight unless he hurried on. The fog was peopled with curious shapes; his flight was like one of those nightmares, so often the subject of a ribald joke (the baked beans, the bridegroom, the surprise party), in which the protagonist, blindfolded or left in a dark room, is surrounded by friends or acquain-

tances who look on coldly while he, innocent of their
presence, makes a spectacular fool of himself. It was as
if, twenty feet away, a line of fateful judges had gathered,
to witness his plight yet take no part in it, neither to direct
nor to help him. He could almost see these figures looming
in the murk nearby, could almost have named them—and
he wanted continually to speak out and say (if only to
reassure himself): I know you are there; but go away,
leave me alone. . . . He ignored them, kept his eyes to
the ground which he could not see, pretended he was
by himself, and reminded himself over and over that no
one knew where he was. . . .

At twenty-four, two years out of college and just beginning his assistant instructorship, he had had his second
affair—if the ten or twelve minutes in bed with the red-
headed Darlene at home at the age of seventeen could be
called an affair at all. He lived in a rooming house on
West 88th Street and his landlady fell in love with him.
She was Viennese, twenty years older than he, still beautiful, a spirited romantic woman with a passionate interest
in the ideas of the young as much as in the young themselves. His inexperience had been no barrier to their love;
she understood it at once and, by a rare intuition, at the
beginning she assumed for him the responsibilities of
love-making. She did not reproach him (as a young girl
might have done, feeling herself unloved) when their first
night came to little; and if she was amused, she kept it
to herself. It was the kind of affair which every young
man should have in his teens; that it had come to him a
good five years later did not lessen its value. The relationship proved an ideal one for him; he benefited enor-

mously by it. Friends remarked the change in him, women especially, who took more notice of his personality than they had been in the habit of doing—though this may only have been because he had not been aware of these things and now saw responses, if not actual invitations, where before he had seen nothing; unlike so many other men, he never took it for granted that he was attractive to women. Curiously enough, his landlady's husband played almost as much of a part in this ideal relationship as she did; he was a casual but lusty European with an extramarital life of his own, and on those occasions when he was at home, the three of them had wonderful companionable evenings filled with good talk and good music, followed by midnight suppers which were an understood prelude to an undemanding love or love-making.

Following this, there was a small succession of other women, never young girls, and none of them lasting long. It was he who saw to that. He had become one of that countless number of young American men who lived their own lives, went their own way with no emotional entanglements, served as the ideal extra man at dinner parties or as a fourth at bridge, to be trusted (justifiably) by mothers in his home town whose daughters were visiting in the city for the first time—popular, uninvolved, speculated about, envied by other men and secretly yearned after by women, and who made love, if at all, only when it was perfectly clear beforehand (to him if not to her) that there were no strings attached. Then, when he was in his thirties, he met Ethel. . . .

The fog seemed to lift, the moonlight began to shine brighter around him; but as the atmosphere seemed about to clear itself enough to show him where he was, it closed again, as if pressed from behind by gusts of night wind. He was wrapped in a thick murk, impenetrable but somehow soothing—except for the large looming figures he seemed constantly to see in his path and whom he kept stepping aside to avoid, only to discover, as he passed, that no one was there at all. Notwithstanding the illusory forms lurking always just ahead of him, he was alone in the enveloping fog. . . .

Ethel Cameron worked in the library at the university. Apart from seeing her there, he met her several times at the home of a fellow instructor. She was twenty-three, not at all vivid or provocative in a sexual way, yet pretty, with a perfect figure and a straight proud bearing. Her modesty and reticence attracted him; it seemed to bespeak a person worth knowing. Because it was the turning point in his life, he would never forget the first time he had asked her to dine with him, at a small Italian restaurant in the Village. He felt very good with Ethel Cameron facing him across the little table, with the fine Chianti, and with the waiter making a fuss over them as if they were lovers; and suddenly he said, impulsively (because he was happy at the moment and she was so attentive, as if he were the most interesting man she had ever been out with): "You know, Ethel? If I were the marrying kind, you're the sort of girl I would like to marry." "Why John, I—" "Though I don't know why I say 'sort,' " he went on, "for there can't be many others like you in this world." "John, that's the nicest compliment I've ever had," she said; "I'm terribly grateful and pleased. But of course we know it'll never happen." "Why not?" "Well, as you yourself said, you—you're not the marrying kind. . . ." "No, I suppose not. . . ." Though denied, it had yet declared itself. That same evening when he sat on her living-room couch—the very moment he sat down beside her and felt her close to him, though he had often sat with her before on other people's sofas—he felt for the first time a small hot sensation plunge downward from his chest, the sensation of desire. Within a week he was making love to her; and before the month was out, they had gone to bed together. From then on he was tied, or sunk, or ecstatically happy about the prospect of marriage, he couldn't decide which—and indeed he had not been able to make up his mind till after they were married.

The ground beneath his feet was uncertain, thick with a kind of turf, no longer the powderlike dust of the pathway. Perhaps he had strayed from the road. Preoccupied with his reverie, he had now not the smallest notion of how far he had wandered in the dark or how long he had been walking. It was as though he had entered a world of time-out or a realm of dream, of which, undreamlike, the evidences were tangible enough—the fog, the constantly changing dark and light, the earth beneath his feet—all but the obscure figures which seemed continually to loom ahead of him in his path. He resisted an impulse to stop and call out: "Who's there!" as the coast guardsman had done last night. He felt the wet hurrying night on his cheek; flecks of damp blew across his forehead and eyes. It was time to turn back before he became irrevocably lost. Yet still he felt impelled to go on. As he stumbled over the uneven ground, he gazed

into the fog above to discover from which part of the
sky the moon shone. Though light of a kind swirled
thickly all around him, he could see nothing.

How much had it been Ethel he had fallen in love
with, how much had it been a desire to find a place in
the world and be the man for a woman like Ethel Cameron? The image of himself as he saw it reflected in her—
it appealed strongly to him and he loved her for it. In
any case they had fallen in love, and it was to be a very
long time before they would question its meaning. The
question, indeed, had only been raised this week, after
ten years of marriage—but with a raw violence he doubted
he would ever forget or recover from, an emphasis of guilt
he could not but accept as his own.

The sea was loud. He supposed the density of the
atmosphere and the fog itself brought the noisy beach
nearer, though such a night as this should rather have
muffled or softened (it seemed to him who knew nothing
of these things) than augmented the sound. Dampness
blew into his face as if it were actual spray from the
breakers; and this too, no doubt, was the tangible and
fleeing mist.

He began seriously to wonder how far he had gone
and where; began to worry. If he had lost his way, it
would be sensible to sit down somewhere and rest, possibly to wait for the fog to lift. He half suspected that
the hotel lay only a few hundred feet off; certainly he
had not gone so far but that, if the night were clear and
there was no blackout, he could see it from where he
was. He had turned back. Sure that he was headed in
the right direction, he plodded on, expecting his feet to

strike the macadam at any moment and thus find his way home again.

But they did not. Tired at last, he reached down to feel the ground, found it smooth and clear, and lowered himself to the sand. He would rest a few moments before going on. Beneath his palms the earth vibrated to the pound of the surf. A yellowish murk moved rapidly over the island, momentarily lifting and closing, never obscuring, never quite revealing, the brilliant sky overhead. He thought: somewhere above that fog tonight is the full moon Ethel has been waiting for. His heart turned suddenly with pity then—for Ethel lying under the harsh electric light with a magazine, while he wandered in the mist with his dilemma. He stretched at full length on his stomach, his head turned to one side and his cheek on the sand. For an instant the light shone suddenly wide and clear; he saw the breaking waves not thirty feet away; he saw a small object glistening on the beach within arm's length. He reached out; it was coated with a sticky grit. Some half-awakened sense within him responded as to a painfully familiar object, and the astonished hand closed on the bottle of sun-tan oil.

He heard the hissing scattering running sound of pebbles as the waves slid back down the beach after the thundering breakers had cast them far up the sloping sand; he felt the cool spray on his face and hands. He held the bottle tight in his now-sticky palm, the irritating grit already under his fingernails. He thought of Cliff.

He thought of himself sitting on the beach in the hot sun of the morning, while Cliff bent over him (as he had not permitted him to do) and touched his shoulders with the oil. In imagination he felt the broad fingers moving down his bare arms, as they had moved down Bill Howard's; and he felt the two strong hands moving over his upper arms, shoulders, and back. It was an act so personal and intimate that he could not have stood it. And suddenly, to his horror, he felt a slow rude pressure growing in his loins, so that he was no longer able to lie face down in the sand; he was obliged to turn over on his back.

What held him helpless on the beach for so long, then, was the realization of the danger he was in. Oh, not with the Coast Guard; he could take care of himself there. If surprised by the man and his dog, he could explain the situation and how it had happened. (But could he?) He could explain how he had been walking in the fog and lost his way. (But did that explain anything?) The coast guardsman would be satisfied. (But what about himself?)

END

E̲ARLY IN THE MORNING, Ethel Grandin sat alone at one of the little glass-topped wicker desks in the writing room. It was probably the one room in all of Dune House where she would least likely be found. She had made a few efforts with the scratchy pens and the black ink which was as thick as glue. But her mind was not on what she was doing. She could not forget the baffling scene last midnight when her husband had got up from the steps of the porch and walked away into the fog as if he were a stranger to her. She was beginning to believe he was a stranger. After he had gone—though she had called after him desperately, as if in a kind of panic for his welfare—she went up to the bedroom and, to her surprise, fell at once into a sound sleep, a sleep of exhaustion.

This morning she had begun and torn up a letter to the University dean, the gist of which was to ask him if

it might be possible for her husband to be relieved of
his teaching duties for the summer. She considered following this with a letter to her parents-in-law to tell them
that their son was in need of a long rest, away from the
boys and herself, and could he spend the summer with
them in his home town? But she rejected both letters.
It did not seem fair to go to such lengths without first
consulting her husband, whom they most concerned. Instead, she wrote the following with the difficult pen:

Dear Alan & Ted:
    Isn't it awful of me not to write you more often?
Even with nothing to do here, it seems impossible to
find time to sit down & write. This morning I came down
early to be sure to get a letter off to you today, for if I
wait till 9:30 or 10, by that time we are off to the beach
& there is no chance.
    Are you having a good time with Grandma &
Grandpa? I know without asking that you are being good
boys. I'm sure you get better swimming than we do here,
for the surf is always very strong & there is a strong
undertow which makes it risky to swim out very far.
But Sconset is wonderful. The beach is glorious & we
have had perfect weather every day. At night there is
usually a heavy fog but the days are lovely.
    Your father & I are having a wonderful time. Last
night we went to a big dance for soldiers & sailors at the
Yacht Club in Nantucket. Which was great fun. Good
friends of ours here are a Marine captain & his wife who
has seen active service at Guadalcanal. He is wonderfully
interesting to listen to & I often think how excited you
would be to know him.

Your father is still asleep upstairs because of our late night last night so I send love for him, & I know he will be writing you himself tomorrow or next day. Do give our best love to Grandma & Grandpa. We send all our love to you both. We miss you.

                              Lovingly,
                                Mother

Curiously dissatisfied with the letter, Ethel Grandin glanced up from the writing desk and gazed about the room. No one else had come in. The walls were hung with a few prettified scenes of whaling in the old days, and two conventional seascapes in oil by artists unknown. Through the window she caught sight of the Howards strolling arm in arm up the road toward Tom Nevershead. She addressed the stamped envelope and immediately forgot it. Her mind was not on the letter at all; least of all was it upstairs in the bedroom, where John still lay asleep. Her mind had wandered off into the murky fog last night in search of her husband; and the worst of it was, she had the awful feeling that it might never come back to her again.

                              II

IT ISN'T WHAT HAPPENS TO US that matters. Anything can happen to anybody. What matters is what we let it do to us.

John Grandin had often heard his father say this. He himself, at appropriate moments, had passed it on to three or four students, and he had often thought it would come in handy when his sons began to grow up. It was one of those sayings which are stock in every family; parents trot them out when other words fail, or when a good homely aphorism can take the place of an awkward or tedious explanation and stop the inquisitive young, to boot, by giving them something to think of. There was no denying the truth of the saying; and its value lay in direct proportion to the seriousness of the event. But he had led an uneventful life and had never given it much thought.

Up to now, that is. Now something had happened that couldn't happen. The point was, what was he going to let it do to him?

The moment he opened his eyes, John Grandin remembered the walk in the fog, where he had gone, and what he had found; remembered, even more graphically, what had happened to his physical person as he held the bottle of sun-tan oil in his hand and recalled the sensual scene earlier which inexplicably had angered him; inexplicable no longer. It was like waking up after a bad dream to discover that the dream had been only too true—was no dream at all and would carry on through the entire day, through many days or weeks, impossible to shake, forget, deny. The sense of shock which had gripped him last night on the beach was gone; in its place, an almost physical depression had taken over, a powerful but impotent protest which, though it cried out that *such things could not be,* was yet made senseless by the sickening realization that they could and were. It was as if he had stood up and shouted in indignant outrage: "Look here, I won't have it! That's not the kind of man I am, do you hear?"—only to be forced to accept the reverberating echo which said: But you are.

But he would not have that sort of thing! Life was too short, life was complicated enough, there was his family, his students, his career; besides, Cliff Hauman, fond of him though he knew he was, no more wanted it than he did.

He could not call it accident; events had shown it to be inevitable, perhaps, and even just. But man was supposed to be a creature of his own will, able to decide for himself what he wanted or did not want, and to some extent the master of his destiny still—willful, unconscious, or momentary impulses notwithstanding. He remembered seeing an Odets play which had affected him deeply, one line of which disturbed him to such an extent that he could not get it out of his mind during the long wakeful night after. At one point the hero had said, "All my life I've been afraid to do something wrong and now I've done it." This thought had struck him with such force that it almost seemed to have been written for him alone, though nothing in his life at the time had warranted such a disturbance over a mere handful of words.

But he had done nothing wrong. He would do nothing wrong. He had been warned, he knew now what had been upsetting him, and henceforth he could and would be on guard. Because he was aware at last of the nature of his relationship with the marine and the dangerous direction it had taken, he felt that Cliff was powerless to affect him further in such a disturbing way. For the first time, Cliff Hauman almost seemed unimportant, except as the means by which he had come to understand.

John Grandin had always believed he knew himself through and through; when he found that he did not, he knew himself at last. Shocking though the revelation had been, Cliff had meant experience, a knowledge of his unconscious, an extension or illumination of his nature. Very well; though he refused to give in to it, he would try to accept—for what else does life hold for us, he asked himself, if not experience? Hard as it may be to take, everything that happens to us should be knowledge, should be useful for the future, should be good.

John Grandin thought of himself as modern and civilized. To some extent he understood the neuroses of his fellow men. Perhaps they could not help themselves. But being uninhibited—the giving in to wayward impulse—is anarchy and chaos. Civilization means control; where would he be if he should let happen what was impossible and abhorrent even to think of? To hell with being "modern," "civilized," or "sophisticated." Actually there was no such thing, beyond a self-induced or superimposed state of mind, unsound and superficial. The "twentieth century mind" was a euphemism which such persons as the glittering Arne Eklund used as a veneer for willful behavior, an excuse for self-indulgence. Even modern man was born a primitive and would always be a primitive so long as he had a feeling heart in his breast.

In view of what had happened, Grandin was a fine one to be placed in the position of adviser to youth. He felt the irony keenly. Professors in personal conference with the young were supposed to serve as examples of behavior, to represent an exemplary manhood: indeed, that is why he had received such an appointment. True, neither the faculty nor the students need know of what had happened, and would not. But what about himself? University prestige notwithstanding, he would feel himself a hypocrite through and through; and as such, he would be unable to meet the students with a free and honest mind. His conscience and his guilt—in short, his new knowledge of himself—would stand in the way of the rapport essential between him and the students. He had no doubt that he could get away with it; what upset him was his own state of mind. For him to set himself up to advise youth in any capacity seemed an outrageous dishonesty.

The strangest part of his dilemma was that in spite of the conflict within, no real conflict existed, in the sense that others were involved besides himself. The problem was, if not of his own making, at least of no concern to anyone else, apparent neither to Cliff nor to Ethel; for them nonexistent. Thus no problem held true, except the inner moral conflict which had been undermining his very spirit—and which yesterday morning and last night had sharply reminded him that, whereas any other man affectionately involved with a serviceman (as so many nowadays) might in a fond or casual moment throw a comradely arm about his shoulder, *he* must not. At last he knew why. And if the overwrought or keyed-up emotions of the times had not created the dilemma in the first place, they had at least brought the thing to the surface, named it, and named him.

But was it any help to realize this; did it do him any good? Would it—could it ever—happen to Bill Howard, for example?

Bill Howard was just lucky, that's all—lucky through no credit of his own that he had been born with the proper distribution of whatever it is (who knows?) and thus had no predisposition to error of this kind. John Grandin was reminded of a conversation only last spring with an old friend down from the University of Maine for the Easter holidays. They had had lunch together, and during the course of the hour his friend had said solemnly: "A very sad thing happened at school, it's distressed us all." "Oh?" "One of the professors," he went on to explain—in all seriousness—"was caught screwing a pig." To the horror of the visiting colleague, Grandin instinctively threw back his head and roared with hilarious laughter. The friend regarded him with shock and disappointment; nor could John Grandin blame him. For in the very instant that he had given way to such a reflex, he had comprehended with genuine compassion the desperate lengths to which the poor fellow had been driven, his utter public humiliation because of an episode of no real consequence whatever, the ruin that would inevitably end his whole career, and his personal tragedy for many years to come.

It was all a matter of degree. Bill Howard was the fortunate man, the untroubled, the world's favored. It was only a question of degree, upward from the professor who screwed the pig (ludicrous though it still sounded), to the teacher or philanthropist or minister or banker beaten up by a sailor in a water-front dive or cheap West Side hotel, to the bedizened pansy who cruised Riverside Drive looking for roughnecks or servicemen, to the brilliant dancer or artist whose neurosis was the very foundation of his art, to the scoutmaster or headmaster in a boys' school whose sublimated passion for boys in knee pants fitted him so completely for his tasks, to John Grandin himself, and to the well-adjusted happy Bill Howard; and from there, downward, it was only a matter of degree again—from Bill Howard, to the husband who must be at his wife day and night, to the sex-obsessed traveling salesman, to the married man who boasted of extramarital conquests amounting to satyriasis, to the seducer of girls barely this side of puberty, to the vicious rapist, and to the so-called sex maniac whose lust for girl children culminated in murder and mutilation. All were pitiable, helpless, or tragic—except Bill Howard, who was just lucky.

Bitterly John Grandin had discovered himself to be the kind of man he refused to become. He wished with all his heart that he could find in himself a bold affirmation which said that his fondness for Cliff Hauman—his infatuation, if it came to that—needed no justification whatever; the fact was enough. But the fact was what he could not accept.

What of his wife; what of his growing sons; what of Billie; what of Cliff himself? Each of them would be repelled by such a turn of events, unable to accept the truth. If they knew, they would cast him out; nor could he blame them. At all costs Cliff must never know; his inmost manhood would be offended (John Grandin could not forget that calm adult rebuff when he had deviously introduced the subject of contraceptives). Nor must Ethel know, who would be wounded possibly to the point of leaving him forever, having discovered that the man she loved was no man at all. Now, for the first time, their violent quarrel took on a sinister but crystal-clear meaning. He knew now

what she had been telling him without realizing it; he
realized why he had been so destroyed by what should
have been (and what would have been, had it been any
other couple) a routine spat between husband and wife,
an episode in the Jiggs-and-Maggie saga. But the quarrel
had been no mere episode; it was the logical climax of
long strain, the very secret of their inadequate relationship—proof enough (before the proof of finding the bottle
of sun-tan oil) that he had been a poor husband for Ethel
beyond the inescapable fact, not unlike the habits of other
men his age, that he had not been coming to bed with her
—and why.

Curiously enough, he did not mind the prospect of
seeing Cliff that morning; it was Ethel he dreaded meeting
far more. His confidence in himself was gone utterly. He
could not tell Ethel. It would be a confirmation of the
first-night quarrel: he was more inadequate as a husband
than even she realized. They could not possibly meet this
revelation; they were not big enough. To tell her what
had happened would be to rip them asunder with a realer
split than any they had had before, perhaps the one true
break they had ever had, a break impossible to remedy
because it was founded on such a fundamental thing as
disparate love.

He got up and dressed. Ethel had left the room early.
When he came in last night, the light was out and she was
asleep. He remembered her sharp anger as he had quitted
the steps and left her standing there unanswered, to walk
off into the fog. If she was still hostile this morning, it was
no time to reveal to her what last night had been revealed
to him. In any case he knew he could never reveal it—

reveal it, that is, and still be able to keep Ethel and the children, which is all he wanted of life, all he had been planning on, all he loved.

III

THE HOWARDS AND CLIFF were lying under the sunshades when John Grandin arrived on the beach. Billie was sitting up, her hands on her hips, in the middle of explaining something with wide-eyed amazement.

"Imagine! I forgot," she exclaimed; "I simply forgot! Isn't it the limit? And to get that autograph was almost the only reason why I wanted to go to the dance in the first place. But somehow, I don't know why or how—"

"Toni Lansing didn't count for very much last evening, it turned out," Sarah Howard said. "And neither did anyone else. Nobody except the boys . . ."

"I don't know about you-all, but I-all wouldn't have missed it for anything," Bill Howard said. "Boy, you certainly knocked 'em dead, Cliff, in that street cleaner's outfit of yours.—Hi, John! Where's the good wife?"

Grandin sat down. "I believe Ethel had some errands to do, at the drugstore. I expect she'll be along later." He did not care to say that he had not found her anywhere in the hotel, though he had waited in the room again after breakfast. "What time did you get home last night, Billie?" he said.

"Oh, not till *all* hours."

"We missed you," Cliff said. "Gee, you didn't even say good night, Johnnie."

"You were having too good a time. Ethel and I didn't want to bother you."

"Bother us! After we all went together and everything?"

"Well, if you don't know what I mean," Grandin said coldly, "I can't explain it."

As once before, he was aware that Hauman was offended; but hurting Cliff's feelings was something Grandin felt he could no longer avoid. That was one of the consequences of getting involved with sentimental all-enveloping people like the marine; they bowled one over with their thoughtless or unthinking attention, and then when one wanted to ignore them or go on with the business of life in one's own way, they were hurt. He knew it was as much his fault as Cliff's; but he also knew it wasn't he alone who had kept the impossible relationship so feverishly alive.

If he was going to turn on Cliff, however, just because he had renounced him, he was a pretty poor sport indeed. He looked at the large blond head turned aside, the strong shoulders, the childlike mouth, and all the incredible life and youthfulness of him. Certainly he knew now that he was fond of the fellow. Yet it was still impossible to say— and would always be impossible to say it—Cliff, I'm very fond of you. . . . The innocence and clean good looks of Cliff Hauman touched him deeply. He should be able to accept him at last, in the best sense of him, with a real understanding of what Cliff had meant to him and would always mean, long after Cliff had passed from his sight and ken. It might be armor enough, then, against entanglement or danger. It might not, too; but at least John Grandin would understand what the relationship was and what it meant—what he *himself* was, what he wanted, and did not want. . . .

IV

ETHEL GRANDIN stood at the bedroom window, looking down over the bluff toward the beach. She had purposely waited in the little writing room downstairs till they had all gone; after the mystery of her husband's alien coldness last night and his sudden walking away from her as if she did not exist, she had to be alone with herself this morning. From the writing room she saw the Haumans come out on the porch, finally, head for the rose arbor across the road, and disappear down the stairway of the bluff; a few minutes later they were followed by the Howards, who had returned from their walk. When at length her husband went across in his torn cotton robe and slippers, carrying his towel over his arm—looking very alone and somehow pathetic, perhaps because he did not know he was being looked at by her—she left the writing room at last, passed through the nearly deserted lobby, and went upstairs to the bedroom. Here she could be sure of at least a couple of hours alone before her husband returned from the beach for lunch.

Through the white haze of the morning, she could just discern the group far down on the beach, lying about under the sunshade; though from this distance she could not tell one from another. Only Pete was clear and plain, sitting on his perch, perhaps dozing in the sun, as, in all probability, none of the guests was in the surf.

Ethel Grandin was at a loss to understand what was happening—oh, not to herself, but to her husband. He seemed to be changing under her very eyes. The least thing said now, and he was gone from her; it would be a long time before she would forget how he had suddenly disappeared in the fog, ignoring her pleas for him to come back. Formerly, even when he was preoccupied with himself or with his work, he had been the most sympathetic of husbands. What had become of that man she had loved? It was as if someone else had arrived on the island in his place; a stranger.

Their difficulties since they came to Sconset had been her fault. Though she could not forgive herself for the way she had turned on him the first night, she hadn't been able to prevent it, either: it had had to come, better then than never. But nothing was good enough. He had either ceased to love her entirely, or what small love still existed between them mattered nothing to him.

Was it overwork? Was it the new book just finished or the likelihood of more intensive work this fall? Was it possibly the prospect of summer school? Would a whole summer off, a summer at home, help any—a summer away from her? For he seemed to be himself with others; it was only when they were alone together that he became alien and strange. She had threatened to go home to Maine and stay there till she had made up her mind what she must do about their marriage; and the one weak thing she was guilty of was not to have gone. It was proving a constant humiliation to stay for the rest of the two weeks with him in Sconset. What unreasonable stubbornness had impelled her even to think of it? In the face of their estrangement,

posed on one knee, his chest drawn up and his stomach pulled in, looking eagerly at Grandin and the camera. The Howards stood self-consciously behind the Haumans; and just as he snapped the shutter, Sarah Howard made a face.

Then Bill Howard took over and the Haumans posed for a series of pictures separately and together. John Grandin sat in the sand and watched the performance—watched Cliff with a melancholy fascination.

Simple and transparent though he was, he knew again he would never know Cliff, never get at him, in the way he had always been able to get at or communicate with those he liked. Cliff gave everything of himself; but what was there, really, to give?—beyond an abundance of good will which in the end proved pointless, all but inane. His flattering attention sprang from nothing more meaningful than a childish desire to please and to be liked, and so make life easier and pleasanter for them all; it seemed to have little to do with the one to whom it was addressed. But to argue the matter was as pointless as Cliff's flattery. He was the child of nature—rare indeed, though so often alluded to—who found life good all around him, who liked any and everybody provided they liked him, and whose simple-minded but truehearted affection (oh, there could be little doubt that it was truehearted) might very well last forever, the more so the less it was tried.

It was hard to think of this big kid as a captain, someone who had been chosen because of his ability to lead other men. In the Marine Corps, Cliff was doubtless a different fellow altogether: stern, reserved, valuable, perhaps even distinguished. He was one of many thousands of young men who had come out of mediocrity to find sudden important niches for themselves in a world of violence, boys for whom the intensity of life had gathered into one consuming purpose all at once. The meaning of many years of living was being crammed into a few months—often into a few hours—and the climaxes of existence, which most people waited all their lives for, these boys were discovering daily. Small wonder that Cliff's honeymoon was proving far less of a relief from strain than an interruption to his one wholehearted interest. His restlessness now was a hint of the eventless future which awaited him when the war should be over—if he survived. To John Grandin there seemed little chance that he would survive; that passion of Cliff's almost certainly marked him for death.

Yet now, for some reason, his belief that Cliff would die seemed like emotionalism of the most irresponsible kind. There was no earthly reason why he should be so sure that Cliff was headed for death. In spite of his confidence that he would get through his physical examination in Brooklyn, it was by no means certain that he would pass. He might very well be rejected, sent back to Billie as a husband, and the two of them would wind up in some little three-room flat in Bridgeport or Stamford, with Cliff settling down to an ordinary job (reluctant at first, but eventually happy) and becoming very rapidly the kind of young man who could not have held John Grandin's interest for five minutes, the aura of the uniform gone, the glamour of the Marine Corps a thing of the past. Or if his hunch was right and Cliff did get back where he wanted to be, never to return again, what could one do about it? Many thousands of young men were dying these days on foreign fields and beachheads. It was the pattern of the times—and who knew but what it might be Cliff's very fulfillment, his end and purpose in life, to be added to that growing number?

Billie had borrowed the camera and was now taking pictures of Cliff. Grandin watched the pantomime. Cliff stood at full length, his feet apart and his hands on his waist. The expression on his face was self-conscious and a little strained. But there was such a sincere desire on his part for the picture to be a good one that he submitted more than willingly to each of Billie's suggestions. He didn't smile outright, it was too serious a moment for that; but he did do his best to look pleasant. In this he succeeded so well that John Grandin found himself looking forward to receiving one of the developed prints. At the same time, he had a sudden odd little prevision of one of those snapshots, curling and yellowed, stuck in the mirror of his bureau, long after he should have heard the last of Cliff Hauman.

VI

THERE WAS a shout below, then the sudden running of feet across the macadam. "Last one down to lunch is a rotten apple!" It was Bill Howard.

Ethel Grandin froze in her chair. In the most intolerable suspense she waited for the sound of her husband coming along the corridor. Time and again during the past hour her impulse had been to get up and run—run—where? From what? Most of all, to what? She had nothing, nowhere to go; she felt herself to be a total zero, of no account whatever in her marriage, possibly even of no use to her children. Now, with the door about to open, it seemed to her that it would take more than she could muster in herself to face her husband—not courage, but a cold hate she was far from feeling. Self-loathing was all she felt. But it was enough; enough to undo her utterly.

He came in, his red-cotton robe half open, his hair wet and rumpled from the shower below the bluff.

"Well," he said, "where have you been? I looked—" He caught sight of the overseas cap lying in her lap and stopped.

After a pause he said quietly: "What are you doing with that?"

She could not face him; she looked down at her lap, the tears already starting to her eyes. "What is this, John?"

His heart sank. "It's Cliff's overseas cap."

"I know that. Why have you got it?"

"He gave it to me."

"Why?"

"Because I wanted it."

"Why?"

He walked to the window. "Yes, why," he repeated quietly. He stood looking out with his back to her. "I saw it in his room, and I wanted it. I didn't know why, then."

"Why do you say that?"

"Because I do now." By an effort of will he turned and looked at her. "I suppose you know that I have grown very fond of Cliff Hauman. If you know anything about me at all, you know that."

"I'm afraid I don't know much about you at all. . . ."

"Please let me finish. . . ."

"I don't want— I don't think I care to listen— I can't— Oh, I can't. . . ."

"You've got to listen," he said emphatically. "This is the last thing in the world I wanted you to discover, but now you've got to." He came over to her chair and tried to take her hands, but she pulled away. "Please look at me," he said.

She buried her face in her palms.

He watched her in silence, his heart wrung with pity for her. After a moment he went on: "I've liked Cliff enormously since we came here. I'd rather—oh, anything —than tell you this, but now I have to. I think I even loved Cliff; I don't know. After we met on the boat I seemed to fall under a kind of spell—almost like falling in love. It was completely involuntary on my part, I swear to you. I didn't even realize it was happening. Had I known— But the point is, I didn't know. Truly I didn't. I wasn't aware of it. It had nothing to do with me at all —or with us."

The hands came down. "Nothing to do with us," she said, so bitterly and so low that he could scarcely hear her, "—how can you *say* that!"

He had the awful feeling that these words were meaningless now, but he felt a compulsion to go on, futile though they were. "It was out of our control, I mean. It didn't affect my love for you in the slightest—except as it bewildered me, upset me without my knowing why, made me touchy and difficult. All right! I've loved Cliff this past week, but at least now I know it."

The conversation was carried out on both their parts

in the quietest of tones, as if each were facing himself alone. It was no moment for shrill reproach or strained defense.

"What does it mean," she said, expecting no answer. "I've been asking myself, ever since I found this, what does it mean. . . ."

"It means what I tell you. You've got to believe me, Ethel. If ever you trusted me, you must trust me now. I admit it was a fool thing to do, taking Cliff's overseas cap. I felt like an idiot at the time, but—I wanted it. It doesn't matter so much now."

"Why do you keep saying 'now'?"

He told her, then, what had happened last night in the fog, where he had gone unknowingly, what he had found, and what it had revealed to him. "I didn't lose my way," he said finally. "I went down there purposely in the dark, as if by design—like a man walking in his sleep, determined to do unconsciously what I consciously knew I must not do. You can put it that I was deranged or out of control, like the shock victim who passes through fright to panic to disorientation. Then I found the bottle of sun-tan oil—I had gone straight to the beach. When Cliff wanted to spread it on my shoulders, you yourself were angry with me for acting like such a fool. I was a fool, nothing worse."

"It's perversion," she said, daring it in her despair.

He tried to master the sudden anger that flared up in him at such a charge. "You'll only be sorry later, Ethel, if you begin to use words like that," he said. "There's no such thing as perversion, anyhow," he added; "everything is either normal, hypo, or hyper. If I've learned anything at all through this, I've learned that much. . . ."

"What is it going to mean? . . ."

"Nothing. I understand Cliff now and the way I felt about him. But since last night, somehow it's all different. I don't want that in my life any more than Cliff does. Naturally I still like him and will always like him—there's no reason why I shouldn't."

"I mean to us. . . ."

"I know it's hard for you to take," he said. "It was just as hard for me, harder, at first. I didn't think it was possible. But don't you see? If it *is* possible—"

"Stop! I won't listen to this."

"Ethel, you'll have to understand! I'll take the blame for it, if you like, if we must 'blame' anyone—but it isn't my fault, really it isn't. This thing didn't occur willfully. These few days in Sconset I've been all at sea—"

"Few days," she said hollowly. "Do you honestly think it's been just these 'few days'?"

"Perhaps not; you may be right. Perhaps it's been due to happen for a long time, I honestly don't know; and it took Cliff to bring it out. Maybe it's a definite part of me, part of my nature. But till now, my love for you has kept it in the background where it belongs. Our love can do it again."

"Love. Do you think you can use me as a—a—"

"Don't say something you'll be sorry for," he interrupted. "I love you, Ethel. I believe you love me. I don't think anything else matters. Does it?—Is Cliff more important than we are? Not to me he isn't."

"You were always good at words," she said. "These are just more of the same. . . ."

Ordinarily he would not have kept on so long. If an

honest admission did no good, then forty such admissions would be futile. But the dilemma had become Ethel's almost more than his own. Out of a sense of guilt he felt impelled to continue, in a desperate effort to communicate to her his fullest understanding of the situation. Boldly, he even resorted to sarcasm now, as if by this device he might restore the argument to the "normal"— to one of the common quarrels of marriage. "Okay," he said, "if you'd rather I said nothing. I could have kept it to myself, you know. Most men would have."

"Didn't you? Didn't you?"

"Only so long as I was unaware of what it was all about. But I'm sure I would have told you eventually."

"I wonder," she said. "You wouldn't have told me anything if I hadn't found—this."

"Well, maybe it's your fault, then, rather than mine. You shouldn't have been snooping in my suitcase."

"Do I hide things from you? No, I don't have to!"

He went to her again. "Give it to me."

"What are you going to do with it?"

"Keep it, of course."

"I insist that you give it back to Cliff!"

"What earthly good would that do? He wanted me to have it. He'd only be hurt if I gave it back."

"And what about me?" she said. "Doesn't it matter at all about me?"

"Ethel—Ethel! If we're going to dwell only on this fool cap and ignore everything else, we'll get nowhere. The cap itself is nothing. My wanting it is what mattered. Now that I understand why, the cap doesn't count."

"Then give it back!"

"You can throw it out the window," he said, "tear it to pieces, burn it—anything you like, I don't care. But I will not return it to Cliff. He wouldn't understand."

She looked up at him; and he saw in her eyes—the eyes he had known so well and for so long—a cold hatred.

With difficulty he tried to recover himself, but his heart despaired as he finally turned guiltily away and went toward the bathroom. "I'm going to dress," he said as nonchalantly as he was able, "and go down to lunch. It's late. Are you ready?"

By the time he came out, she was packing her things. "What are you up to?" he said.

She did not answer. There was a finality about her silence, about her every move, which told him she was through. Apart from his grief at such a turn of events, his pride was affected. "You don't mean to tell me you're leaving?"

There was still no word from her whatever.

"How do you expect me to explain this to the others?" he cried in frustration and anger. "How on earth can I possibly account to the Haumans for such an abrupt departure?" Even as he asked the questions he realized their futility. What did it matter in view of the realer, the more serious issue? Ethel was leaving him. Unwilling to believe it to be true, however, he went downstairs.

Self-conscious in the extreme, he explained to Billie and Cliff that Ethel was indisposed. Because of the scene he had just been through as well as the suddenly oppressive presence of both Haumans, he excused himself from the table as soon as he decently could.

After lunch he did not dare go to the bedroom to find

out if Ethel had left. Packing her bags had probably been a feminine dodge, he told himself; but in his heart he knew only too well that she had gone or was going. If Ethel was still upstairs, the least he could do was go up and try to stop her, tell her he was sorry, or even say good-bye. Instead, he went for a walk alone in the direction of Tom Nevershead, the road he should have taken and thought he was taking last night in the fog, all the way.

Though he had no intention of giving it back—indeed, as he had tried to explain to Ethel, what good would it do?—John Grandin realized he had made an incredibly stupid mistake ever to take the cap in the first place. But as he reviewed the situation now, trying to find a way out, his whole dilemma seemed founded on mistakes.

From the very start of the holiday, each time it had been given him to make a decision, select a choice of two actions, or exercise judgment of any kind, he had invariably chosen the wrong one, almost the fatal one—willfully, perhaps, though he didn't know it at the time. It had been a bitter comedy of errors from the beginning.

Moon or no moon, it had been a mistake to choose this period in preference to the longer holiday he could have had later, at the close of summer school. It was a mistake to buy the sandwiches and cokes for Cliff Hauman in the cafeteria: he didn't even know him at the time; but it had been even more of a mistake to invite the Haumans to join them on the upper deck. It was a mistake to offer them the use of their room at Dune House, when they came out to Sconset to swim. Baiting Ethel about her distress ("I suppose it's a moral question") had been a very serious mistake indeed. It was a mistake to have let the Haumans take them over so completely; and he should never have permitted Miss Fly to seat them all at the same table. He should not have attempted to question Cliff so personally in the shower, he should have avoided him as much as possible (what, indeed, did they have in common?), and he should not have attended the Yacht Club party where, from the beginning, he had felt he did not belong. As it turned out, it had been a serious error to have left Ethel's bottle of sun-tan oil on the beach, though this was an oversight merely; but he should not have abandoned her on the steps of Dune House to go wandering off by himself on a disastrous midnight walk in the fog: purposely or not, he had headed straight for the beach against the regulations of wartime. But perhaps the greatest error of all went far back: he should not have married.

Why had he married? He had loved Ethel Cameron, or at least thought he had; but as he looked back on it now, his feeling for her seemed to him to have been whim rather than passion. He had wanted to belong, fit in, find a place in social life which he could have found only in marriage. Well-intentioned though he had been, did one have the right to play with another's life in such a fashion? Out of a kind of will to do good, an unconscious dread of the errors to which his bachelorhood had been susceptible, he had involved Ethel in an insoluble problem of his own making and dragged her down with him. What could he do about it now? He had committed another deadly error in allowing Ethel to leave the island by herself. In the dangerous state she was in, who knew what she might not do? Yet he had stood helplessly by and allowed her to go. Why? Pride, perhaps. Certainly it had little to do with Cliff Hauman. Since the upsetting revelation of last midnight, he had positively ruled out even the remote probability of getting anywhere with the marine.

VII

EXCEPT FOR PETE, he was the first one on the beach. The sun had not yet reached its full power, but already the day was scorching. It might be his last morning in Sconset— it should be, if he had any sense at all (though in his heart he knew it wasn't)—and he wanted to get the most out of it, even though it was no fun alone and he was far from being in the mood to enjoy himself. Ethel had left yesterday afternoon; he couldn't very well stay on much longer without her. Already their quarrel was public enough; but curiously this didn't seem to matter any longer.

Pete had raked the beach clean and was now setting up the sunshades. "You're early this morning, Mr. Grandin."

"A little."

At dinner last evening he had explained to the Haumans—and later to the Howards—that Ethel had received a wire from home, something about the children, and had had to go; she had asked him, he said, to say good-bye for her. Whether Cliff and Billie wondered or not—whether the Howards surmised what was up—he was past caring. The one thing that mattered was that Ethel had left him, their holiday was ruined, perhaps even their whole future, in spite of the fact that he had done his very best to be honest with her.

He had to accept it. When he came down to breakfast alone this morning, Miss Fly for once didn't try to cajole him with bright amenities; on the contrary, she seemed peculiarly embarrassed and, when she came near him, she was almost gloomily silent; she avoided his table as much as possible and ostentatiously spent a quarter of an hour visiting with the Eklunds, mother and son, chattering a little too loudly, it seemed to him, though they answered back fully as loud, in a vain effort to make themselves understood. He looked at Arne Eklund but received no answering look in return. He was not surprised; for by not introducing him to the Haumans, he had long since done himself out of that young man's friendship. Immediately after breakfast he got into his shorts and robe and went to the beach.

He lay on his back in the full sun. There was no one he wanted in the world but Ethel Cameron. If their marriage was to come to nothing, all he had been living for and building on since before his thirties was wasted; he wanted nothing else in its stead and did not know how he could go on alone. Losing his sons was bad enough; but worse by far seemed his loss of Ethel. The boys would grow up and leave, eventually pursuing lives of their own, remote from his; and that was as it should be. But to lose Ethel—to think of trying to go on without her—meant no future for him whatever. In a few weeks, perhaps, he could make another attempt to recover her and so restore their marriage; but failing that (and there had been an

awful certainty of purpose in her attitude which suggested
darkly that he would fail), what should he do with his life?
Move on to some small college, live out the rest of his
anonymous days alone? And what of Ethel? Would she
find another man to love, to give her the love which perhaps he had not given always to his fullest? But Ethel did
not discover other men easily. Having found the one man
she loved—having given herself up to him—it would be
impossible to do so with another. With Ethel, love came
only once. So it did with him—the kind of love he and
Ethel had had, the only kind he wanted in his life.

It had been despicable to let her go without making
any real effort to stop her; dangerous, too. Because of
what had happened, he knew that Ethel was all but irresponsible for whatever she might do now; the blow that
he had been expecting to fall may not have been last
night's fateful revelation, after all—it might well come
through Ethel, something she might do because of the
desperate lengths she had been driven to. Even though
he was aware of this, he had stood by as if all were well;
had turned his head and looked the other way, so to speak,
and let Ethel go off in her misery alone. Why had he let
her do this; what kept him here, helpless? It was certainly
not because of Clifford Hauman. He felt so strongly
about Cliff at the moment, almost with a kind of anger,
that he would gladly have accepted the fact that they were
never to meet again. There was only one way to ensure
this; he could leave the island, as Ethel had done, and the
Haumans would pass out of his life forever. But because
of some inexplicable reason he still stayed.

In the early weeks of their courtship, even during

the first months of their marriage, he had had a fear of losing Ethel; he could almost think of it now as a kind of premonition of what had happened to him this week. As a fiancé and bridegroom he had tormented himself with the thought: Did she love him enough, would she tire of him, lose interest and cease to care? She did not. The longer their marriage lasted the more he became assured that she loved him deeply. It had been a wonderful feeling, the very basis of his happiness. For his own security, it was what he most needed to know. Yet what had happened? *He* was the one who had grown careless, taken their love for granted, been attentive to his marriage duties only when it occurred to him to do so, and thought of love (if he thought of it at all) as something that was there regardless: like the apartment, like the children, like his job. Indeed, he had got in the habit of spending more time with the children, far more time and thought and devotion to his work, than to Ethel. He could not forgive himself now for this neglect; he longed with all his heart to make it up to her, as he had longed on the train; but it was not neglect that had precipitated this last serious quarrel. Neglect, yes, but only in so far as it involved a passing infatuation for Cliff Hauman, a falling under his youthful charm and spell. Had Ethel turned from him months ago, he might have taken it and understood, knowing her justified; but for her to base their separation on his preoccupation of a few days with a young man he would soon be seeing no more of—a preoccupation which had not been willful or indeed understood until it was too late—was unfair.

He was not trying to rationalize the matter or excuse

himself. He had always (he believed) understood Ethel, and that understanding on his part had been one of their strongest bonds. He understood full well how a woman of Ethel's limited experience, temperament, and single-minded devotion—or indeed any woman—would require a considerable period in which to readjust to this momentary excursion of his into another kind of love, which she could only feel to be a blow to her inmost pride, a blow at her very womanhood, impossible to withstand. He knew that and understood it; he could almost think for her through her ordeal, articulating her problem, whereas she herself was only speechless in a floundering daze. But how could it in the long run affect her—*them*—because he had been briefly sidetracked in an impossible infatuation which he at last understood?

He was not so foolish as to think that Ethel would say, Go ahead, love him—for that was not what he wanted of Cliff; and he would have bitterly questioned Ethel's love for him if she had advanced such a proposal. The fact that she was upset, perhaps beyond any possibility of his recovering her, proved without a doubt that she loved him truly. But could that be any consolation to him now, if, in the realization of such a fact, he was at last to lose her? His falling under Cliff's spell was no more important than if he had had a holiday flirtation with a young girl; less so, in reality, for the one might lead to a secret if brief fulfillment, while this could never lead to anything. If he loved Cliff—very well, he loved him, and that was that; the thing ended as soon as it was accepted. Or had he been the kind to want or need physical love with another man, that would have been all right too, provided the love was real and inescapable; for what is is, and truth is truth, no matter what form it takes. But he was as unprepared by both temperament and experience to love Cliff as Cliff was to love him. Let them be fond of one another, if necessary, and forget it, as he was prepared to forget it. It was an episode, a passing thing, a sign of the times perhaps; Ethel could not—could not in her most extravagant imagination or deepest hurt—believe it meant anything more. But the fact that she did left him with no defense whatever, beyond his futile but honest explanation yesterday noon—oh, honest as he was able—of his understanding of what had happened to him.

A few guests had come down from the hotel but he lay with his eyes closed as before, ignoring them as if asleep. Presently he heard familiar voices coming across the sand.

"Look, kids, there's the Herr Professor, baking himself to a turn. What'll we do, heap ashes on the scholarly head?"

He opened his eyes and sat up. Bill Howard approached with Billie and Cliff Hauman.

"Is it fun being a bachelor again?" Howard asked.

"No."

"*My* wife is writing letters. At least that's what she said; but between you and me, I'll bet she's gone back to bed. Never saw anybody in my life who enjoyed sleep as much as Sadie."

"Oh, that reminds me," Billie said, arranging herself under the sunshade. "Do you know I haven't written a single thank-you note for all those lovely wedding presents? Not a single one!"

"Good god," Bill Howard said, "you've only been married three or four days. Plenty of time later when the long grind begins."

"But four days!"

"I'm sure nobody expects you to interrupt your honeymoon to write thank-you notes for a dozen pairs of salt-and-pepper shakers and a couple of totally useless Lazy Susans."

"Oh, but brides always do!"

"Forget it, beautiful. Come on, how about a quick dip first, just to get it over with."

"I'd love it, Mr. Howard."

"You too, Cliff? I won't trouble the learned doctor."

"Guess I'll get some sun first," Cliff said absently. "Maybe later."

Bill Howard and Billie ran hollering down to the surf, and Cliff sat in the sand. Grandin lay down on his back.

"How do you feel, Johnnie?"

"All right."

"I suppose you miss Eth."

"Very much."

Surprisingly Cliff asked, then: "Rather not talk?"

"No, not especially."

"I've been thinking of you, Johnnie," he said. "I'm sure going to miss you, gosh, when we go away from here."

"I shall miss you too, Cliff."

"You know who you remind me of, Johnnie, kind of? Not really, but in a way. Just happened to think of it last night. One of the swellest men I ever met, the nicest kind of guy you could ever want to meet."

"Who is that?"

"When I was in college my best buddy and I had a heck of a time trying to pass English. He played football too, and of course we couldn't play in the big games unless we passed—you know how they are about those things. Well, there was this English prof Joe and I had, by the name of Scott," Cliff went on; "Scotty, I called him—and he gave us an awful lot of his time trying to help us out. Gee, he was a great guy, Johnnie, when you come to think of it. Wonder whatever became of Scotty. . . . Why, there wasn't anything he didn't know about. He knew everything in the world there was to know about books and things like that. He read more books! It was a real education just to be around him, honest it was. You and he would have gotten along great.—And listen to this, Johnnie, do you know what he used to do for Joe and I? Why, nights before exams he used to sit up with us almost all night long helping us cram so we'd be able to pass—going over the whole course with us, over all those little things Joe and I had been too dumb to get in class," he added, with a laugh. "You wouldn't believe how much he used to do for us, you wouldn't believe it! Why, we owed everything to him, Joe and I did. I know darn well that neither one of us would have *grad*uated even, if it hadn't been for Scotty. I can't begin to make you understand the time he gave us—the time alone!"

His arms folded over his eyes to shield them from the sun, but listening keenly, John Grandin understood it all too well.

"But I'll tell you what," Cliff said. "One night when we were sitting at the desk in his apartment, just he and I

—I'd gone over to his place so he could help me study— do you know what he did? Scotty put his hand on my knee, his whole hand, and left it there for a second. Can you beat that, Johnnie? Can you beat it?"

Grandin said: "And what did you do?"

"Do! Why, what do you suppose I did!" Cliff answered sharply. "I said, 'Uh-uh, Scotty, none of that!'— You should have seen his face."

After a moment Grandin said: "And was that all there was to it?"

"Sure, I couldn't have anything like that. After all!— And do you know what," he went on; "he tried the same thing on Joe once too. Joe told me. Can you beat it, Johnnie? Gee, it was too bad, because he was really a wonderful guy, honest. You wouldn't think so from what I've told you, but he was. Why, Scotty would have done anything for Joe and I, anything in the world. . . ."

Grandin sat up and drew off his robe. "I think I'll have a swim," he said.

Cliff said nothing. Very unlike himself, he seemed strangely preoccupied and moody. He sat in the sand, his arms over his knees, staring out over the water. At length he said—but after so long a pause that there seemed no connection at first: "Of course I was a lot younger then. . . ."

For a moment, John Grandin wondered whether he had heard correctly. If so, what was the meaning of that afterthought—or was it, indeed, an afterthought at all? But he refused to puzzle it out now. He got up and walked down to the surf.

He felt the need for action, exercise; but he stood for

a moment at the edge of the sea studying the waves, as if testing their power in advance. A strong wind blew in from offshore, sending the great green rollers thundering far up the beach. His heels sank deep as the water swirled around his feet, undermining the sandy support beneath his soles; he felt the spray sting his face. Sharp though it was, it refreshed him. He walked into the surf, waited for one of the breakers to rear up, and plunged headlong through it.

Emerging on the other side, he was drawn rapidly out by the pull of the backward-racing water. He swam for the next breaker just beyond, gathering itself to strike again. He rose to the top and went over before it folded and collapsed. In a few moments he was far out.

It was exhilarating being tossed about on the gray-green billows, rising and falling among the roaring changing long hollows rolling and always rolling landward, always to the shore. He gave himself up to the rough lull and rocking of it. . . . *Hurry me out of sight of the land; Cushion me soft, rock me in billowy drowse; Dash me with amorous wet—I can repay you.* . . .

Presently he saw that Cliff was swimming nearby, but farther out, already ahead of him. Now and again he caught sight of the dark wet head, so tawny when dry, drawn rapidly up the slant of a broad green wave to its crest, passing then from sight, to reappear, when the wave had passed, afloat in the hollow of one of the rolling troughs. He swam with grace and power; it was a keen pleasure to see him master the buffeting waves.

But Cliff had had enough. He turned and headed inshore, stretched out flat, threshing violently to keep pace with a racing breaker, then riding it rapidly toward the beach. He shot Grandin a look of happy triumph as he rode past. In another moment Grandin turned back also.

But it was not so easy as Cliff made it appear. In a very short time, much too short for ease of mind, he found it hard going. He kept his eyes fixed on the sandy shore and the people lying about on the beach, whom he saw only intermittently from the tops of breakers, as if a curtain rose and fell, rose and fell, on the view of his goal; the beach seemed as remote as before, regardless of how desperately he fought for progress.

The thing to do was to look away: forget the shore and the distance, whether near or far, and concentrate on the thing to be done, here, now, by no one but himself. He swam on, but easy as possible, relaxed, conserving strength, forgetting fear and fatigue, inching gradually but (he thought) ever more surely and safely home. He bent his head sideways, breathed quietly, and by an effort of will allowed his limbs to attain their maximum reach and strength with the smallest possible strain. When he dared to look again, he was no nearer than before; but what aroused in him the keenest panic was the fact that those on shore—Billie and Cliff, Bill Howard, the other guests, Pete himself dozing on his perch—were completely oblivious of his distress.

Then came over him the most unaccountable sensation of all, a fury beyond his comprehension or experience, more destructive, far more dangerous, than panic. This was the surprised and surprising feeling of having been made a fool of—by no one but himself, which somehow seemed the intolerable part of it—for getting himself into such a humiliating position; for surely he could never save himself now, he was far too spent. He was furiously angry and ashamed. How different was this sensation from what he had always supposed the thoughts of a drowning man to be, when, in the last moments before going under, the victim's entire life is said to pass rapidly in cinematic review before his agonized eyes. No such thing happened now. Grandin's whole being was filled with an anguished passion of protest that *this* was the way it was to be. It was insulting to his dignity and to all that he had been preparing for during his whole life, which, if not comfort or privilege or esteem in the world, was at least not an ignominious end like this—all merely for having been so foolish (oh, nothing more reprehensible than that, nothing deserving of this punishing and final humiliation) as to swim out beyond his strength to get back. While his friends sat there not more than a hundred feet away, he must here go down, with no one knowing, no one aware of his difficulty, no one to whom he could say, not goodbye, but: Isn't it silly—isn't it outrageous and silly that this is the way it should have had to end?—He was not even to be allowed to explain. . . .

He could cry out and help of some kind would come at once, but the infuriating part of the whole circumstance was that he could not cry out at all. He found he could not bring himself to utter a syllable of protest aloud, no, not even if it meant his death. Rather than draw such humiliating attention, he would rather succumb wordless and—while it lasted—unnoticed.

Something of this sort (though far more keen, bitter, and unbearable) passed through his mind as he fought to keep afloat. It was ironic and frightening that the everyday I'd-die-rather-than-ask-for-help was here literally, crazily true. Then his heart almost gave way as he saw that Cliff had turned, was looking toward the sea, was watching and listening, attentive with a quiet alert concern. Breathing hard, his brow barely above the wet, Grandin caught his glance. Cliff moved from the group to the edge of the surf. By a discreet pantomime he simulated across the distance which separated them the silent cry, the precious but unspoken words: Are you all right?

He could not answer, he could not even shake his head; he could only by a superhuman effort thrust himself forward perhaps another dozen inches—to be pulled back again by the outward-rushing water beneath him; but through the spray his exhausted eyes, rapidly losing interest in all which his vision encompassed, saw Cliff tensely still at the edge of the beach, frowning, studying the situation, before, like a released spring, he struck out through the surf.

He remembered nothing of what happened then; he only came to as Cliff lowered him to the dry sand beyond the reach of the waves. He lay on his back, gasping, and looked up at Cliff—who stood, his hands on his knees, bending over him with a worried expression.

"Don't talk. You're all right, Johnnie, just don't talk."

He turned his head and saw that Billie and Bill Howard and now Sarah Howard too were sitting under their sunshades, some little distance from where he lay in the sand. He looked up at Cliff again, touched by what he thought had been a remarkably sympathetic consideration.

"This is where we landed," Cliff said. "We were carried downshore by the current. You fought, Johnnie. I had a heck of a time."

Relief swept up in him; nothing in all the world could be more important at this moment than the fact that he was alive; and for the first time since his early youth, life suddenly seemed to offer possibilities hitherto undreamed of. He was humbly grateful that Cliff had carried him to shore at a distance from the others, but he could not speak of it.

There was no need to. Cliff did the talking.

"You were still on top when I got there, still battling away, Johnnie, but a little slow. I think you were ready to give up. You wouldn't of, would you?"

"No." He smiled, enormously gratified and pleased with Cliff. "Let's go back now."

"Wait a little."

"I'm all right. Besides, I don't want them to know."

"Give me your hand, Johnnie." He pulled him to his feet and they went across the sand.

"Anybody got the time?" Cliff asked, perhaps a little too heartily, as they rejoined the group.

A few moment later the Haumans and John Grandin started across the arid expanse toward the bluff. Sarah Howard, left behind with her husband, watched them go. Suddenly she turned about. "Well, I'm damned," she said in quiet astonishment. "All along I thought it was Billie. But it's Cliff, my god."

"What's Cliff?"

"That John Grandin is in love with."

"No!" her husband said.

"Yes."

"The poor guy . . ."

In his bedroom alone, resting before lunch, John Grandin knew why he had let Ethel go without making any real move to stop her, and why he allowed himself to be held helpless here, when common sense if not self-respect should have impelled him to leave the island with his wife. This is what he had unconsciously been waiting for, what he must have known—through some unnamable intuition—was bound to happen. It was almost as if he had been certain all along that Cliff would yet make the impossible statement, the words which no one in the wide world could have anticipated: "Of course I was a lot younger then." Till then, Grandin had done his best. Now he would resist no longer. With a full knowledge of the danger which lay ahead as well as the improbable pleasure. he was glad at last that he had stayed on.

VIII

THROUGH THE SMOKY WINDOWS of the daycoach, the Cape looked like a wasteland. One could even wonder why so many people chose this barren and isolated strip of land between two waters for their summer homes. But Ethel Grandin regarded the flat sandy wastes, the swampy fields, the stagnant inlets and self-conscious dwellings of the rich vacationers almost without seeing them at all; the trip up to Boston was a time-out during which she must get onto herself; it didn't matter about the landscape, whether interesting or not.

It was flight. She had engaged the one Sconset taxi and caught the boat from Nantucket just after lunch, arriving in Woods Hole in time to connect with the Boston train. She could not even remember the trip across; it had been a period of utter misery, not because she was alone and had left her husband behind, but because, apart from her serious split with him, she did not know what she was fleeing from, still less what she was running toward. The boat had not been crowded; it was not at all like the morning steamer which carried so many vacationers back to the mainland to catch the early train to New York. She had sat in a folding chair on the heaving deck and heard the cries of the sea gulls which followed the boat like lost spirits, listened to the churning wash alongside the prow, paid no attention whatever to her dull or indifferent fellow passengers absorbed in their own inane pleasures and problems, and all but froze in the icy breeze that blew mercilessly along the exposed deck. She could have gone inside, but for some reason she had to be in the open air, chilling though it was.

When the Boston train chuffed in at Woods Hole, as if impatient to start, she boarded it automatically, forgetting her arrival only a few days ago, the meeting with her husband, the silly way she had got off the wrong side of the car and the strain of the boat trip when, more often than not, she was on the verge of tears. The Haumans had then been a pleasant diversion, but only because they had served as a postponement of the crisis due to come up sooner or later. Now, all she remembered of the whole stay

in Nantucket, aside from the shattering scene yesterday
when she had found Cliff's service cap in her husband's
bag—and the insulting way he had tried to rationalize it—
was that she had never once, no, not once, spoken to him
of her pleasure because his book had been accepted for
publication in the fall by Scribner's. What he must have
thought of her for completely ignoring this turning point
in his life did not matter to her now. Nothing mattered
but the tragic fact that, as she believed, she had lost her
husband for good.

She did not care what the Howards might be thinking
of her sudden departure, what Cliff and Billie might think,
or even what her husband thought. She had had to get
away; and thank God, she had courage enough to act on
her own at last. It had been a cruel abasement to her to
have stayed in Sconset as long as she had; to stay longer
would have been to vitiate all she had been trying to tell
him during that dreadful first night, the gist of which she
only understood now for the first time. She wished she
could have pitied her husband during his fruitless attempts
at "explanation" yesterday; instead, to her horror and
despair she had hated him with a real hate. Never before
in her life had any man—above all, her husband—reduced her to such a feeling of nothingness. She was nothing to him henceforth, could be nothing ever again, and
consequently her pride as a woman was wounded to the
quick, her love unneeded, even flouted in her face. What a
lucky woman indeed was Sarah Howard who, though Bill
lacked John's intelligence and fineness, was at least loved
by her husband. They were in love with the passion of
youth; so much so that she could no longer tolerate their

presence: it was an oppression to her spirit which, in view of the disillusionment of her marriage, she could not take. As for the Haumans, Billie was a pitiable figure, perhaps, but at least she would learn in time to love the man she had married. Ethel Grandin felt no worry whatever about their future; it was her own future, only, that seemed bleak and without promise.

Much as she had loved him, she hated her husband now for letting her go off by herself. If he had had the slightest feeling for her, the slightest understanding of her despair, he would not have stayed on, alone. It was outrageous to her feelings as a woman that perhaps he had lingered because of Cliff Hauman. The thought itself was intolerable, even hard to believe—in spite of all his wordy discourse on the meaninglessness of his having had Cliff's overseas cap in his possession, like a cherished thing, an intimate keepsake, the handkerchief of a loved one.

IX

THOUGH HE HAD TWICE BEEN ANGERED BY HER, John Grandin felt himself obliged, perhaps out of a sense of duty, to discuss Billie as objectively as possible. He and Cliff lay in the shade of the sun umbrella, and they were as much alone together as if they had been on a desert island. Grandin was keenly aware of the intimacy, but for the time being he tried to put it from his mind.

"It's none of my business, Cliff," he said, "but there's something I've noticed."

"What's that, Johnnie?"

"Well, Billie doesn't seem to realize the seriousness of what's ahead for you—or for her. It's your responsibility to make her realize it."

Cliff gazed unhappily over the water. "Billie and I—" he said—"we can't talk about these things, that's what's the matter. When I try to, she almost acts like she doesn't know what the heck I'm talking about. Gosh, I don't like speaking this way behind her back, but it's the truth."

"You must remember, Cliff, your experiences have been different from hers. There is no way for Billie to grasp them."

"But she doesn't even take the war seriously, do you know it? I mean Billie doesn't seem to know what's going on. When I talk about the war—"

"She feels left out. It's something she has had no part in. You've been away, living an exciting life of your own, and maybe you're even going back to it."

"You're darn right I am, but she acts like she doesn't believe me at all."

"She believes you, Cliff. Only—"

"Only what?"

"Perhaps she'd rather not believe. Billie doesn't want to hear about it. Like many people, she'd rather not know. When something doesn't fit into their scheme of things, they simply pretend it isn't so."

"That's it! That's just it, Johnnie," he said emphatically, astonished that someone else could express for him what he himself hadn't been able to put into words. "She'd rather not know—Billie doesn't *want* to know . . ."

"She's young, Cliff. You happen to have been through a good deal lately; but Billie— Everything's been happening to you; nothing to her." He finished lamely: "You know it isn't her fault, don't you?"

Cliff gazed moodily into the surf, his forehead troubled and frowning. "Gee, sometimes I even think—" He broke off, as if disgusted with himself.

"Better not say it."

Surprised, he turned. "What was I going to say?"

"Some such thing, I suppose, as—that you should have waited till after the war."

"Gosh, that's exactly—"

"Well, you mustn't even think it." .

"I've got things to do, darn it," he said vehemently. "I can't settle down yet, not while the war is on!"

"I've noticed Billie doesn't believe you're going to get back into the service. Not even yet."

"I am, though, I certainly am. I've got to!"

"Then"—without even caring, Grandin wondered how much he had any right to be saying this—"then you've got to make her accept it and know it. Otherwise, it's not fair."

Cliff's feelings came out in a rush of words. "Johnnie, that's the whole trouble, that's the very thing that's been on my mind, I can't get rid of it, I simply don't know what to do about it. You're right, you're absolutely right—men understand these things; women don't. When I tell Billie I'm serious about going back, I run up against the same thing every time. How can I make her believe when she won't? Like you said, she doesn't want to. And so we— we talk about something else, or—don't talk at all. . . ." After a moment he went on again, but in another voice entirely, low and serious: "There only one thing that helps. I love Billie. I've always loved her. We used to have swell times together. She's the best girl I ever had. There's nobody I'd rather be with. We always had a wonderful time. From the day I went away, we planned to get married. I was the happiest guy in the world to think she'd even have me. And all through boot camp and the 'Canal and the months in the hospital, I thought of Billie and couldn't wait to get back to her. Well, now we're married. . . ." He fell into a gloomy silence, then, as if he had nothing more to say.

Grandin felt an infinite sympathy for him and wished he could have been of some help. Life was pretty poorly ordered, he reflected, when all one could do in such a case was stand aside and feel sorry.

"I don't know, Cliff; it's your problem," he said. "But there's one thing you can do. Why, my lord, you and Billie may be separated for six months, or several years, possibly even forever. You've got to make her face it, Cliff. She's headed for a dreadful unhappiness otherwise. It's not your fault—your whole interest is taken up with getting back into the service, and I can't say I blame you. But if you don't see to it that Billie accepts the fact right off, then I think—and mind you, I don't like to say this, because you haven't got a mean hair on your head—I think you're being very cruel to her. . . ." Then, because this kind of talk was making Cliff uncomfortable, he changed the subject to one nearer his heart. "Tell me about you and Guadalcanal, Cliff. You never have, you know."

At once Cliff seemed relieved. "You know something," he said, turning with a charming and touching

freshness toward Grandin. "Every night just like clock-
work, those rascals came over. Sure as it got to be one
o'clock, right on the nose, they'd start slamming down
out of the sky. If we got any sleep at all, it was only before
one o'clock or after three."

"What did you do during those hours?"

"Do! There wasn't anything *to* do. When we heard
the siren we'd scram out of our holes and beat it for the
antiaircraft. Then we just stayed there till they went
away, that's all."

But Grandin was unsatisfied. Here was firsthand experience, yet he was getting nothing out of it. "Didn't you
send up planes yourselves?" he asked.

Cliff laughed, delighted. "Heck, we didn't have any
to send up. We didn't have anything. Those were the days
when we had just moved in, before the Army came or the
Navy or anyone else. All we had was what we brought in
on our backs. Gee, last night I laughed right out loud, to
think how those rascals always waited till we hit the sack
before they started coming over. Billie wanted to know
what I was laughing it."

"But when the Japs were overhead—" Grandin urged
—"when they were actually dive bombing—what was it
really like?"

"Like?"

"For example"—he felt foolish indeed suggesting anything so obvious, but it might lead to some tangible revelation—"there must have been a lot of noise, certainly?"

"I'll say! There was a heck of a lot of noise. Talk
about excitement! But gee, it all happened so quick you
didn't begin to think about it until it was over."

"Couldn't you—well, see anything?"

"Nothing but a lot of gun flashes. Of course the searchlights poked around the sky and once in a while they found a plane but most of the time they didn't. Anyhow it was pretty as— It was very pretty, specially if it was a nice night."

As he had often realized before, John Grandin noticed again how the man of action seems unable to recapitulate what he has been through. Cliff's stories consisted largely of great gaps, nothing was really accounted for, nothing narrated, so that one had to ask a dozen questions to find out—and even the questions produced answers which answered nothing. It was almost as if the dramatic things of life (at least for the purposes of "story") happened to the wrong people; they were seldom able to communicate the event. They did not remember the telling detail which, reproduced, would have made the experience come alive again, recognizable as truth; and if they were unable to call up the significant touch, it may well have been because they had not experienced the thing in any real sense, the sense of getting something out of it— had not, so to speak, been aware of what they had been through. The revealing episode which one recognized as having actually happened without question, and which would have enabled one to identify oneself with the story, was always missing. Perhaps, he reflected, "experience" requires more than experience: perhaps it takes imagination as well.

"I should think that after you'd got settled down," Grandin suggested, "you'd have been mad as hell for being called out every night?"

"Mad? I don't know, maybe we were, Johnnie, I can't remember. But when everything got going at once, we forgot about it. A little excitement never hurt anyone, you know. We were kept so hopping busy we never had time to think whether we were mad or not. Gee, it was fun, in a way. I mean exciting."

"Fun?"

"Well, I suppose it wasn't fun, maybe. Maybe that's the wrong word." But it was obviously the right one. Cliff's zest in talking about it told all too plainly that it had been fun, great fun; and that if he were given the choice right now between a night like that and a mild Nantucket evening, there was little doubt as to which he would choose.

Even had he been more articulate, nothing n to be learned from Cliff's account. It was a comm tive, nowadays. One read it in every paper, heard it on all sides. Boys home from the fronts told more or less the same thing—one could have anticipated almost everything they had to say, and even, in many cases, told the story better than they did. Why was it, then, that John Grandin listened with such admiration, attention, and interest? He wondered himself why he should be hanging on every word of a recital which, in these times, was by no means unique. One of the things which held him was Cliff's eagerness to share an experience which the marine knew could never be Grandin's—and because of which, possibly, he pitied him. In a sense that he was not aware of, Cliff was trying to give him something of his youth, or at least of what it was like to be young in 1943. John Grandin was touched by the effort and the gift, even though they made him feel more remote from Cliff than ever.

"Johnnie," he said suddenly, "you're a wonderful guy, do you know it?"

"Why, I—"

"No, I mean it, I really mean it. You can't imagine what it means to me, Johnnie, to be able to talk about these things. Ever since I came back I've been thinking about them a lot. Out there, I don't think a single thought ever entered my head; but lately—well, what I've been through, what all the other guys are going through, it's something you've got to speak of, once in a while. You're a good listener, Johnnie. I guess that's why I pick on you."

"I'm interested, Cliff."

" ̄ ɲow it, that's what I feel about you and it means   ̄" He scooped up a handful of sand and began ⸌ ⸍t over his knees. "You're the kind of guy who understands things. I feel I could talk to you about—well, about a lot of things."

"I'm very flattered, Cliff, but—it probably has little to do with me. You'd find others the same. Don't you think it's largely, perhaps, because you haven't talked with others before?"

"Maybe you're right, Johnnie, but women—they never understand. When you come right down to it, I guess men are the only ones you can talk with. You even more than most."

"But we scarcely know each other, Cliff."

"Gosh, I don't feel that at all. Do you, Johnnie? It isn't the first time I've wanted to talk," Cliff said, studying the sand he was filtering through his fingers. "I've wished

I could talk to you seriously before, but it takes a long while before I begin to make up to people. I mean I'm not the familiar type. I like to judge people awhile before I make up my mind about them."

Again John Grandin felt the prying inquisitiveness about Cliff's personal life which he had experienced outside the shower a few days ago and which he knew he had no right to ask about. More than ever, but with a sinking sensation, a helplessness, he felt impelled to ask questions of this sort now. It was an acute discomfort on his part for wanting so unreasonably to know. His compulsive curiosity made him realize— and he didn't give a damn now— that some sinister process operated within him beyond his control.

"What about your friends on Guadalcanal?" he said. "Didn't you have some congenial companions you could talk with there—share ideas with?"

"I had some wonderful buddies," Cliff replied effusively. "But I don't remember that we ever talked much. But gee, we had some great times! Some of the swellest fellows I ever knew. My best buddy was Walt Farnsworth. He's a prince, Johnnie, a prince! You couldn't ask for a better buddy in the world. Jeepers, you should have seen him eat! Why, he could eat more than ten fellows put together. It did you good just to see him stow it away! The amount of chow he put under his belt made you feel good just to watch him. I was crazy about Walt, and you would be too. From the time we shipped out of San Diego, right up to when I was sent back, Walt and I went through everything together, and on leave, boy, the times we had, in Sydney and Melbourne and some of those places!"

Though he remembered too well the rebuke outside the stall shower, John Grandin could not help asking what about Sydney and Melbourne? He knew the danger, but he didn't care now; recklessly he even hoped Cliff got the idea.

"What about those times," he asked, "in Sydney and Melbourne?"

"What about them, Johnnie?"

"Did you and Walt— I mean, didn't you—"

"If you mean did we have a high old time, we sure did. Boy, we had a circus! The food that Walt tucked away, why it would have done your heart good to see it."

"But what about girls, Cliff?"

"Why do you ask, Johnnie?"

"I suppose I mean, after such isolation on Guadalcanal with the troops, sex must have meant—meant—"

"Oh, sex," Cliff said with a smile as if they had been talking about nothing more serious than the weather. "Well, I guess sex has its place, but I never thought of it much. Jeepers, you don't have time. Anyways, isn't it the same everywhere?"

X

ETHEL GRANDIN arrived home just after supper. The children were already in bed but her father and mother were still at the table. They were not talking. It had become habit with them by now to spend hours on end together without conversation. When Ethel walked in, their simultaneous thought was: What are you doing here?

Ethel avoided their look. "I suppose," she said, "I should have let you know."

"What's the matter?" her mother said.

"Nothing."

"But—what about John? What are we supposed to— What will people think?"

"I don't give a damn what people think," Ethel said, turning away. "Don't I count for something?"

"And don't we?" her mother said. "Don't we have a right to know if—if anything's wrong?"

"We didn't have a quarrel, if that's what you mean. John's going back to New York and I came home. We didn't happen to care for Sconset or Nantucket: that's all there is to it."

"Would you like some coffee?" Mrs. Cameron said.

"No thanks."

"Really, Ethel, you don't look yourself at all."

"I'm not myself!" she said, and hurried from the room.

While she was unpacking in her bedroom, her mother came in.

"I know it's none of my business," Mrs. Cameron said, "but I want to know what happened."

"Nothing happened."

"Then what are you doing back so soon?"

"I told you nothing happened! There's nothing more to say, Mother."

"It couldn't have been very nice for your husband to cut short your vacation like this."

"It wasn't very nice for me either! Now please . . ."

Exasperated, her mother went back downstairs.

After Ethel was undressed, she went to the bathroom across the hall. She opened the medicine cabinet to find some toothpaste, and the first thing her eye lighted on, placed well forward on one of the glass shelves, was a bottle of nitric acid. She did not remember having seen it there before. Thoroughly frightened, she stared at the bottle. Then, scarcely knowing what she was doing, she stepped into the hall and called her mother from below.

"Mother!"

"Yes?"

"What's that bottle of nitric acid doing in the bathroom?"

"Why, nothing. I was cleaning some gloves."

"That's no place to leave it! The children—"

"Really, Ethel, there's only one bathroom in the house." Her mother came part way up the stairs. "Ethel Grandin, what on earth's the matter with you?"

"My name is not Grandin," she said, "it's Cameron. It's always been Cameron. It always—it always—" She fled to her bedroom and closed the door behind her, frightened through and through.

XI

JOHN GRANDIN idled at Dune House as if he hadn't a care in the world. He was only too conscious of the distress Ethel was probably going through at home, but he purposely put it from his mind: it was the last thing he wished to think of. All he wanted to do, in his new acceptance of his fate, was to daydream about Cliff Hauman—dwell sensually on the improbability which could never come to pass.

Fortunately, the Howards were preoccupied with themselves and their tours of the island and had little time for him; now when they met, briefly, Bill Howard was cordial and sympathetic though somewhat strained, and Sarah was aloof. This was understandable enough in view of the fact that they had formerly been two married couples together; but his status now was the equivalent of a bachelor. The Haumans were busy with their bicycle riding or spent long hours on the beach—where, for some reason, John Grandin did not care to go now. One evening during their usual awkward session at the dinner table, Cliff suddenly announced—with an ecstasy of happiness that made John Grandin's heart turn over: "I got my wire, Johnnie. I report in Brooklyn Monday morning bright and early for my physical! We'll be leaving tomorrow. This is it, Johnnie!"

Billie ostentatiously paid no attention. She had brought to the table a package of considerable size—her wedding pictures, she explained happily. She spread the large photographs on the tablecloth and John Grandin examined them one by one, while Billie commented on each group or pose. The pictures showed the bridesmaids in their long frocks, arranged on either side of Billie and Cliff on the lawn; the modest, smiling, rather stout parents, wearing glasses, looking curiously alike, and a little nonplused by so much grandeur occasioned by their offspring. There were several poses of Billie alone—cutting the enormous cake, waving at the camera with a grin, descending the staircase with her white-gloved hand rest-

ing with self-conscious grace on the banister and her left
foot on the step above, standing against a bower of smilax
with her arm upraised in the act of tossing her beribboned
bouquet; and one of Cliff. He was buttoned to the chin
in his resplendent white tunic and looked so worried that
John Grandin almost laughed with pleasure at the awkward charm of the picture.

Nevertheless, a strange depression fell upon their
table as Cliff drew the telegram from his pocket and
opened it—a depression shared even by Cliff, though on
his part there was a new and happy tension, a restlessness
and eagerness to be off.

Afterward they went out onto the porch in the evening air—constrained, all of them—to say their farewells.
Sarah and Bill Howard came out and went down the
steps as if they knew no one on the veranda, and disappeared, arm in arm, in the direction of Tom Nevershead. Billie and Cliff Hauman were to go to bed early,
they explained. A taxi was to call at six in the morning in
order to get them to Nantucket in time for the seven-
o'clock boat to Woods Hole. They would arrive in New
York late that afternoon; and on Monday morning—the
examination that would decide everything. Cliff's eyes
shone as he said this, but he was not himself; he was not
thinking of them or of anyone else. The farewells meant
nothing; he would much sooner have left at once without
a word.

Now that it was the end, John Grandin stood about
awkwardly on the veranda, facing the Haumans somewhat
formally. Cliff was not so much self-conscious as preoccu-

pied; he was very quiet, and said little during the few moments they had left. Billie, remembering her manners, smiled dreamily.

"And what are your plans, Mr. Grandin?" she asked politely. "Maybe we'll be seeing you and your wife in New York sometime," she added, with listless indifference.

"I have to be in New York for the opening of summer school, a week from now, but Ethel is staying at her mother's in Maine where the children are. I may be alone a month or so—it does them so much good to be in the country . . ."

With a sudden concern, Billie said: "You mean you and Mrs. Grandin won't be seeing each other for a whole *month?*"

He smiled. "When you've been married as long as we have—" He gave a small laugh. "I suppose it sounds dreadful, doesn't it? But it's one of the facts of marriage."

Billie wasn't listening. Absorbed in some troubling thought of her own, she took Cliff's arm in an abstracted fashion almost as if she were unaware of what she was doing. Instinctively she moved close to him, holding his thick arm with both hands, and gazed fixedly at Grandin. In a small worried voice as if she were thinking aloud, addressing no one in particular, she said: "Oh dear, I couldn't be away from Cliff that long. . . ."

They went upstairs together. At the top of the first landing they parted, the Haumans to go one way down the long corridor to their room, Grandin the other.

Cliff, he wanted to say (and the tears came into his eyes at the thought): I've grown very fond of you. Cliff;

good luck—all the best. . . . But it was something he would never be able to put into words. He stood there a moment longer, watching Cliff go down the long hall, walking with a self-conscious toughness because he knew he was being observed.

It was ended. He had done his best, his willful dangerous best, and nothing had come of it. The thing was over, he was free again (they were both free—free to love and ignore one another, as one does even with the best of friends), and his inexpressible relief that both he and Cliff had escaped danger was so all-embracing that he began to love Cliff Hauman all over again, as he should be loved. Watching him for the last time going off on his destructive natural way—so out of place in the colorless hotel corridor when his proper setting was the company platoon, the LST, or the beachhead—he could not but wish him well from the depths of his heart. . . . Good luck, Cliff; God bless you; so long! . . . They wouldn't be meeting again, no, not tomorrow or ever. Too bad, too, for in spite of his frustration, there would be more point in it now than there ever had been before. But he had his work to do and Cliff had his, and their paths were not likely to cross again, no matter what the future might bring. He wondered whether Cliff would remember or think of him. He doubted if he would very often think of Cliff, though he knew he would never forget him. . . .

In his room at last, his lonely room now, he took up a pencil and a sheet and envelope of the fancy hotel stationery, and did what he knew to be either a very futile or a very reckless thing. He wrote:

My dear Cliff:

I am confident that you will pass your examination in Brooklyn like, as you say, a breeze. Anyone whose heart is so set on a thing as yours is on this, deserves to get it. I wish you well with everything I've got.

But now that our relationship is over, I can't help but feel a little sad, foolish though it may be of me, and still more foolish though it may be to say it. In this connection, it has occurred to me that you might or might not be interested to know that I will be home, alone, on the Monday following your trip to Brooklyn. I say alone because, as you know, Ethel is to stay on in Maine for a while and I will be most awfully in need of company. I think you know how happy it would make me to see you again. The address is 532 West 116th Street, the telephone number is Cathedral 6-4324.

Affectionately,
"Johnnie"

I might as well admit that I've always felt somewhat silly when you called me Johnnie. No one but you has called me that since I was a child. And yet, to be absolutely honest with myself—and to you—I can't help feeling a little flattered, too.

J. G.

He descended the stairs to the lobby, left the letter in the Haumans' box and went back up to his room again, to spend a sleepless night.

XII

AFTER THE HAUMANS HAD LEFT THE ISLAND, he did not know what to do with himself. The Bill Howards seemed too preoccupied with their own excursions to have any time for him. Nor did he need or want their company. He missed Ethel keenly; that is, he worried about her—she was so much on his mind—yet he did not once write a letter to Maine, not even to his sons. Most of all, and passionately, he missed Cliff. He felt his presence everywhere, avoided those places and scenes where they had been happy together, and found himself dreaming of him at night. It was a not unpleasant indulgence, the more so because Cliff Hauman had paid his matter-of-fact farewell and nothing would ever come, now, of that impossible, upsetting relationship.

A few days after the Haumans had gone, John Grandin knew—as surely as if he had received a telegram to that effect—that Cliff Hauman had passed his examination in Brooklyn, was once more the Marine Captain which had long been his ideal in life and was probably already lost to Grandin forever. So the melancholy days passed—not ungrateful, not unhappy, till his last night on the island. After dinner he cornered the Howards long enough to say good-bye and even went out of his way to bid farewell to Arne Eklund, toward whom, he found, he had become utterly indifferent, even to say good-bye to. It was a formality, nothing more; worst of all, his polite farewell to Sarah and Bill Howard was a formality too.

The Sunday before his summer-school classes were to

start, a taxi drove him from Sconset to the Nantucket steamer at dawn; and by seven o'clock he was on the ocean again, sailing back to the mainland. He sat in his chair on the cold open deck and watched the island fading away in the early morning mist, the island where he had been so happy and unhappy. But luckily, Sconset and all that had happened there (or not happened) were farthest from his mind; he found himself preoccupied with thoughts of school. The shrieking cries of the sea gulls, sounding like chalk scraping on a blackboard, went unheard; he concentrated on the duties which awaited him tomorrow, and still more on the new but not unpleasant responsibilities of the school year that would commence in September.

As always, before the opening of a new semester— even though it was only another summer school, with more or less indifferent students—John Grandin was somewhat nervous at the prospect. He wondered what the new classes would be like. If he had as many as half a dozen students to whom the courses meant one-tenth of what they meant to him, it would be worth it. He was aware that he had been deliberately putting Ethel from his mind, unwilling to think of her misery. What he thought of now, as a kind of diversion or distraction, was the promotion that awaited him in the fall and the publication of *The Tragic Ideal*, which might bring him a recognition at last, however slight.

The lighthouse, off from Nantucket, was already far behind him. Sea birds followed the steamer as if it were the only object of reality in their unreal world. A chilling wind blew across the deck; John Grandin wrapped himself as snugly as possible in his topcoat and longed for the lonely voyage to be over, though it was not nearly so lonely as the earlier trip in company with his wife, when they had been estranged to the point of hostility.

He boarded the train at Woods Hole shortly before ten, in a chair car as before; and once again there were the fascinating place names of Falmouth, Pocasset, Buzzards Bay, Onset, Taunton, to say nothing of Providence, which now seemed to connote an almost Biblical rightness. In spite of the fact that his romance with Clifford Hauman had got him nowhere (for romance it had been), it was strange but somehow comforting and comfortable to sense how rapidly the island holiday was behind him; for truly it had never been a holiday to begin with. During the train trip he fell back into the matter-of-fact considerations and details of daily life. Perhaps he had or had not lost Ethel; but Clifford Hauman, thank God, no longer existed. Certainly he would never see him again. . . .

The atmosphere was stifling, sultry, enervating, as he came up the ramp into Grand Central. After the continual breezes of Sconset, he felt he could scarcely breathe. It was no better when he stepped into the humid street; but during the ride uptown, wind of a sort did blow in through the lowered window of the taxi. Arrived at his apartment, he raised all the windows at once and replaced the fallen firetongs against the frame of the hearth. Halfheartedly he considered phoning Ethel in Maine to tell her he had arrived home; in another hour or so it would be time for the evening rates of long-distance. Would Ethel care, for one minute, where he was? Perhaps she would be interested to know, but he could not afford the risk of having her hang up on him.

XIII

EARLY DAWN. The windows showed blue rather than white. Alan and Ted lay sprawled in the wide bed.

Ethel Grandin appeared in the doorway. She stood there hesitantly for a long moment, and then came quietly in. She went to the bed. Erect, lost in thought, she looked down at the sleeping children.

Ted was flat on his back in innocent immobile sleep. Alan slept on his right side, one knee bent and one leg thrust straight down, the left wrist and hand dangling loosely over the edge, exactly like his father. A faint dew of perspiration lay upon their clear foreheads and upper lips.

It was the climax of a dreadful week. Like most of the other nights, her night had again been utterly without sleep, a wakeful nightmare so charged with uncertainty and fear that she could not remember going to bed or getting up. It had been like an agony of birth, and the one reborn was herself. For now with the light of morning growing at the windows, and the sight of the soundlessly sleeping sweaty children, her fears vanished: unaccountably she felt rested and released.

Here is where her love lay and would always lie; through her sons she felt her love for her husband more keenly than ever, more finally, almost as if she had never truly loved him till now. Gazing at her two little boys, she knew how much she wanted him, and that she could never be unwanted again—by them or by him.

What, after all, had happened? Among her husband's things she had found an overseas cap, the overseas cap of a young man they had both been fond of. Nothing more— no more than that. When she confronted him with it and voiced the awful charge, he had explained what it meant and did not mean; and in her fright, she had refused to believe him. She believed him now, she pitied him with all her heart, and she loved him. He was the one who had understood, been fully aware of the danger, and himself rejected the impossible infatuation. Had he gone recklessly on, with no thought of their marriage or of her, then she would have had cause for leaving him indeed. But he had not. "Is Cliff more important than we are?" he had asked; "Not to me he isn't." And even though she had gone off and left him there on the island, with every opportunity of seeing Cliff alone, she knew that Cliff was an episode already past: neither of them would ever be seeing him again.

She returned to her room, took up pencil and paper, and in a few moments she had composed the letter which should have been written days ago. An hour later, it was on its way, air mail and Special Delivery; and by mid-morning, herself again, she had organized her parents and children for a picnic at Old Orchard beach.

XIV

JOHN GRANDIN WAS SORTING out his books to select those which he would need for his opening class when the telephone rang. The automatic dialing system filled the living room with an insistent *zing*. For a moment, he thought of letting it go. Then he told himself that this would be an indication of fear—fear of answering and fear of finding out. After a second or two of hesitation he picked up the receiver.

The young baritone voice sang over the wire, hearty as always but with an unwonted nervousness or tension:

"Johnnie? It's me, Johnnie—Cliff. I'm in the station at Bridgeport, just coming into New York; can I see you, Johnnie?"

"What is it, Cliff?"

"Oh, nothing special—I just thought if you were in—"

"Wait a moment, Cliff, I hear someone at the door. . . ."

John Grandin put down the receiver and walked to the middle of the room. Why should Cliff want to see him, or he Cliff? He knew full well why. If Cliff wanted to call on him—if the two of them were to have the opportunity of being together in the apartment, with no one knowing—what, indeed, was there to decide. It was a fortuitous meeting in private—for what?—such as he could not have dared to hope for. He stalled a moment longer and then went back to the phone.

"Sorry, Cliff, it was the laundryman. Now, what was it you wanted?"

"Wanted? Well, it isn't that, Johnnie, but I'm coming in town and if you're not busy—"

Grandin looked ruefully at the books he had chosen for the first-morning class. "All right, Cliff."

"I'll be there in about an hour and a half," said the

eager young voice, "say about ten-thirty at the latest. I'll
come straight to your apartment, Johnnie, shall I? That
all right?"

"Yes.—You know where I am?"

"Oh sure! I've been keeping that note you stuck in
our box before we left Nantucket. I bet I've been calling
you a dozen times. Though I don't know why, 'cause I
knew you wouldn't be back till today. Still, I just thought
maybe you might be in earlier. . . ."

"Wait a moment, Cliff." He found this difficult to say,
but it was something he had to ask: "Is Billie coming
with you, by any chance?"

"No, just me."

As he came away from the telephone, Grandin
realized with a sinking feeling that he had not given himself time really to think if this was what he wanted. Once
again Cliff Hauman had completely taken over his day.

He sat by the open window and waited. He saw the
worn briefcase on the living-room table, its open flap and
straps hanging down over the edge, ready to be buckled;
he had been about to put in his books for the morning
class. But this was all right, he told himself: class or no
class, it was far more important that he settle this thing
now—one way or the other, for good and all.

But he was filled with an almost physical apprehension of Cliff's coming. There was no sense in kidding himself. Maybe nothing would happen; but he knew what he
himself would go through merely to have Cliff sitting opposite him in the same room, with no one in the world
knowing what they were doing or not doing, no one
knowing where they were. Cliff's calling him on the tele-

phone had not been accident. John Grandin knew only too well, after the note he had left in the Dune House box, that he himself was to blame; Cliff had not even needed to look him up in the book. Nor was this the first time he had called, according to Cliff's own words. What was the meaning of the projected meeting? What did it intend on Hauman's part? For the first time, Grandin had the feeling that he was being played with; and for once he didn't give a damn. Let school and the first class of the summer semester go to hell. Let Cliff come; let what might happen happen.

The hot morning seemed interminable. In spite of his decision, he could not but feel a real guilt to think that the new students would be assembled and waiting— wondering what had become of their professor on this, the first day, while he remained here in the apartment, indifferent to them and helpless in himself. About ten-thirty, the buzzer rang.

Before answering it, John Grandin gave a last look around the living room, thinking, as he did so, that it was a ludicrous and irrelevant thing to be doing; he had tidied it thoroughly the morning he left for Woods Hole. Assuming a calm he was far from feeling, he stepped to the door.

Cliff came in breathless, but with a radiant smile, a smile of complete health and charm.

"How are you, Johnnie? Gee!"

He seemed irrationally delighted to be here, happy— not at all restless (for the moment) as he had been during their farewell in Sconset on that last unhappy evening, an evening unhappy for John Grandin because he thought he would never be seeing him again.

But as the minutes passed, Cliff began once more to create an impression of strain as he had during the boat trip when they first met, even a kind of anxiety. Scarcely looking at Grandin, he walked about the apartment admiring things too enthusiastically. John Grandin watched him. Then, as Cliff became aware of this, he went to a chair and sat down with a kind of self-consciousness.

John Grandin took out a cigarette. Cliff, turning his gaze from the pictures on the wall, hurried across the room to light it for him; then, instead of sitting down again, he resumed his tour of inspection.

With his back to John Grandin, he put his broad hands on his waist, craned his tawny head upward, and gazed at the packed bookshelves reaching to the ceiling. Grandin saw two damp spots in the armpits of his khaki shirt, the first sign of sweat he had ever noticed in the immaculate Clifford Hauman; it must be because of the humid New York heat.

"Gosh, I never saw so many books in my life. Wouldn't my daddy love this? He reads more books! Regular bookworm. . . ." He wheeled about and said, as if it were an afterthought—as if it had just occurred to him: "Say, Johnnie, would you mind if I took a bath? I'm just stinking hot. Dirty too, I guess. . . ."

Without waiting for consent, Cliff found at once the small bathroom between the living room and study, and a moment later Grandin heard the noise in the shower and Cliff sloshing about in the stinging spray.

. . . You son-of-a-bitch, Grandin reflected, not with-

out pleasure in spite of the violence of his thought. . . .
I will not be played with in this fashion, I will not be made
a monkey of. If he had any sense at all, he would have
quitted the apartment at once, leaving Cliff to find his way
out by himself. But he knew he couldn't and wouldn't.
He stayed. To his dismay, he even discovered he liked it.
He himself would never have dreamed of suggesting that
Cliff should take a shower; it would have been so obvious,
such a cheap invitation to sexuality, that he could not
have brought himself even to hint of it—nor, for that
matter, had it occurred to him. Yet when Cliff had expressed such a desire on his own, John Grandin had been
helpless to refuse him.

In less than ten minutes, Cliff was again in the living
room. He was fully dressed as before, shining and fresh;
his field scarf looked as if he were wearing it for the first
time; the damp dark spots under the armpits were gone.

With a rapidly sinking heart, a thumping heart which
gave him actual pain, John Grandin sat rooted in his
chair. He looked up at the broad back and the straining
shoulder seams of the khaki shirt. He loved Cliff Hauman.
Understanding this fact was not enough, however. He felt
he had to declare himself, somehow, some way: the time
was now. But he was unable to do anything but wait. His
mind touched fleetingly on the first morning of summer
school, while he sat here, and ruefully he realized how
the new students would be already in the classroom,
wondering what had happened to their professor—wondering, even, if they had got the date or the hour wrong
and consulting their schedules to find out.

Cliff finally sat down opposite him, but at a considerable distance. For some reason of his own, he had chosen a chair on the far side of the room. As Grandin made conversation to prolong the unhappy happy visit and smoked cigarette after cigarette, Cliff each time sprang to his feet and came rapidly across the room to light it for him; then he would recede at once to his distant chair. The older man noticed how he sat leaning forward, on the very edge of the chair, his elbows on his knees, in the exact position in which he had sat throughout their first meeting on the boat to Nantucket—tense, restless, ill at ease. In spite of his good looks and freshness, with his tawny hair darker with damp but well combed, he was so unlike the natural happy careless fellow of the Sconset holiday that Grandin was keenly struck by the difference. Cliff seemed torn between a restless desire to get up and go, and a kind of worry or unease because, possibly, Grandin might have lost interest in him.

By an unexpected but groundless intuition, John Grandin suddenly got the notion—why, he couldn't have said—that Cliff Hauman had failed his physical examination in Brooklyn and was hanging on for dear life to anyone who still thought of him as the Marine captain he wanted to be. If this were true, Cliff had no need to worry. John Grandin had by no means lost interest in Cliff: on the contrary, in spite of his knowing better, he felt an all but passionate desire to put his arms around the fellow. But what good would it do him; or Cliff? Such an overt move would most certainly mark the end of their relationship forever. . . .

"Gee," Cliff said with a strained unhappy eagerness, "I'd give anything to have you know my buddy Walt, and him to know you. You'd like him a lot, Johnnie. He's a swell guy to pal around with. Christ almighty, the circus we used to have in Melbourne! I wish Walt could tell you about it some time, he could tell you so much better than I could. I don't think either one of us ever laid a dame on leave that we didn't do it together. He loved it and so did I, but it was never any good, I don't care how hot she was, unless Walt was there too. We used to keep it up all night—not just once or twice, you understand, but seven or eight times."

Absorbed and alarmed, John Grandin took out a cigarette to recover himself. Cliff at once started up from the edge of his chair on the other side of the room, but Grandin shook his head. "Never mind, Cliff, I've got it."

This would never do; no, not at all. Never in a thousand years. Fond of him though he might be, John Grandin was disappointed and saddened thus to be made a fool of. He wanted to say: You've got the idea all right, Cliff, but oh, you've got it all wrong, too. . . .

"Say Johnnie," Cliff went on, "did I ever tell you about the times a couple of guys and myself went up to Hollywood from San Diego? We had three-day leaves from the hospital—"

"Just a moment, Cliff," Grandin interrupted.

"Yes, Johnnie?"

"I thought you were seriously wounded. Billie couldn't go out to California because you were too sick to see her—wasn't that it?"

"Oh well, sure." He laughed. "But Christ, they had to let us out once in a while or we'd have gone nuts. I wasn't so sick *all* the time but what I was good for a piece of tail now and then."

"I see. . . ."

"Anyhow, these two buddies and myself went up to Hollywood to look over the place. You know how the movie stars make a fuss over you just because you're a serviceman, specially a marine. Jesus, you can lay almost any of them if you're in uniform. Like I started to say, we went from the canteen one night to the home of Marina Colfax out in Bel-Air—you know, swimming pool, butlers, all that stuff—and almost before we had time for a drink, my buddies and the other two dames disappeared. Marina looks at me wise and says, 'Well, what are you waiting for, kid?' Can you beat it, Johnnie?" He laughed nervously; then he added with a grin: "We went up-stairs, and before midnight I laid her three times."

At this moment Cliff seemed heartbreakingly pathetic. The fellow didn't know what he wanted, any more than Grandin did. Cliff certainly didn't want what he seemed to be inviting, consciously or not. He was a lonely affectionate kid who was hanging on at all costs, trying to stimulate or hold the other's interest by a conversation which must have been as distasteful to himself as it was outrageous, fascinating, and upsetting to John Grandin. Like the destructive young man he had become, he was destroying, in his innocence, the very thing he thought he wanted. Grandin, looking back, began to believe that very possibly Cliff had been exploiting him for days. He was both saddened by the thought, and, curiously, intensely relieved. He got up and walked deliberately across the room like a man in a daze.

At his approach, Cliff rose from his chair and looked about him with an anxious worried smile. Though he was past caring—and indeed scarcely saw him at all now— John Grandin yet felt so sorry that he wanted to put his arms around him and say, Don't worry, Cliff; you'll be back in the service one of these days and everything will be all right. . . . But he knew this was untrue; Cliff's happy days in the Marine Corps were probably already over. Aloud he said the impossible, the utterly unthinkable words, the declaration of love no one could have told him he would ever make: "Cliff, I've grown very fond of you, I can't help it. . . ."

There was no satisfaction in having said it at last; but the release he felt now gave him a purpose and a deliberation he had not experienced in years. Cliff was leaning awkwardly against the fireplace mantel, uncomfortable and self-conscious to the point of pain. John Grandin stood before him, very close. He placed his two hands on the solid but slender waist; beneath his fingers he felt the live flesh and charm and power, the whole potent youthfulness of him. Involuntarily Grandin's hands moved around him and locked, and he drew Cliff tight against him.

For an instant the tense body froze; then it reacted, violent and automatic, as if by reflex.

Even as John Grandin saw the blue eyes suddenly blaze, the hand reach back, the brass-handled tongs go up and swing sharply down toward the flat of his face, he knew Cliff was not to blame, knew he had brought it on himself, asked for it. . . .

XV

ETHEL GRANDIN lay face down in the sand, her cheek resting on her crossed arms. They had had their picnic lunch on the beach some time ago, and now the children and her father were going in for a second dip, while her mother watched anxiously. She herself was content to lie in the sand, freed of the care of her boys for the time being, and think of her husband. Perhaps the letter had already been delivered at the apartment, or would be very soon; in any case, she was certain to hear from him tonight by telephone, and she looked forward to the call.

She could hear the boys squealing with delight and thrill as their grandfather led them by the hand into the small surf, and from time to time she heard her mother call out to them to be careful.

For the first time in her life, Ethel Cameron was aware of why she had been attracted to John Grandin, why he alone, of all the men she had met, was the one she had been able to give herself up to. Perhaps his susceptibility to the influence of Cliff Hauman was the very thing which made him the man he was; it was one and the same with that sensitiveness of his which, unaware, she had loved him for from the beginning. Was there such a thing as the absolute male or female? If so, there could only be clash between them, not love. Had John Grandin been all male, they would not have met on common ground ever.

None of this had she written in her letter, of course. Nor had she mentioned Cliff's name. She could not have brought herself to say what she still felt so keenly—that if

her husband saw Cliff again, she could not return to him
—but it was implied in the letter and she knew her husband would know it. Besides, she felt it unnecessary to
mention Cliff: she believed her husband, now, when he
had said it was finished, finished because understood. The
whole letter might have been expressed in the one sen-
tence: *I know it meant nothing.*

XVI

THE LATE SUN SENT level rays of yellow light straight
across the room to the bookshelves. It was still daylight,
though shortly to become dusk. The buzzer began to ring.
For some time, John Grandin did not hear it. But as the
last insistent buzz died in the room and left a final challenging silence, he roused from his painful sleep.

He opened his eyes. At first he could not see. Then he
wiped the blood from his brow and face and eventually
was able to believe in his surroundings. He could not
trouble himself to wonder who was at the door; he was not
even sure the buzzer had been ringing. From his position
on the floor with his head just under the gate-leg table,
the room looked distorted and unfamiliar. Then he recognized his topcoat on the piano bench, the fire tongs lying
on the carpet near him, and the books. At the same
moment he saw a letter being slid under the door. Foot-
steps walked off along the hall and after a pause he heard
the door of the cagelike elevator slam to, followed by a
whining groan as the lift descended.

He did not try to get up from the floor. The effort

was too much. He lay still and tried to collect his thoughts; and the memory of what had happened that noon came back to him. . . .

The yellow light streamed horizontally through the windows, so that John Grandin, on the floor, lay in a half-dark, fully conscious, now, but with a violently throbbing head. He thought of the summer-school class he had missed that day and would miss tomorrow. He thought of the fall semester, the new appointment, the students he would be expected to advise, and the publication of the work which had occupied him for so long. Bitterly he thought of the turn of events which had reduced him to a beaten man bleeding here on the floor. He had paid for an old flaw or error, paid twice over, far beyond his deserts; and in all justice, everything was as it should be. Luckily Ethel and the children had been spared the knowledge or the sight of this. But only for the time being. Like the students, they were certain to find out. It was a small world, the life of the university, and his family was even smaller. Disaster had struck him down, but it was nothing to the disaster of the uncertain future.

At length, because it was something to do and must be done, he raised himself on his hands and knees and crawled across the carpet toward the door and the letter showing underneath. It was minutes before he was able to slit the envelope and extract the letter, minutes before he could read it, minutes more till he had registered its contents. Involuntarily his head sank lower and lower to the floor; and his sole emotion was a passionate regret that Cliff had not finished the job.